I0675217

GLASTONBURY TALES

FACE BLIND

JL MERROW

RIPTIDE
PUBLISHING

Riptide Publishing
PO Box 1537
Burnsville, NC 28714
www.riptidepublishing.com

This is a work of fiction. Names, characters, places, and incidents are either the product of the author's imagination or are used fictitiously. Any resemblance to actual persons living or dead, business establishments, events, or locales is entirely coincidental. All person(s) depicted on the cover are model(s) used for illustrative purposes only.

Face Blind
Copyright © 2022 by JL Merrow

Cover art: L.C. Chase, lcchase.com
Editor: Carole-ann Galloway
Layout: L.C. Chase, lcchase.com

All rights reserved. No part of this book may be reproduced or transmitted in any form or by any means, electronic or mechanical, including photocopying, recording, or by any information storage and retrieval system without the written permission of the publisher, and where permitted by law. Reviewers may quote brief passages in a review. To request permission and all other inquiries, contact Riptide Publishing at the mailing address above, at Riptidepublishing.com, or at marketing@riptidepublishing.com.

ISBN: 978-1-62649-969-0

First edition
October, 2022

Also available in ebook:
ISBN: 978-1-62649-968-3

GLASTONBURY TALES

FACE BLIND

JL MERROW

RIPTIDE
PUBLISHING

TABLE OF

CONTENTS

CHAPTER ONE

I t was later than Adam had thought, and gathering clouds chased the setting sun. Maybe he wouldn't go up to the top of the tor to visit the tower, the sole remnant of the church built by his namesake. Abbot Adam of Sodbury, and hadn't the other lads had fun with *that* name when they'd all been in school?

It wasn't really a place for laughs, though. A later abbot had died there, hung, drawn, and quartered for his faith, along with two of his monks. A death like that had to leave echoes through time. It was easy to imagine their ghosts haunting those blood-soaked stones.

Unusually, there was no one else around. Then again, Adam had taken the less well-trodden, steeper path from the east rather than follow the tourist trail up from Chalice Well. And it was a chill day turning into a cold evening, the lowering clouds threatening a return of the day's rain. Maybe he should have put on something better suited to the weather than his worn leather jacket. He'd never had the knack of thinking ahead like that.

What would it be like to have the sort of mother who always insisted on you wearing a waterproof and taking an umbrella? Who wrapped a hand-knitted scarf around your neck before they let you out of the house? Adam huffed a bitter laugh as the first raindrops hit his face. He could remember those same lads from school complaining about being smothered, when at fifteen, sixteen they were clearly grown men who didn't need their mums anymore.

Even then, he'd felt a shameful twist of longing for that sort of care. His mum, when he'd told her he was going out, mostly used to give him a blank stare or a nod. But every now and then, he'd get a *"Don't be late back"* that had actually sounded like she meant it, like she cared about him—until a switch would flip, and she'd go back to her usual, distant self.

The rain was coming down in earnest now. Perversely determined to make it to the top after all, Adam hunched his shoulders and lengthened his stride. Raindrops stung his cheeks as the wind tugged at his jacket. Should he have done more to mend their relationship? Tried harder? Tried *sooner*?

The ache in his legs from the steepening climb was a welcome distraction from the turmoil in his heart. It wasn't like she'd ever given him any encouragement, was it? The last time he'd come up from London to see her stood out vividly in his memory, like a single painting in a gallery targeted by vandals. She hadn't smiled when she'd opened the door to him. Hadn't shown any interest in his life.

When he'd moved back here a month or so ago after nearly a decade away, he'd wondered if it would be different. Would absence have made her heart grow fonder? Or would all maternal affection have withered away, dead from lack of nurture?

He'd never know now. Maybe it was better that way. He could tell himself the terms of her will meant she had loved him; she just hadn't been able to show it. Tell himself it wasn't guilt that had made her leave everything to him.

Head down against the driving rain, Adam almost walked straight into the tower, stopping himself in the nick of time. The stone was slick when he touched it with wet fingers, proving it was really there. That he was. Still trailing his fingers on the stone, he rounded the corner of the tower to the more sheltered side that looked down towards the town. The old structure felt warm at his back as he gazed over pocket-sized fields and a toytown Glastonbury, made hazy by the weather. As he stood there, a thick mist blew over the ground below him, and within seconds it was as if he were cut off, standing on an island in a cloud.

A man could almost believe in the legends that surrounded the tor, at a time like this. Could imagine, as he had as a child, the wild hunt setting out from under the hill, the fairy horde led by Gwyn ap Nudd, the horned god of the underworld.

Adam smiled to himself and shook his head. Time to head back. His hair was soaked, water dripping into his face and down his neck.

He'd need a hot shower and a good meal when he got back home—if those gits he lived with hadn't used all the hot water and occupied all the rings on the stove already.

The rain had slackened to a heavy drizzle as Adam started down the path, moving quickly so as to warm himself up. Mist shifted and swirled in front of him, now thicker, so that he could barely see a few paces ahead; now thinner, allowing a view almost to the bottom of the hill. It was strangely quiet, as though sound were deadened, but then, there was no one else here to make a sound.

Or was there? Casting his gaze around, Adam caught sight of a dark figure some way distant, near the other path—the two were more or less at right angles this high up—and was blindsided by a sudden shock of familiarity.

"Mum?" he whispered—but it couldn't be, could it?

Christ, that was her coat, the long dark one he'd seen only hours ago in the downstairs cupboard. And her hair, worn loose and flowing over her shoulders, like when he'd been little.

For a moment, he could swear she was singing: a song he'd forgotten, until now, brought from the Scottish Highlands of her birth: *I left my baby lying there . . .*

Then the mist rolled over the hillside and she vanished from his sight.

His pulse throbbing in his ears, Adam ran across the grass. But when he reached the spot where he'd seen her, there was no one there. He scrambled farther, feet slipping in the wet grass. How could she have disappeared? He stopped, panting, and gazed all around, willing the mist to clear.

There. A figure on the Chalice Well path.

Not Mum, though. Disappointment dropped like a lead weight in Adam's stomach. It was a man, walking alone, head down, probably keen to leave the tor before darkness set in. Adam slip-slid down and around the hill to him. "Did you see her?" His voice came out rough. Harsh.

No wonder the man took a step back, eyes wide. "What?"

"There was a woman. Older. Uh, about sixty. Just now. Did you see her?"

The man stared at Adam. He was attractive, Adam noted distantly, with broad shoulders and gelled-up hair. For all his modern looks, there was something strange about him, as though he'd sprung from the legends that surrounded the tor. With the height of him, and that solid build, maybe even something dangerous.

"I haven't seen anyone here. Apart from you," the man said at last, his gaze still oddly intent. "Did you . . . lose her?"

Christ. Adam shook his head. He was going mad. His mum was dead, and her coat was in a bag waiting to go for recycling. "No. Sorry. Mind playing tricks."

The stranger flinched—or was it simply a jerky hunch of the shoulders?—and took a step back. Adam was put in mind of a stray cat, unsure if the outstretched hand would mean a pet or a blow. He didn't say anything. Well, who *would* want to talk to someone who'd admitted to seeing things?

"Sorry to bother you." Adam turned away to make the weary slog back around the hill and down to where he'd parked the Yamaha.

He kept his eyes open on the way. But his mum, if she'd ever really been there, had gone.

CHAPTER TWO

Rain had been falling steadily that afternoon, and Corin had been relieved to have reached Glastonbury in one piece. The drive down from Wiltshire had taken the best part of two hours, instead of the one-and-a-half Google estimated. Although he hadn't needed to use any motorways, there had still been some idiots driving way too fast, and he'd stopped a couple of times to let them go by.

Having pulled into what he hoped was the correct parking space, he hauled a few bags out of the Volvo and up the external staircase to the two-bedroom attic flat that was his new home. The woman who opened the door to his knock introduced herself as the landlady. She handed him the key, gave him a quick rundown of the quirks of the boiler, and left, unfurling her umbrella, with a parting, "We're just down the road if you need anything, my lover."

"Thanks." Corin remembered to smile, and shut the door behind her. Then he slumped down on the sofa. It sagged in the middle, as if used to someone heavier. Corin wondered who'd had the flat before him. Why had they left? Moving on to something better?

Or running away from something worse, like him?

He stood up again and gave himself a mental shake. He'd chosen to leave Avebury, and he still believed it was the right decision. The flat might be smaller than the one he'd left, but it was light and airy, and he'd been sold on the place as soon as he'd seen the view from the windows. Up high in the attic, he could see over his neighbours' rooftops to the tor beyond. Or, if he preferred, he could gaze down into the street to watch life going on below. Corin had originally thought of getting a place out in the countryside, but here, he could have the feeling of being away from it all while still being handy for the shops. The fact that the flat had a reserved space in the residents' car park was the icing on the cake.

If he was being spectacularly honest with himself, he could admit that hiding in some lonely hermitage wouldn't have been the best idea for his mental health, so it was probably just as well that the only country homes on the market had been ridiculously large houses with equally ridiculous price tags.

And running up and down the stairs to the front door will keep me fit, he thought ruefully as he braved the rain several more times to fetch the rest of his boxes and bags. Amazing how much stuff one single man could accumulate. The larger bedroom, the one he'd be sleeping in, had a fine view of the roof and tower of St. John's Church. Corin hung up the few items of clothing that warranted the attention in the cheap fitted wardrobe and shoved the rest into the chest of drawers, an antique pine monstrosity that dominated the room and failed to match with anything else. Then he took towels into the bathroom, making a mental note to buy some soap.

As he hung a hand towel by the sink, his gaze fell on the mirror fixed to the wall with capless screws that were rusting contentedly in the twilight of their lives. He froze, still not used to a stranger's face staring back at him. The stranger had mid-brown hair, cropped aggressively at the sides to blend in with his three days' beard. The top was gelled up, except for where the rain had flattened it. Corin ran his hands through it, forcing it to stand up for itself again. Did the stranger look better after that? Corin's judgement was an unreliable beast, these days, but he'd made an effort. "See, Declan? I still care," he said aloud.

His brother didn't answer, because he was back in Swindon, probably trying to explain to all their friends why Corin had left so suddenly. And why he was so bloody stand-offish these days.

It had been hard in hospital after the accident. Harder yet when they'd sent him home with a bundle of information about prosopagnosia—face blindness—and a list of coping strategies to practice. At least when somebody had come up to his bed in the ward with a determined smile and maybe a small gift, he'd been able to be fairly sure they were someone he knew, even if he hadn't been able to tell who they were—often until they'd been talking for several minutes. There had been one visitor he'd never managed to identify, putting the young man off after an awkward conversation with claims of tiredness that hadn't, in fact, been faked. It was exhausting straining for every clue to who a person, apparently of some importance in his life, might be.

Coming out with a flat *Who are you?* didn't help. He'd only done it the once, and the woman had flinched as if he'd slapped her. Then she'd pasted on a smile, identified herself as a neighbour in a slow, high-pitched voice as though he were a child or an elderly dementia sufferer, and left.

Returning to Avebury, his home village, had been a nightmare. It was a small place, where he knew dozens of people well enough to say hello to. He'd never realised how little there was to distinguish them from one another. Everyone wore dark, casual, practical clothes, suitable for walks in the countryside or playing with the kids. Corin had seemed to have an unfailing knack for guessing wrongly which ones he should greet, and those who'd eye him strangely for it. Even when he got it right, it still *felt* wrong—as if by losing their faces, he'd lost all connection to the people he knew.

When he'd found himself eating baked beans without toast for lunch to avoid having to go out, Corin had decided enough was enough and started searching for a flat in a town where every visit to the local shops wouldn't be a social minefield.

So here he was. And, hopefully, things would be better here, where he could look forward to going out, rather than dread it. He'd been planning to celebrate his new home with a takeaway for dinner, so Corin threw on a jacket, shoved on his trainers, and set off, with a stop at the car to grab his umbrella.

There were two takeaways on his street—a small, family-run Chinese place, and a larger Indian that was also a restaurant. *Chinese tonight.* The place had an inviting air, with a short, white-haired lady behind the counter and a bright-red lucky cat waving in the window. He would give the chow mein a try, after he'd had a bit of an explore. Or maybe the crispy beef. Hell, why not both? He was celebrating, after all.

Corin took a meandering walk through the centre of town with his umbrella and let the rightness of coming here seep into his bones. Glastonbury's many old buildings spoke of its rich history—the George and Pilgrims' Hotel, and the abbey itself, to name but two. Maybe after he'd lived here for a while he'd get tired of the wacky witchiness of the shops that surrounded them, but he doubted it. He didn't have to buy into the new-age spirituality of the town to appreciate its uniqueness—so unlike the majority of cookie-cutter towns across the UK, all with the same chain stores and restaurants. In a place like this, he wouldn't be able to forget where he was.

And then there was the tor, rising to the east. That conical hill topped with its square, blocky tower had been the first thing he'd seen, driving into Glastonbury. Its height made it visible for miles around. The rain had finally stopped, and Corin had a sudden urge to go there. To plant a flag on the local landmark, as it were. Not having internalised how big Glastonbury was, Corin debated whether it would be sensible to go back to his flat and fetch the car. In the likely event his damaged brain couldn't find the way back home unaided, it'd be easier to use the car's GPS than the one on his phone. Especially if the rain set in once more.

Against that was the fact he'd driven two hours to get here, and he *really* didn't want to get back in the car again today. Okay, so he'd been fine on the A roads coming over, and traffic in town wouldn't be moving very quickly . . . No. Just thinking about taking the car was sucking all the joy out of the idea. Corin took another glance at the tor to get his bearings, and set off on foot.

For once, his luck was in. Aided by the brown signs around town, he found the start of the tor footpath without too much difficulty, a short distance past the Chalice Well as his tourist map had promised.

The footpath was wide and well-maintained, swept clear of fallen leaves from the trees that bounded it. Another brown sign promised he'd get there in fifteen minutes—good news, seeing as the sun was now close to the horizon. The way was steep, and Corin could feel it in the backs of his legs and his buttocks, which apparently reckoned they'd had quite enough of a workout moving his things into the flat. A set of long, shallow steps led up to a kissing gate, and once through it, he was out in the open, the green hummock of the tor rising before him.

A dark figure on the other side of the gate was bundling up a sleeping bag. Corin had his hand in his pocket before he heard the predictable "Spare some change?" in a weary, toneless voice. He didn't envy anyone living on the streets as the days grew colder.

"Here you go, mate." Corin dropped a couple of quid into their hand. In the twilight, it was hard to make out any details of the black-clad figure with their hood pulled down low over their face.

The rough sleeper didn't speak again but gave Corin a sketchy salute in thanks before returning to packing up their few goods.

The path led on up through a field of sheep to another gate, which seemed to mark the base of the tor proper. A few trees grew there, one of them adorned with colourful ribbons. *Prayers? To which deity?* The gradient became steeper, and there were steps to aid the weary climber. Corin halted for a moment to turn and view the way he'd come. Glastonbury town lay before him, and beyond it, the sun sunk low in the sky.

But now rain was setting in. Putting up the hood of his waterproof, Corin headed onwards, following the path on its winding route towards the summit of the tor.

As he neared the top, the rain slackened again. The wind, by contrast, picked up sharply. It ruffled Corin's hair as he stopped once more to put back his hood and turn in a slow circle to gaze over the Somerset Levels—all cosy English countryside these days, with villages and patchwork farmers' fields, but thousands of years ago he'd have been surrounded by marshes. Glastonbury Tor would have risen out of them, high and dry, a true island. No wonder they called it the Isle of Avalon to this day.

St. Michael's Tower, at first half-hidden by the brow of the hill, grew taller as he approached. Its sandstone stood out darkly against the grey skies visible around and through it, the arched doorway at the front going straight through to the back. Corin shivered. Those strong winds had ushered in a rolling mist and the light was fading fast.

Better get a move on if he was to make it to the tower and back before dark. Corin increased his pace, half jogging up the low steps of the pathway. By the time he reached the tower, he was warm with the exercise and relished the wind on his face. There was no one else around, which had to be a rare occurrence for a place so iconic. He wanted to make the most of it.

A moment later, a sinking sensation came with the realisation that he wasn't, in fact, alone: a lean figure was visible on a second path heading down from the tower. Corin must have just missed meeting him at the top. Further unease greeted the view—or rather lack of it—of his own path. Damn it. He'd have to cut short his walk here if he didn't want to risk getting lost in the dark and the fog. Still, he had all the time in the world to make a return visit. Telling himself to be philosophical, Corin started to make his way back towards civilisation.

He hadn't gone all that far when he was startled by a shout from only a few feet away. Corin whirled. How had he not heard anyone approaching? "What?" he managed, heart racing.

The man standing there was dark-haired, wet, and bedraggled, dressed in a black leather jacket that didn't appear to appreciate the soaking it had got. "There was a woman. Older. Uh, around sixty. Just now. Did you see her?"

The earnest, almost desperate way he spoke was arresting. His accent was unexpected—more London than Somerset. Corin gazed at him in a futile attempt to find something visually unique about the man. Something memorable. But his features were entirely regular and his build well-proportioned. Useless, in other words. "I haven't seen anyone here. Apart from you. Did you . . . lose her?"

The man seemed to hunch in on himself, and Corin wished he could offer comfort. "No. Sorry. Mind playing tricks."

It hit him like a blow. *God, you too?*

"Sorry to bother you," the man said before Corin could bring himself to voice the admission, and ran back in the direction he'd come from.

An inexplicable sense of loss assaulted Corin. Why should he care that a man he'd never met before—and wouldn't know if he saw him again—had gone? What was it to him if the stranger did or didn't find the woman he was looking for? If she even existed, that was. Rattled, the relaxation from walking on the tor totally gone, Corin increased his own speed back towards the town. Back towards the sanctuary of his car and his flat.

As he reached the gate, his unease intensified. Damn it, had the strange man been seeking the homeless person? Corin had forgotten all about them in the stress of the moment, and they'd now disappeared, hopefully to somewhere sheltered. Not that Corin would have been able to give any useful information about them. And while he was the last person to trust his judgement on these things, they hadn't seemed anything like as old as sixty. Nevertheless, the nagging sensation that he should have done more followed him all the way down the path.

Walking back through town five minutes later, pathetically reliant on his phone's GPS, he wished he'd brought the car, after all. Everything looked different in the twilight, and the gung-ho spirit that had prompted the excursion had vanished with the sun.

And you don't run into unexpected, demanding people in the car, either.

At least, not unless you're driving without due care and attention.

CHAPTER THREE

Before he went walking with ghosts on the tor, Adam had spent the day at his mum's house. They'd buried her the previous Thursday, on a bright sunny afternoon that had made the few flowers shine bright with jewel tones. It had sparked a rare memory of the living room curtains when he'd been little, and how she'd used them to teach him the colours of the rainbow.

As he'd parked the Yamaha outside Mum's house way too early on that damp Sunday morning, Adam had thought of those curtains again. When had they come down? The ones hanging there now were in the muted, drab tones he recalled from his teens.

His sister Evie's VW was already there, and as he pulled off his helmet, she got out of the car and came to join him. "Managed to get up on time, then?" she greeted him.

Adam made an effort not to take offence. "Wasn't easy. The lads were up drinking till late last night. And no, I didn't join them, but they weren't exactly quiet. Why didn't you go on in?"

Evie gave a tiny shrug. "Thought I should wait for you, that's all."

She turned away from him, so he couldn't tell if that was a dig or not. Maybe wouldn't have been able to tell even if he'd seen her face. With a nine-year age gap, they'd never been close, and all his time away hadn't helped.

He was only beginning to get to know her again.

Mum's house was one of the smaller, older houses on the Roman Way. It and its semi-detached neighbour were reached up a flight of thirteen stone steps from the street, and the elevation meant the tor was visible from the front garden. Adam stopped for a moment to appreciate the familiar view, then turned a critical eye on the garden itself. The front lawn needed mowing, but the shrubs at the side appeared healthy.

"She looked after the place okay." Was Evie's tone defensive? Or accusing because Adam hadn't been there to help Mum out?

Or was he projecting his own feelings onto her? "I'm sure she did. It's not like she was *old*, old."

Evie drew in a breath as though she was about to speak, but didn't, so Adam strode up to the front door. His newly cut key stuck in the lock, and he jiggled it, suppressing a curse.

"Shall I do it?" Evie asked, her breath warm on the back of his neck from where she'd huddled into the tiny porch with him to escape the drizzle. Apparently she still saw him as the little kid who needed help with everything.

"No, I think I've got—" The key turned all of a sudden, and Adam bashed his knuckles on the door jamb. Biting his tongue once again, he pushed open the door to his childhood home. The narrow hallway was much as he remembered it from the last time he'd visited—shit, was it over three years ago now? His conscience, which had already been prodding him, stabbed him in the chest.

But it wasn't like Mum had wanted him there, anyway, had it? She'd dithered and fidgeted, making him a milky cup of tea as if she'd somehow forgotten he'd hated the stuff all his life. He'd choked it down anyway. It had given him something to do.

Evie had been there that time too. Had Mum asked her to come as a buffer between him and her? Mum had talked to her about local things and people they both knew—and spoken to Adam as though he were a stranger. Give Evie her due, she'd done her best to include him, but Mum hadn't budged. In the end, she'd stood up, said, "I must get on," and made it clear Adam could kindly sod off.

He'd been meaning to visit again, since he'd moved back home to Glastonbury in August. Had asked Evie to mention it to Mum, get her prepared for it. He'd thought he'd had plenty of time.

Mum's heart hadn't agreed.

"I cleared out her fridge last weekend and donated all the cans and things to the food bank," Evie said, snapping Adam back to the here-and-now.

"So you were fine coming here without me last week?"

She reddened and folded her arms. "That was before we read Mum's will."

"That wasn't what I . . . Look, I don't care what the will says. This house is as much yours as mine. More, even."

Evie didn't look at him. "Anyway, I thought we'd start with her clothes. They'll need sorting and bundling for the charity shop, if they're good enough, and textile recycling for the rest."

"Right." Adam could do businesslike too. "What about furniture? Is there anything you want there? Or is that all for the charity shop too? We can get them to collect, and they can take the clothes as well."

"We've got a house full already." Yeah, and her and Paul's taste in furnishings was worlds away from Mum's mishmash of stuff bought second- or third-hand. "But what about you?" Evie went on. "Won't you want to keep it?"

"Me? I've got *one room* in a shared flat. The *smallest* room. Where would I put any of Mum's stuff?"

Evie pushed her glasses back on her nose. Large and squarish, they shouldn't have suited her but somehow did. "You don't have to sell the house. The mortgage is paid off—if nothing else, Dad was good for that. You could live here. It's just as convenient for where you work as that flat of yours."

Adam fought down the anger on Dad's behalf. She had good enough reason to resent him, whether she knew the truth or not. "Yeah, but if I sell the place, I can give you half." He'd had it all sorted in his head—he'd use his half of the money to get a flat somewhere he didn't have to share a kitchen and bathroom. He hadn't imagined getting a whole house to himself.

"That's not what Mum wanted. And I don't need the money. Paul and I are doing quite well between us."

"Yeah, but it's not fair."

"It's fine." She coloured. "And maybe I'd like the house to stay in the family, have you ever thought of that?"

"Is it really that important to you?"

She turned away. "It doesn't matter. It's your choice."

Should he give her a hug? Adam hesitated but gave in to the impulse anyway. Evie took a sharp, startled breath, but then relaxed into his embrace.

"I'll think about it," he told her. "I wasn't expecting it, you know? And I haven't got a lot of great memories from living here."

Evie sniffed, then broke free from his arms. "You were always her favourite, when you were little, do you remember that?"

Adam shook his head. "Nope. Don't all siblings think the other one's the favourite? What I remember is the way Mum's gaze used to slide off me, like she wasn't sure I was really there. Or ought to be, whatever." He'd been a constant reminder of her guilty conscience, hadn't he?

"She wasn't always like that. Something changed," Evie said slowly. "I'm not sure what, or when. But it doesn't matter now," she added briskly, right when he'd made up his mind to tell her.

Did it matter now? Maybe it didn't. They were both grown adults, not kids—okay, one kid and one uni student—trying to work out why Dad had left them. Why things had been so bad in the months—years, maybe?—before he'd gone. That time was all jumbled up in Adam's head, memories telling him things had happened before they really had. Pictures in his mind that had never been real. Echoes in his mind of childhood nightmares, most likely.

Evie was already heading upstairs, so Adam hastened to follow her. "Do you know where Mum kept her jewellery?" he asked. "We should sort that out first, in case there's anything valuable. Don't want to leave it lying around in an empty house."

"I, um, did that last week too. I've got it at home." She hesitated, tucking a strand of blond hair behind one ear. "I know legally speaking it's yours, but there's a couple of rings I'd—"

"Bloody hell, Eves. Of course you should have them. I mean, all of it. What am I going to do with Mum's jewellery? Give it to the girl I'm never going to marry?"

"Just because you're gay doesn't mean you won't have a daughter one day."

"Could say the same for you. Uh, apart from the gay thing."

Evie shook her head firmly. "No. Not going to happen."

"You might—"

"*Don't* say it. I mean it. I'm not going to change my mind, and Paul's fine with that."

"Right, then if you're that worried about cheating my hypothetical kids out of their inheritance, leave it to 'em in your will. Seriously, it's yours."

"Okay." She looked down. "I wasn't sure you were going to be so, well . . ."

"Reasonable?"

"*Nice*, I was going to say."

"What, cos I'm usually such a git?"

She rolled her eyes. "No, but . . . It's not like we've ever been close, or anything."

"Sorry," he said awkwardly.

Evie stared at him, her mouth open. "I'm not blaming *you*. I'm older. I should have made more of an effort to stay in touch."

"Hey, I was the one who left."

"You were a teenager, and you had your own problems. I should have made allowances for that."

Did she mean the coming-out-as-gay thing? Or Dad? Or Mum? "It was difficult for both of us. But it's different, now."

She nodded, then bit her lip. "I'm glad you came back. It's good to have you here."

Adam hunched his shoulders. "Yeah, well. It's home, innit?"

Evie flashed him a smile. "We should get started on the clothes."

Adam hesitated. "Uh . . . Been meaning to ask—did you sort out her, uh, papers too?"

"Apart from the will? I found the house deeds and her other important documents. She kept everything neatly filed. I've put them on the dining table so you'll be able to find them easily."

"No—I meant, letters and stuff?"

"From the solicitor?"

Certain his face was red, Adam avoided Evie's gaze. "Private letters. From . . . people she knew years ago. Stuff like that."

"I don't know what she did with those. If she ever got any. I mean, there were always a few Christmas cards from Scotland, but they got recycled."

"What about older stuff? Like, before everyone started using email?" He risked a glance at Evie.

Her eyes were wide. "That would be back before you were born. Why are you so interested?"

Adam had to turn away again. "I thought it might help me connect with her, that's all. Find out about what her life was like when she was young."

Evie laid a gentle hand on his arm, and he felt like a total git for lying to her. "If I find anything like that, I'll give it to you. But there's been nothing turned up so far. I know she used to burn receipts, so it's possible she burned letters too. She could be a bit . . . funny about privacy."

"Yeah." Adam took in a deep breath and let it out slowly. It had only ever been a faint hope that he'd find a letter or a photograph that would explain things. Explain *him*. "Come on, let's sort out those clothes."

It didn't take much time to clear Mum's wardrobe and chest of drawers, and the mundane task was . . . not quite *soothing*, as so many items sparked memories, but grounding, somehow. Helped him focus on the present. The practical. "Not a lot here, is there?" Adam said idly, folding a skirt so long out of fashion it'd probably come back in again.

"You know Mum. Never bought anything new unless something old had worn out, did she?" Evie, kneeling down by the bed, rocked back on her heels. "God, the arguments we used to have when I was growing up. 'You already have a pair of perfectly good jeans. What on earth would you want another pair for?'"

"Yeah?" It didn't ring a bell, but then there was no reason why it should.

"I suppose you were too young to remember. That's why I started working weekend jobs from when I was fourteen—so it was my money and she couldn't say a word about it."

Adam grinned. "And there was me thinking you had a fantastic work ethic. Right—just the coat cupboard downstairs, now, unless there's anything under the bed?"

"Not even dust bunnies. Oh—tell a lie. Here's her slippers." Reaching far under the bed, Evie brought out a pair of warm, woolly slippers in bright red. She sighed. They looked brand new and unworn. "I bought her these last Christmas."

"Going to keep them?" Adam said softly.

"No, they're not my style, and they'll only make me sad. Someone will love them, though." She dropped them carefully into the top of the charity shop bin-bag. "Come on, then. We're cracking through, here."

The two spare bedrooms—his and Evie's—turned out to have very little clearing to be done. Half the drawers were empty, and the rest held only spare linens, which they left where they were for now. What had happened to his childhood tat, old books, souvenirs of school trips? Charity shops, presumably, or landfill somewhere. "Did she chuck all your old stuff too?" he asked.

Evie shrugged. "Anything I really wanted to keep, I took with me when I moved out for good. How about you?"

"Same."

"What, all in one rucksack?"

Adam shrugged. "If I've managed ten years without it, I'm pretty sure I don't need it." He'd never been one for holding on to stuff. At least, not since he'd left home at sixteen with only what he could carry in a backpack.

"Nine. It was nine years ago you went to Dad's." Evie was silent for a moment. "She didn't even tell me until the next time I visited and I asked where you were. I was all, 'Is Adam out with his mates?' And she said, 'No, he's living with your father now.'"

Adam fought down a surge of annoyance. So Mum hadn't told Evie he was gone. Was he supposed to feel guilty for that too? "Let's move on," he said, and jogged down the stairs.

Evie followed at a slower pace.

The downstairs coat cupboard was hardly bulging at the seams, despite also being home to the ironing board and the hoover. Mum had a decent-quality waterproof that appeared almost new, a light mac, and a big, chocolate-brown wool coat, worn thin in places. The only other things hanging on the rail were the peg bag and a long, dark-grey man's overcoat, which Adam pulled off its hanger in amazement. "Was this Dad's? Why did she keep it all these years?"

Evie frowned. "Maybe she was waiting for you to grow into it? Try it on."

Adam laughed, and slipped his arms into the sleeves. His hands failed to appear out of the ends. "How do I look?"

"Like a little kid playing dress-up. Come on, I'll add it to the charity shop stuff. How is Dad?" Evie asked as she shoved it in the bag, her tone only slightly forced.

"He's okay. Still working hard and golfing harder." Adam hesitated. Should he tell her?

No. This wasn't the time, with Mum barely cold in her grave and the two of them reconnecting after so many years. And if she knew already . . . he wasn't sure he wanted to find out right now.

Adam pulled out the next item: Mum's winter coat. "She must have had this, what, twenty years?"

"Not that long. Ten, twelve, maybe? Not more than fifteen. She had a lovely red coat when I was little. Bright, with black buttons."

"You sure?" The dark brown coat was the only one he recognised. It felt lighter than he'd imagined. Or remembered, maybe. His mum had worn it to pick him up from school on dark winter afternoons, on those treasured occasions she hadn't left him to make his own way home, and there was a picture in his head of her wearing it one bonfire night too, with the rare treat of a hot dog fresh from the barbecue.

Hadn't it smelt smoky for weeks afterwards? Adam couldn't recall a lot of his childhood. But there had been rainy afternoons when he'd pretended to be a small creature hibernating, snuggled up under Mum's coat, with a book on his bent-up knees to read by torchlight.

Books had been his world. He'd spent hours in the library, first the one at school and later the one in town, poring over tales about magic and fairies. Myths, legends, and stuff people had made up. He'd first met Gwyn ap Nudd in those stolen hours, safe in his fortress of books. Finn MacCool and Beowulf. Merlin and Arthur too, although since he'd seen them in films and on TV, they didn't seem so real to him somehow. Stories of courtly lovers and knights doing battle with monstrous beasts. Trickster elves that would twist your words and snatch a child from its cradle to leave a changeling in its place.

He'd wondered what it would be like to be a fairy child, his true parents far away and yet so near, in Avalon, under the hill. To search them out, once he was a man, to proclaim proudly, *Look, I've found you. I'm worthy.* To be welcomed in with open arms to a world of wonders.

Of course, real life wasn't like that, was it?

"It's hard, isn't it?" Evie said softly. "The memories kind of hit you, don't they?"

Adam nodded, his throat unexpectedly tight. "Think this is good enough for the charity shop?"

Evie made a face. "Probably not. It's had a good innings, though."

It was crazy to feel a pang as the coat went into the bin bag. It was only a thing, right? Adam had never set much store in things.

Evie did, though, didn't she?

"You know you can take anything you want, don't you?" Adam tried to let his voice show his sincerity without betraying his crippling guilt. "I don't even know why Mum left everything to me. It doesn't make sense."

Evie shrugged. "I'm sure she felt you were most in need of the money."

"Yeah, but I'm not, am I? I've got a job. I do all right."

"Not exactly running the business, are you?"

"It takes time, okay? Nobody starts at the top."

"I don't . . . Adam, don't take this the wrong way, but why didn't you stay in graphic design?"

Adam huffed. "I got fed up of all that soulless corporate stuff I was doing. Arguing over one stupid logo after another. Tattooing's . . . freer. And it's getting more mainstream, so don't look at me like that. It's not all death metal fans and bikers these days. Not that there's anything wrong with them."

"*Mainstream.* You mean women having a midlife crisis?"

"Why, you having one now? Could do you a discount." Not that thirty-four was middle-aged, but when they'd been kids, she'd never let him forget that she was almost ten years older and, supposedly, wiser. Payback was sweet.

Evie raised an eyebrow. "Sure you can afford that? Designing logos may not be inspiring, but I bet you earned more than whatever you're getting from the illustrated woman."

Adam surprised himself with a snort at that description. "Sasha's a good boss. And I've only just started. I can't expect a huge salary."

"Why didn't you stay at that tattooist's in London until you'd got . . . certified or whatever it is?"

"It doesn't work like that. I mean, yeah, I did a course in London, and I was pretty much at the end of my apprenticeship, but body-art licences are local—I'd have had to re-register with the council here anyway. With Sasha, it's about learning how she runs her studio and her keeping an eye on me until she can trust me to know what I'm doing." Adam shrugged. "And it felt like it was time, that's all. Time to come home." Not to Mum's, but to Glastonbury. He'd felt the tug of the place, but that would sound crazy to Evie, so he didn't say it aloud.

"I am sorry, you know," Evie said.

"What for?" Adam could think of a few things she might be sorry for, but he didn't like to presume.

"That you didn't get to see her before she died."

Yeah, that was one of them. "Hey, it's not like you physically stopped me coming here." It was one of the reasons his own conscience was working overtime.

"No, but . . . I kept telling you she needed more time before she'd be ready to see you."

"And I trusted your judgement. You weren't to know what would happen. She was only fifty-nine—what age is that?" He paused. It wasn't only that he'd lost the chance to reconnect with Mum. He'd lost the chance to ever ask her about his father too. "Although . . . six weeks was a bit longer than I was expecting."

Evie coloured. "Yes, well, she'd got a lot worse, hadn't she, since you last saw her."

Adam blinked. "What do you mean, *worse*?" From what he could remember, she'd always been fine with Evie. It was only him she couldn't seem to relate to.

"You know. Funny. Not . . ." Evie shook her head. "Not normal. People used to come and tell me about things she'd said. Acting all concerned. As if."

Yeah, small towns. You had to love them. "What kinds of things?"

"She had this obsession with doubles. Doppelgangers. She used to say she'd seen them going into people's houses when they were out."

"Christ." Adam's face felt weird. Screwed up. "I didn't know."

"It's not as though you could have helped." She didn't say it unkindly. Just factually. Maybe that was worse.

"Do you know what was causing it? Was she on, like, medication for it?"

Evie's lips were tight. "She wouldn't go and see the doctor, would she? And I wasn't about to have her sectioned."

What if something had happened? What if she'd harmed herself? Adam didn't ask. It was too late for questions like that to be useful, and in any case, did he have the right?

And yeah, she wasn't wrong about Mum and doctors. Soon after he'd started secondary school, Adam had been in agony with an ear infection and had only got medical attention in the end because the school nurse had insisted. Strange how he couldn't remember it being an issue when he'd had his accident. Of course, Dad had still been around then. Maybe he'd put his foot down.

"I thought maybe it was early-onset Alzheimer's, although not all the symptoms seemed to fit. Maybe it was that combined with some depressive condition?" Evie said quietly. "She'd aged, too. She looked more like seventy, and it wasn't simply that her hair was all grey. She *moved* like she was old. I was worried . . ." She broke off and fiddled with her shoulder-length blond hair, tucking a strand behind her ear. "I was worried what you'd think when you saw her."

Christ. *Had* he seen her? Adam had wondered, when he'd come back here to live, whether he'd bump into Mum in town one weekend or lunchtime. He'd never seen her in the crowds—but how much attention had he paid to the little old ladies with their shopping trolleys? "Did you think I'd blame you?" he demanded to cover the way his stomach had dropped.

"*No.*" Her tone verged on snappish. "I thought you might be shocked, that's all."

"Sorry." Adam sent her a rueful smile. "Think I am. Shocked, I mean. I remember her with brown hair. She wasn't grey when I saw her . . . three years ago, was it?"

"She stopped dying it soon afterwards."

He blinked. "I didn't know she dyed her hair."

"She'd be pleased to hear you say that. She wanted it to look natural." Evie sighed. "Come on, let's do the living room. Even if you decide to stay, I don't suppose you'll want all Mum's knickknacks."

"Dunno. Any of them, like, family heirlooms?"

Evie snorted. "Tat she picked up at car boot sales, more like."

Sure enough, the ornaments on mantelpiece, shelves and windowsills were an odd collection. Adam wondered what she'd seen in them to make her shell out the 50p or a pound or whatever they'd cost her. Was the Toby jug in memory of a family member who'd used to collect them—her gran, maybe? Had the hand-whittled wooden figure borne some resemblance to someone she'd once cared for? They'd never know now. Adam hadn't met any of his Scottish relatives, although he was fairly sure his grandparents on that side had still been alive when he was born. It was like Mum had moved down here and decided to make a clean break with her past.

Speaking of clean breaks . . . "It must have been pretty rough on you," Adam said awkwardly. "I mean, Dad leaving right when you went away to uni."

Evie thrust a vase into a box with unnecessary force. There was no crash of shattering china, so hopefully it had survived. "You know what? I was glad when he left. I wished he'd done it sooner."

"What?" Adam stared at her.

"Oh, come on. You know what it was like back then. It'd been awful for, God, I don't know how long. The last happy time was when I got my GCSE results—you remember, we went out for pizza to celebrate, and you ate too much garlic bread and were sick?"

Adam rolled his eyes. "Yeah. Happy times." He didn't recall it, actually, but sue him, he'd been, what, six? Seven, maybe, since his birthday was in July and results came out in August.

"After that, everything seemed to go wrong. I got dumped by Nathan-the-bastard, you had your accident, and Mum and Dad's marriage went to pot. And he kept going on about wanting to move."

"What, Nathan?" Adam was losing the thread here.

"*Dad*, obviously. It was like he wasn't happy with anything anymore. It was just after his company really took off, and he got the Mercedes. Suddenly nothing was good enough for him at home. Not our house, not Mum, not even us."

"Hey, it was a stressful time for him, okay?" It sounded weak even to Adam. None of what she was saying seemed familiar—the car, yeah, and Dad being busy at work a lot, but not the rest. It must have all gone over his head at the time. He couldn't even recall the talk of moving, which must have been Dad casting about for any way to make things better, to make a fresh start, before finally giving up and leaving them.

"It was all right for you, wasn't it? You could stick your nose in a book anywhere." Adam winced. She didn't seem to notice. "But all my friends were here, and I was right in the middle of my A levels, and all he could go on about was moving to the other side of the country. Like it didn't matter how I felt about it. Or how Mum did. All so he could have a big flash house and a better postcode. And then he went off without us anyway. I hope he's happy now."

Was he happy? Dad seemed to have a fair degree of contentment. Then again, he'd never remarried. Probably too wary to trust anyone that far, after what Mum had done.

"He couldn't even be bothered to come to the funeral," Evie went on, her voice cracking.

"Hey, it wasn't that he couldn't be bothered. He just . . . didn't feel right about turning up." Couldn't face the daughter he'd left behind, most likely, but Adam didn't think telling Evie that would make her feel any better.

"I'm not mad at you for being on his side," Evie said after a moment. "I get it. I really do. Things weren't great with Mum, so you went to live with Dad. And I'm glad it worked out for you. But I'm never going to forgive him for breaking up our home, and I never want to see him again."

Shit. He should tell her, shouldn't he?

What, so that then they could all play happy families, only without Mum? Feelings weren't that simple. *Grief* wasn't that simple, especially when it was this new and raw.

"Anyway," Evie said, standing up. "It's time we had a tea break. Or coffee, for the philistines. Are you sure you're British?" she went on, striding to the kitchen. "Sometimes I think the fairies left you."

A flash of memory: Evie, much younger and angry with him for using her pens. She'd said the same thing to him then, and he'd dreamed about it for days. Adam stared after her for a moment, unsettled, then shook his head and followed her to the kitchen.

As they left the house, the sun was setting in streaks of red and orange. The skies had cleared a little while they'd worked, and Adam turned to gaze at the shadowy mound of the tor. He'd always loved that they could see it from here. He'd been so envious of Mum having the front bedroom, so she could see it from her window, while he'd had to make do with a view of the back garden and the fields beyond.

He should take a walk up there. It had been too long since he'd paid his respects to Gwyn ap Nudd, king of the underworld. Adam gave a low huff of amusement. He might no longer believe in fairies, but the tor called to him, even so.

"Something funny?" Evie asked, getting out her car keys.

"No, just thinking about taking a walk. Getting some air in my lungs."

She gave a faint smile. "Good idea, after all day cooped up indoors."

Was she angling for an invitation? "You, uh, want to join me?" Adam asked, hoping it didn't sound as awkward as he felt. Much as he wanted to reconnect with his sister, he needed some time on his own.

"No, I'd better get back. Thank you." Now she seemed awkward.

Maybe we've got more in common than I thought.

Adam tried to show the rush of affection he felt for her as they said their goodbyes, and from the warmth in her eyes, maybe it'd got through.

That was one long-neglected relationship rekindled. Time for another. He got on his Yamaha and turned it in the direction of the tor.

CHAPTER FOUR

Corin woke up Monday morning wishing he'd taken the day off, but the move really hadn't warranted it and it was too late now. So he made himself some toast and coffee, and steeled himself to sit at his desk. Getting down to work felt strange. Same old routine in entirely different surroundings. He'd worked mainly from home since before the accident, the company having drastically downsized their office workspace the previous year. Some of his colleagues had complained about feeling isolated, but it'd never bothered Corin, although he'd used to look forward to meeting up in person with his team every so often.

Now it was his worst nightmare. With the reduced office space had come hot desking, meaning anyone could be sitting anywhere at any time, and there were no family photos or mascots on desks to give him a clue to their identity. Another plus to the move here: with luck, his manager wouldn't expect his physical presence in the office so often, and he could use the distance as an excuse to avoid social events altogether. At least in online meetings everyone had a name tag so he knew who he was talking to.

He had an online meeting at eleven, which would be a test of his new wi-fi. Given his profession as software engineer, it would be embarrassing if the setup failed, so he spared some time before the meeting to check his upload/download speeds. All seemed to be performing well, and he clicked on Join Meeting at one minute to eleven with reasonable confidence, then carried on drafting an email while he waited for the others to turn up.

"Hi, Corin." A female voice.

Corin glanced at his screen and briefly panicked. "Hi, Sophie's mum," he forced out, hoping it sounded more droll than desperate.

"Oh, did I not change that? Sorry!" The woman laughed, and a moment later, the name tag changed to *Claire*.

Corin's heartbeat eased off a little. It was stupid of him to get so worked up about it—who else could she have been anyway? There were only the three of them supposed to be in this meeting—but damn it, he'd *relied* on having that name tag. Although he knew he should get into the habit of identifying people by voice and other cues, the jarring disconnect between the familiar sound and the unfamiliar face always seemed to throw him. "That's okay. How are you?"

"Fine, thank you. How did the move go? All unpacked yet?"

"Getting there. So, uh, Sophie's your daughter?" Claire had only recently joined the team, and he hardly knew her. And they had to talk about something while they were waiting for Peter to turn up, late as usual, and Corin would rather it wasn't about him.

"Yes, she's three. My oldest. The other two are twins, Ollie and Luke, and they're nearly a year now."

"Must be a handful."

She laughed. "You're not wrong there. Do you have— Oh, here's Peter."

Peter's prematurely bald head appeared, and he waved. "Hi, Claire. Sorry I'm late. Hi, Corin. It's me. Peter," he added with gentle emphasis.

"Yes. Thank you, Peter." He was clearly trying to be considerate to the disabled person on the team, but Corin would have preferred he hadn't made it quite so obvious.

Claire's hand shot to her mouth. "Oh, sh—sugar. I should have introduced myself, shouldn't I? Sorry, Corin. I forgot."

Corin had blanked his own face on his screen, so couldn't tell if the flush that crept over him was visible. Human resources must have sent a memo round about him. *Be kind to the man with brain damage.* "No, it's fine. Shall we get down to business?"

Peter coughed. Possibly as a subtle reminder that *he* was the designated team lead, despite Corin's pre-accident seniority. "Excellent suggestion, Corin. Right, so, we've had a customer note an intermittent error on the rendering..."

The conversation turned technical for a while, and Corin relaxed. Until they got onto a discussion of base code.

Claire pursed her lips. "I thought we were supposed to be standardising? That was all everyone was talking about before I went on maternity leave."

"Yes, but that was Blair's baby, wasn't it? Er, pun not intended. And since we lost him . . ." Peter reddened. "Um, sorry, Corin. Painful subject for you."

"For all of us," Claire insisted. "I was on his team back when I started working here. I couldn't believe it when I heard the news. He was such a lovely man. So, well, *lively*."

"Yes, but Corin was in the car when it happened," Peter went on doggedly, as if any of them could possibly have forgotten that.

"It's fine," Corin said shortly. It wasn't fine—they had no idea how bloody fine it wasn't—but he could be professional.

"The memorial service was lovely," Claire put in. "Such a shame you couldn't go."

Peter cleared his throat and leaned forward, his bald head looming large on Corin's screen. "I'm sure Corin would have been there like a shot. If he hadn't been in hospital with a brain injury."

She rolled her eyes. "I just thought he might want to know about it. You were friends with him, weren't you, Corin?"

"Yes." Hopefully his curt tone would finally clue her in that he did *not* want to talk about Blair's death. So what if it was a lie, and Blair and he had never really been friends?

Lovers, yes, if you could call it that when one of them had held a totally different view of their relationship to the other. Enemies . . . that too, in the end, although it ripped at his heart—or was it his guilty conscience?—to think of it. But never friends. And no force on earth could have dragged him to that memorial service.

"Corin?" Peter's voice startled him.

He swallowed. "Sorry, I missed that. Connection froze." God, if he was hooked up to a polygraph right now it would look like an earthquake had hit it.

"Really? It's been fine on my end," Claire said blithely. "Maybe you should check your setup? I was having a moan about the analysis tools—I'd forgotten how bloody useless they always are. So I've been making a few tweaks, trial and error . . ."

By the time the meeting finished soon after twelve, Corin was more than ready to take a lunch break—emphasis on the break, rather than the lunch. As he was about to sign off, though, a private message popped up from Peter. *Can you stay online for a minute?*

Hopefully Corin's sigh hadn't been audible. *Fine*, he messaged back.

Once Claire had cheerily waved goodbye and it was just the two of them, Peter cleared his throat. "Corin, I've been wanting to have a private word. I hope you're okay with me as team lead. It's only until we're sure you're, ah, up to speed with things you've missed."

"It's fine. Meena spoke with me about it." *"Best to ease you back into work,"* Corin's manager had said. Corin had mentally added *until we're sure your brain isn't totally fucked.*

"I know, but are you sure you're okay with it? We've always got on well, and I'd hate to fall out over—"

Corin forced a smile. "It's fine, really. It's the sensible course of action." Team lead had the most client contact, for a start. And maybe he wasn't totally fine with his effective demotion, but it wasn't Peter's fault, was it? "Don't worry about it."

He wasn't sure but thought Peter looked relieved. "That's great. That's a load off my mind. Thanks for being so good about it. It can't be easy for you, with all the . . ." Peter made a vague, handwavy gesture that was presumably supposed to convey *Traumatic Brain Injury*. "Right, lunch then. I'll see you Wednesday—unless anything comes up, of course. You know you can always get in touch if you're . . . Yeah. You know."

"Of course." Corin kept the smile going until he'd turned off his video and left the meeting. Why did an hour of interacting with his colleagues feel so long—and so draining—when a day coding could go by in a flash? He saved his work, then grabbed a jacket and headed out without pausing to check the weather.

Luckily for him it was a cool autumn day, the skies grey but not threatening as Corin clattered down the metal staircase and out into the streets. He wandered through Glastonbury, marvelling anew at its eclectic selection of shops, so unlike the usual UK high street.

Maybe in somewhere like Tintagel, which had its own King Arthur connection, you got this mass of crystal emporia, hippie clothing stores, and general weird and witchy stuff, but the majority of places were very similar to Swindon, with its chain stores and restaurants. His old home village of Avebury, with its Neolithic stone circles, had its Henge Shop, but Glastonbury, being far bigger, could accommodate whole streets catering to those in search of spirituality.

Corin wasn't certain why he liked it so much—God knew he was never actually going to shop at any of these places—but somehow the uniqueness of the town lifted his spirits. Maybe it was the reassurance that there was somewhere for everyone, including those who didn't precisely fit into the norm? Corin must look incredibly boring and normal to the new-agers who shopped for dreamcatchers and pyramids, but he'd never really felt like he fitted in. Even before the accident.

There were also plenty of tattooists' studios. Passing one, Corin was struck with the idea of getting himself inked. Giving himself some kind of identifying tag he could latch on to, so he could be sure whose face he saw when he looked in the mirror. Well, at least when he had his shirt off—he wasn't quite desperate enough, or unconventional enough (see: boring and normal) to get a tattoo on his face or neck.

As he paused, the woman inside glanced up and caught his eye through the window. She was striking, with her hair bright scarlet except where it'd been shaved on one side, and a large septum piercing that glinted in the sudden ray of sunlight that had emerged from behind a cloud.

She raised a challenging eyebrow, and Corin realised he was staring. She probably thought he was judging her on her appearance. Or he fancied her.

Oh, what the hell. He pushed the door open and went in.

Close to, the woman's eyebrows resolved into a series of tattooed-on dots, and there was a death's-head moth inked onto her throat. Her earlobes were stretched out around hoops approaching an inch in diameter.

Corin found himself smiling. He'd know her again, no problem. "Morning. Uh, afternoon, now, I guess."

"Ah, who's counting? Thinking about getting some ink?" She matched his smile, and her tone was warm. "I've got a waiting list myself, but Adam could do you in a couple of weeks if you're not choosy as to your artist."

Adam? He must be the guy in the back of the shop working on a young woman's shoulder. He was dark-haired, with no visible ink or memorable features. Corin's heart sank.

The woman was still talking. "He's cheaper, too, cos he's new, but he's a good artist, no worries there. Did you have something in mind, or do you want to have a flick through the books? I'm Sasha, by the way."

"Corin. And I'm not sure . . . Just moved here, actually." As if that was relevant to anything.

"Oh yeah? Where are you from, then?" She sounded genuinely interested.

"Swindon." It was close enough, and he didn't feel like being more specific. Saying he'd lived in Avebury would only lead to assumptions about him having druidical leanings, where in fact anyone wanting a meaningful discussion of the Web of Life would find Corin sadly disappointing. He'd liked the place, that was all. And it had been convenient for work.

"Bloody hell, my lover, you're going to find it a bit different around here, then. But the scenery's lush. You seen much of it yet?"

"No." It came out harsher than he'd meant it to, and he softened his tone. "Haven't had time—I only moved in on Sunday."

"How did you choose to move here, then, if you don't know the place? Stick a pin in a map?" She laughed and carried on without waiting for an answer. "I've got a sleeve coming in now, so how about you take a look in the books and see if anything grabs you?"

Even as Corin took the proffered file, she was turning away to greet a large, heavily bearded man coming in the door, dressed like a biker in worn black leather. He walked like a biker too, with an easy, wide-legged gait. "All right there, Scratch?" she said cheerily.

The bearded man stepped forward with a scowl, and Corin could see the spiderweb tattoo on his neck. "Sasha, you tart, you been cheating on me again?"

Corin took an involuntary step backward.

Sasha laughed. "Sit down in that chair and stop frightening my customers away, you daft bastard. This is Corin. He's new around here."

"You don't waste your time, do you, girl?" The man—*Scratch*?—turned to Corin, and the scowl was now a grin. Coming from a man of his muscular bulk, it wasn't any less intimidating. "A virgin, are we? Don't worry, she's always gentle."

Corin hoped he was talking about tattoos. "I was only thinking about it," he said, handing the file back to Sasha. "I'll let you get on."

"Hang on a mo, I'll introduce you to Adam. Adam!" She yelled it out before Corin could tell her not to bother. "You got a minute?"

The man in the back glanced up. "Just finishing up here. Gimme two secs?"

"Uh, I'd really better be off." Corin cursed his failure of courage—God, he'd never be able to come in here again—but he'd met two new people in the space of five minutes and his anxiety was rocketing at the thought of a third. Especially this Adam, who seemed to have no distinguishing features at all. He was white, with short, dark hair and a tall, lean build—the sort of build Corin had always found attractive, which made it even worse. Presumably, given where he worked, he must have tattoos, but they were covered up by a long-sleeved T-shirt and jeans.

The man's—Adam's—expression changed, although Corin wasn't sure what it meant. "Shit. Hey, please wait? I won't be a mo, and I want to apologise."

Sasha whistled, badly, between her teeth. "Oh, like that, is it?"

Corin didn't have a clue what either of them was talking about, and he hated it. He'd have left, but Adam was already coming over, his customer waving him on.

"No, Sasha, it bloody isn't, all right? Look, mate—"

"Corin," Sasha supplied.

"Right. Corin." Adam stopped in front of him. "I'm not mad, okay?"

That sounded like he thought *Corin* was the one who should be apologising, although God knew what for. But wasn't there something vaguely familiar about that voice? That earnest, pleading tone teased at Corin's memory, the recollection never quite coming close enough to catch. "That's . . . good?"

Adam was nodding. "I— My mum died recently. Got my head in a mess, that's all. Don't normally go around seeing ghosts in the mist."

The pieces slotted into place. Corin let out a breath as relief cascaded through him. "Oh, it was you on the tor?"

"Uh, yeah." Adam's face had reddened. "Sorry. Guess it didn't make as much impact on you as it did on me."

"No, that's not— I'm not good with faces."

"Too busy looking at other bits of him, were you?" Scratch put in and laughed.

Corin froze. God, had he been so obviously checking Adam out?

"Simon Greczik, you shut your mouth and get your shirt off," Sasha hissed.

"If only you were always this eager to get me out of my clothes." Scratch mock-sighed and shrugged off his jacket.

Corin scrubbed his face with his hands. This was all getting too much. "Sorry. I mean, I'm sorry about your mum. Although I'm glad you hadn't actually lost someone on the tor?" It came out sounding like a question, as he realised it might not be the most tactful thing to say in the circumstances, however much the news reassured him personally. The thought of an elderly woman wandering in the mist on the tor had been nagging at him. "I should be going. Sorry."

"Tell you what," Adam said, and his voice had softened. "Why don't you sit down for a minute? I'll settle up with Jodie, and then I'm free for half an hour, so we can talk about what you might want me to do for you."

"I hope you're talking about the ink," Scratch, now shirtless in Sasha's chair, said with an audible leer.

This whole situation was absurd. Corin let out a despairing laugh and sat down on the leather sofa by the window. At least the tattoo art file gave him something harmless to focus on. He flicked through a bewildering variety of designs. Some were photos of customers, and some were sketches. They mostly seemed far more extensive and elaborate than anything he could imagine for himself.

"You okay, mate?" Adam said five minutes later, after the girl had departed, her cling-film wrapped shoulder now hidden under her hoodie. "Can I get you a cup of tea?"

"No, thanks. I'm fine," Corin said, and wished a moment later he'd said yes. Then again, juggling a hot drink and the heavy ring binder seemed like a recipe for disaster. And he didn't want to prolong this encounter, did he?

"Okay, cool. Uh, so, I'm guessing we're both equally crap at making good first impressions?"

Corin laughed despite himself. "Technically I've been making a bad second impression. Unless you're saying you didn't really notice me on the tor, either?" Which was a stupid thing to say—after all, Adam had recognised him. Envy twisted briefly in his gut.

Adam smiled. "If you're fishing for compliments, I'll warn you, I'm crap at those too."

"That's okay, I'm terrible at accepting them anyway." God, were they actually having a conversation? A flirtation, even?

No. He mustn't read too much into this. Especially with how bad he was at reading people these days.

"But, yeah, I noticed you," Adam said.

Was Corin imagining the emphasis in his words? He searched Adam's face for any clue but found nothing. Christ, it was far too warm in here. "You, um, go up there often? I mean, I imagine as a local it's nothing more than part of the scenery to you." Oh God, kill him now.

"Nah, I've always liked the tor. And I've only recently moved back here—lived in London for nearly ten years."

"Oh, that makes sense. With your accent." Corin hadn't consciously noticed it, but there was barely a trace of a Somerset burr in his voice. "Did your family move away?"

"Something like that." His tone didn't invite further enquiry.

"Sorry, none of my business." Corin was an idiot. Given the recent death of his mum, family would be the last thing Adam wanted to talk about with a stranger.

"No, it's fine. Just complicated. Now, did you see a design you liked in the books?"

Safe ground. Corin told himself he was relieved the conversation was no longer personal. Although wasn't choosing an image to be permanently inked into his skin intensely personal? "I'm not sure.

I don't want anything big. Or intricate. Something clear." He was explaining this badly. "More stylized than photographic?"

Nonetheless, Adam nodded. "Celtic symbol, maybe? They're pretty popular." He grabbed a piece of paper and a pen from the front desk, and sketched a couple of quick, three-pointed designs. "There's the triquetra or the triskelion. Symbols of a triune deity—doesn't have to be the Christian one. Or there are other Celtic knots. The tree of life is another popular one—you probably know what that looks like, right?"

Corin nodded. He'd seen it in several shop windows on the way here. "Not that one." He wasn't sure he could sit still while someone etched a symbol of life and wholeness on his skin. "Any others?"

"You've moved here recently, right? So maybe you want something to symbolise a new stage of life? Like, a transition? If you're going for Celtic symbols, there's this. It tends to be more women who go for it, mind." With impressive ease, Adam sketched a stylised butterfly, its wings reminiscent of the knots of the triquetra.

"Yes. That one." Corin had rarely felt so certain of anything recently.

"Yeah? It stands for rebirth, transformation. People often choose it if they've been through a difficult time. Like, an illness or getting out of a shitty relationship. But, yeah, more women than men."

Was he trying to talk him out of it? "I'm sure."

Adam nodded. "Okay, cool. Where do you want it?"

"Here." Corin placed his hand high on his chest, above his heart. Where the tattoo would be hidden by his shirt, but he could easily see it by pulling the collar aside.

"No problem. Had any ink done before?"

Wasn't it obvious? Most likely Adam was simply being tactful. "No."

"Okay, then you'll be glad to hear you haven't chosen the *most* painful place. With your build, it'll be sitting on muscle, not directly over the bone. And with a small design—I'm assuming you'd like it pretty much the size I drew, right? A couple of inches?"

Corin nodded, relieved that on this, at least, they could communicate clearly.

"Then that'll be pretty quick, with solid lines and no shading. Shouldn't take more than an hour, depending."

"Depending on what?"

Adam laughed. "On how good you are at sitting still, and whether you need breaks. How are you with pain?"

Corin shrugged. "Okay." He'd had constant, severe headaches for weeks after the accident, and got them occasionally even now, when stressed. He could cope with an hour or so under the needle.

"Right, then. We can make an appointment for you in around a month, if that's okay?"

"Not sooner? Your, uh, colleague seemed to think you'd be able to fit me in in a couple of weeks."

Adam's mouth twisted. "Thing is, it's going to be on your skin for a long time, so you want to be sure it's what you want. Best to take a while to think it over, and no worries if you change your mind, either about the design or about having a tattoo at all. I mean, you seemed like you were rethinking the idea, earlier—and there's no shame in that."

"I won't change my mind." Why would he? It wasn't as if anyone else was ever likely to see it. Corin had never been one for going around with his shirt off simply because the sun was shining, and as for lovers . . .

He'd deleted the dating app from his phone. It hadn't brought him anything but grief, and now seeing an endless succession of indistinguishable faces seemed like a mockery.

"No offence, mate, but there's been plenty of people who've said that and had to eat their words later on. Tell you what, we'll split the difference. Three weeks. That okay?"

Corin nodded. "Fine. Thanks."

"Great, let's have a look at the diary. And, uh, so you know: Sasha's not so much my colleague. More my boss. She built this studio up from nothing, and I'm just the new boy. Uh, not that you need to worry. I've been a tattoo artist for over a year now, and before that I was in graphic design, so I know my art. Christ, sorry about all this. You don't want to hear my life story."

Didn't he? "Is it very different?"

"What, tattooing from graphic design? Is it ever. Don't think I was cut out for all that corporate stuff."

Corin wanted to ask why he'd gone into it in the first place, but it was none of his business. He coughed. "So, uh, three weeks?"

"I'll get the diary." Adam went over to the desk and returned with an actual paper book, then flicked through its pages. "Midweek okay? It'll be more like six weeks if you want a Saturday."

"I can take a half day off. You know you could do all that electronically," Corin couldn't help adding as Adam picked up the pen he'd used before.

"Not my call. But I like the old-fashioned way. Probably why I didn't get on as a graphic designer—it's all digital art these days. Everyone wants to save the trees, but who ever thinks about the poor electrons forced into a life of servitude?" He grinned, a wide, easy smile with lines at the corners of his mouth that showed it was a common expression for him. "Mondays okay for you generally?"

Corin blinked at the sudden return to business. Except it hadn't been sudden, had it? That was what he was here for, not to get lost in the smile of a man he wouldn't know the next time he saw him. "Uh, midweek would be better, actually. I'm on my lunch hour at the moment." And in danger of seriously running over at this rate. He'd have to work late tonight to make up.

"Cool. Wednesday the twentieth, then? Two o'clock do you?"

"That works for me." Corin didn't point out that it was closer to two weeks away than three. Maybe Adam had accepted that Corin wasn't the sort to change his mind.

Maybe he wants to see you again sooner, a treacherous voice whispered in his head as he paid his deposit. Corin stamped down on that thought hard. It wasn't like that, and it never would be. His spirits sank. "I'd better be going," he said quickly. "I'll see you on the twentieth."

CHAPTER FIVE

"L iked him, did you?" Sasha asked approximately two seconds after the door had closed behind Corin.

"He liked you all right," Scratch put in over his shoulder. "Couldn't keep his eyes off you."

"Hold still," Sasha snapped. "You want this blurred?"

"He's . . . interesting," Adam allowed. And no, he hadn't minded being the subject of that intense gaze. Not at all. "Seemed a bit nervous. Which you weren't helping with, mate."

Scratch laughed. "Shows he likes you."

"Did he tell you anything about himself, Sash?"

She shook her head. "Only that he's just moved here from Swindon."

Swindon? Adam hadn't pictured Corin as a city dweller. Maybe he'd lived somewhere on the outskirts. "He reckoned we should go electronic with the diary. Think he works in IT?"

Sasha pursed her lips. "He didn't look like a nerd."

"Oh?" Scratch demanded. "What does a nerd look like, then?"

She grinned. "Skinny, pale, big heavy glasses. And hunched shoulders from being bent over a screen all day and a games console all night."

"So you wouldn't call me a nerd, then?" Scratch continued more mildly.

"No. You're a metalhead."

"But he likes Doctor Who and comic book stuff," Adam reminded her. "And gaming."

"My point exactly." Scratch nodded sagely.

"Keep still. That makes you a metalhead with side interests. Not a nerd."

"So your definition of a nerd is that they're short-sighted, too thin and have bad posture?" Adam raised an eyebrow. "Okay, then, I agree with you. He doesn't look like a nerd."

"See? I knew you fancied him." Sasha grinned, and Scratch laughed.

"Shut up. I hate you both."

Adam thought about him later, as he rode his Yamaha home from work. Corin. The nervous new guy with the intense dark eyes and the athletic build. And the great smile when he forgot to be nervous. Corin had liked him too; he was sure of it. But for some reason the guy had hesitated, as if he was wary of getting too close. He'd been like that up on the tor—God, when Adam had made such an idiot of himself.

No prizes for guessing why the bloke was skittish, then. Who'd want to hang around with the weirdo who saw dead people? Adam was lucky Corin had still agreed to let him do his ink.

The shared house he roomed in was along a narrow street turned into a cul-de-sac by a metal barrier across the middle. It'd presumably been put up to stop drivers using the residential street as a rat-run into town. At some point in its life someone had absent-mindedly tried to do that anyway: there was a massive dent in the middle, and the metal had rusted all around it. There was a bunch of kids kicking a football against it right now and the continual dull *clang* made Adam's shoulders bunch as he trundled his bike up the overgrown driveway and under the unbroken part of the corrugated plastic lean-to. Then he cursed—

someone had smashed a pint glass out here and not cleared up the shards.

Great. A puncture would be just what he needed.

He opened the front door with the usual combination of shoulder push and kick to free it where it stuck, and nearly fell over a girl sitting on the floor. She was all bare legs and shoulders like cold weather only happened to other people, and laughing her head off while she smoked a roll-up. The sickly-sweet reek of weed was overpowering.

Next to her, his equally skinny legs stretched out to form a further trip hazard, was Bry, one of Adam's housemates.

Adam sighed. "Do you have to do this in the house?"

Bry gave an exaggerated eye roll. "Well, *duh*. Live next door to the feds, don't we? Can't do it in the garden."

"One. We live next to *one* copper, who's not even home right now." The car had been gone from PC Williams' (pristine) drive, and no lights were on.

The girl held out her roll-up. "C'mon, chill."

"No, thanks." He'd tried cannabis on two separate occasions, and each time he'd ended up anything but *chill*. The first time he'd put the racing heartbeat and gut-wrenching anxiety down to worry that his dad would catch him, but his second attempt while at uni had convinced him he was better off sticking to the beer.

"Bo-ring!" Bry's expression was of friendly contempt.

His girlfriend laughed. "Aw, will Mummy be cwoss if you do drugs?"

Adam froze. His pulse thudded in his ears.

"Uh, babe?" Bry said slowly. "Not good. His mum just died."

She gave a nervous giggle, and somehow it broke the spell. With an effort, Adam's fists unclenched. He stepped over Bry's legs and made his way into the kitchen. Time to grab that beer and take it to his room.

Except the beer—*his* beer, his last one—was gone from the fridge, and the leftover pasta he'd planned to have for his tea had vanished too. Adam cast a furious glance over at the sink and yeah, there the container was. To add insult to injury, it was still half full, and had a fork sticking out of it.

As he stared in seething disbelief, someone started blaring thrash metal upstairs, the base notes throbbing through the ceiling. Bry bellowed out, "Keep it down, you wanker!"

His girlfriend shrieked with laughter and yelled, "Your music su-ucks!" Someone banged hard on a wall.

Christ. Adam closed his eyes briefly. He was paying rent for this? When he owned a whole flippin' house that was empty and waiting for someone to move in? He was an idiot. Evie had had the right idea all along.

Adam strode back out into the hallway and fixed Bry with a determined glare. "I'm moving out."

Then he stomped upstairs to pack, the faint strains of "What? Why, dude?" barely audible above the din.

CHAPTER SIX

"Oi, Corin, ain't it?" The call came from the side street Corin was passing on his way to get some food for his tea.

He turned to find a hefty biker type beaming at him through an unruly beard. But he knew Corin's name, and there was a spiderweb tattoo on his neck, like the man in the tattoo studio a couple of days ago. "Scratch?" he hazarded.

"That's right. Fancy a pint? Welcome you to Glastonbury, like?" Scratch ambled over to him and bumped shoulders in what seemed like a friendly way.

Corin took a side step to regain a little personal space, grateful he'd managed not to stagger. "Uh . . . I was about to get a takeaway. Haven't eaten yet."

"Get a plate of chips in the pub, mate. 'Less you've got someone waiting for you at home?"

Corin shook his head. "No. I live alone."

"Well then," Scratch said, as if he'd won the point.

He probably had, Corin realised, as he found himself falling into step with the man. Scratch was leading him back the way he'd come, but as long as there was food at the end of the road, he didn't care. "I can't have more than a pint. Work tomorrow."

"Yeah? Where's that then?"

"I work from home. Software engineer."

"Living in town?"

Corin waved a hand at Archer Street, which, with uncanny timing, they were about to cross. "Just down there."

"Good, innit? Me, I live back up the high street. Above one of them hippie shops. Handy for Sasha's, and not too far to stagger at the end of the night." He laughed and jostled Corin again with his leather-clad shoulder.

Was this a pickup? Corin hoped not. Not that he had anything against Scratch—he seemed pretty friendly, and easygoing with it—but Corin couldn't imagine fitting in with a biker crowd. And anyway, he wasn't looking for anything right now. Not a relationship, and definitely not a one-night stand. The thought of not being able to recognise a man he'd hooked up with the morning after had him breaking out in a cold sweat. "So what do you do for a living?" he asked, trying to keep his tone polite but casual.

"Locksmith. Gimme your phone."

Corin hesitated, but he didn't want to be rude, so he pulled out his phone, unlocked it, and handed it over.

Scratch tapped in his number. "There you go. If you ever lock yourself out, give me a bell. Or if you got a safe that wants cracking. All right if I send myself a text so I'll know who's calling?"

Again, it felt impolite to refuse. "Uh, I guess. Thanks." Corin accepted his phone back, hoping Scratch was joking about the safe. "Have you lived in Glastonbury long?"

"All me life. Well, 'cept for a couple of years. Moved to that there London for a while, but it wasn't for me. Dunno how Adam stuck it so long. Gimme some hills any day, not wall-to-wall bloody buildings and six million strangers. Can't get to know people in a place like that."

Corin huffed under his breath. Maybe *he* should move to London.

Scratch was talking again. "More'n your life's worth to ride a bike around London, too. Pedal bike, like. Don't know how the couriers survive."

"You're a cyclist, then?" Corin asked, because it seemed the obvious thing to say.

"Oh yeah. Got a hog for the roads, but round town I'm on my mountain bike most of the time. Keeps you fit, saves the planet, and no worries parking in the summer when the hordes invade." They'd reached the end of the high street, at the Market Cross. Scratch turned up a side street.

"Bad, is it, when the festival's on?" That was undoubtedly an issue Corin should have looked into before moving here, but he'd been so desperate to get out of Avebury he'd taken the first decent flat he could find and figured he'd get to know the area when he got here.

"Ain't just the festival. All the airy-fairy tourists and wannabe witches on their holidays. Communing with the spirits of nature, healing crystals in one hand and a spliff in the other. Not that there's anything wrong with a good spliff, mind." He peered at Corin from under bushy brows. "You ain't into all of that New Age bollocks, are you? Cos, you know, apologies and all if I've been dissing your sacred beliefs."

He sounded sincere rather than sarcastic. "I'm more into hard facts," Corin reassured him.

"That's all right, then. Here we are."

The pub was in a colourful part of town, with brightly painted murals on several walls nearby. Corin would have to come down here in daylight to see them properly—if he could find the place again. No, no, he'd be fine. Straight down the high street, turn right and keep going until he got there. He could do that. It was a few doors down from an Indian restaurant. The rest of the street, as far as Corin could tell in the dim street lighting, was a jumbled mix of residential housing, offices and independent shops. White-fronted and adorned with old-fashioned carriage lamps, the Prince of Wales sprawled widely, as if it had cannibalized a couple of neighbouring properties over the centuries it had been standing. Chalk boards advertised pub grub and live music nights.

Inside the door, it had a rough-and-ready ambiance, with a large area to the left that was mostly empty, just a bare plank floor and a few wooden chairs and tables scattered around. Presumably this was where the live music took place. Scratch scuffed his heavy boots on the doormat and headed right, where there was a much warmer feel: carpeting and upholstery, and softly glowing lights. Corin followed him to the bar.

"All right, my lover?" Scratch greeted the middle-aged barmaid with henna-coloured hair.

She gave him an indulgent smile. "Here's trouble again. What can I get you? Pint of Becket's?"

"You know the way to a man's heart." Scratch turned to Corin. "What's your poison?"

Corin shrugged. None of the tap labels meant anything to him. "Guess I'll try the Becket's?"

"Good man. Make that two, then, Ange, and we'll have a couple of menus."

The menu was short and equally split between traditional pub grub and vegan dishes. Scratch ordered fish and chips, while Corin went for the vegan burger with sweet potato fries.

"You vegan, then?" Scratch asked. "You're in luck here. Half the caffs in town, they look at me like I'm a serial killer when I walk in wearing leather."

Corin gave a rueful smile. "No, but I've been eating too many takeaways lately. Thought a couple of vitamins couldn't hurt."

Scratch laughed. "Long as you don't overdo it. Come on, there's a table free over in the corner." They sat down with the pints, and there was silence for a minute or two as they each took a long swallow. The beer was strong and good, with a surprisingly tart citrus flavour.

"Ah, that hits the spot. So: young Adam." Scratch leaned forward, wiping the froth off his moustache with the back of his hand.

Corin blinked, startled, and waited for him to get to the point, but apparently Scratch thought they were already there, as he didn't say anything more, just fixed Corin in the eye. There might be a significant expression going on, but it was wasted on Corin. "What about him?" he asked in the end.

"He ain't had an easy time of it, see."

"With his mum dying, you mean? Were they very close?"

Scratch snorted, confusing Corin further. "Not so's you'd notice. Strange woman, Adam's mum."

"You knew her?"

"Oh, yeah. Me and Adam were at school together."

"You were?" Corin couldn't keep the surprise from his tone.

Scratch laughed. "Wouldn't think so, would you? It's the beard. Makes me look older. Less than a year between us, if you can believe it."

"But he doesn't talk like you." Corin flushed. "I mean, his accent's not so, um, local."

"Spent too much time in that there London, didn't he? He was in his teens when he went to live at his dad's. Not an age you want to be sounding different to everyone else."

"I suppose not. Is that why you went to London—to be with him?"

"Yeah—later on, that was. He got his dad to give me a job. He's got his own company. Construction. Too much like hard labour for me, though. Course, I knew I had to start at the bottom, but I reckoned I didn't much fancy making it to the top, neither. Came home, got meself an apprenticeship in locksmithing, and here I am." Scratch sat back and took a gulp of his beer, then sighed in satisfaction. "But where were we? Oh, yeah. You want to tread softly with our Adam."

Corin was thrown by the sudden change of subject. "Who says I want to . . . *tread* at all? Look, I've just moved here. I'm not after a relationship."

"Suit yourself. But let him down gently, all right?"

"You really think he's interested in me?" Corin couldn't keep the doubt—or the eagerness—out of his voice.

"Why not? You're fit enough. I'd do you!" Scratch was grinning, as far as Corin could tell through that heavy dark beard.

"You'd do anyone," the barmaid—or a similar one—said in a fond tone, putting their plates in front of them.

Scratch let out a loud laugh. "You'll ruin my reputation, you will."

"Can't ruin what's already in tatters," she returned, and left them.

Corin frowned. "I thought you and Sasha were . . ."

"Me and her? No, that's just joking around. We're mates, is all. Footloose and fancy free, that's me." There was a hint of regret in his tone, although Corin wasn't sure if it was for Sasha or for the general state of being single.

Unsure again if he was about to be hit on, Corin focused on his plate and hoped that would send a subtle message. They ate in near silence for a while, Scratch dousing his fish and chips with around half a dozen sachets of tartare sauce that had to be eating into the pub's profit margin. Occasionally he'd break off chewing to enthuse about the bands who played here regularly, none of which Corin had heard of.

Corin's burger was decent enough, but he found himself missing the meat.

"So was Sasha at school with you too?" he asked, once he'd reached the picking-at-the-fries stage.

"Her? No. She went to some posh girls' school in Bath. I met her a few years ago now, when she started up Furious Ink. She's a good girl, she is." Scratch picked up a stray chip in his fingers and dabbed it into the pool of tartare sauce remaining on his plate before chucking it in his mouth, whole.

"Has she done a lot of your ink?"

"Oh, yeah." Scratch's voice was muffled as he spoke around his chip. He swallowed it down, took a swig of his beer, and put his pint back on the table with a flourish. "Lemme show you the last one she done, before she started working on my sleeve."

Without ceremony, right in the middle of the pub, he pulled his sweater and the T-shirt underneath up to his armpits to show off a pretty decent set of pecs. "It's the one on the left. My left, not your left."

A little taken aback, Corin dutifully peered at an intricate design based on what he vaguely recognised as a Viking compass. Someone on the other side of the pub wolf-whistled.

"Ah, piss off, you're only jealous of my manly chest!" Scratch yelled back good-naturedly.

"In your dreams." The whistler walked up to their table, shrugged off a leather jacket, and sat down. He turned to Corin. "Sorry about him. He'll flash his tits at anyone. How's it going?"

"Fine, thanks." Was Corin supposed to know this man? He had a lean, attractive figure, with white skin, short dark hair and dark eyes. Clean-shaven and dressed casually, with no visible scars, tattoos, or piercings.

The stranger shifted backwards on his seat. "Uh, it's Adam? From the tattoo studio? Sorry, you were looking at me like we'd never met, so . . ."

Scratch was staring at him. Corin swallowed. "Sorry. I'm *really* not good with faces." God, this was mortifying. "Sorry. It's, uh, time I was going anyway. Work tomorrow." He stood, nearly knocking over his chair.

Adam's eyes widened. "Hey, you don't have to go. I'm not, like, offended or anything." He gave a twisted smile. "Guess I've got one of those forgettable faces."

Corin shook his head. "No. It's not you. I— I'll see you around." He turned and walked out of the pub.

Then he stood there in the dark, trying to remember which direction they'd come down the street.

Sod it. There was a fifty-fifty chance he'd hit the high street within five minutes or so, and if not, he'd simply have to do a U-turn. And hope he wouldn't bump into Scratch or Adam on the way back.

On the bright side, he probably wouldn't have a clue if he did.

CHAPTER SEVEN

"Cheers for that, mate," Adam said with heavy sarcasm. "Find the bloke I fancy and then flirt with him, why don't you?"

Getting angry with Scratch was a lot less painful than dwelling on how Corin had first forgotten Adam existed and then practically run away as soon as he realised who Adam was.

"I wasn't flirting!"

"With your shirt off, flashing your tits?"

"I was showing him Sasha's ink." Scratch shrugged. "Anyway, he's not looking for a bloke. He told me."

Damn. Adam's eyes narrowed. "Why did he tell you that if you weren't flirting with him?"

"Ah. Might have given him the idea you were interested."

"You did *what*? Jesus, Scratch, I don't believe it." God, this was a nightmare. And he was supposed to ink the bloke in a couple of weeks—in the very unlikely event Corin didn't cancel the appointment. "Did you read a manual on how to be a shit friend?"

"Maybe?" Scratch rubbed his beard. "I'd have put my life on it he fancied you. I was trying to let him know he was in with a chance. Egg him on a bit."

"Fancy me? He doesn't even bloody remember me from one meeting to the next."

"Maybe he ain't been looking at your face?"

Adam glared at him. "We talked. He looked at my face. He just didn't find anything worth remembering about it."

"You ought to get a few piercings, that'd make you stand out in a crowd. Or get Sash to ink you up good." Scratch frowned. "Funny, though. I'd have sworn blind he'd have taken a photo if he thought he'd get away with it."

The weird part was, so would Adam. He glanced around, gauging the lighting. It wasn't that bright in here—but then again, it wasn't that dim, either. "So what were you doing having a drink with him, anyhow? Did you meet him in here?"

"No, bumped into him on the street and asked him if he fancied a pint."

"So he knew who *you* were, then." Because it was Scratch, who he'd known all his life, Adam didn't try to hide the bitterness in his voice.

"He remembered my name. Course, he's only been here a couple of days. Can't be that many metalheads in town who know him." Scratch rubbed his beard. "Took him a minute, mind. Then I said his name, and he worked it out. Odd, though, him not knowing you. I mean, we spent the last hour talking about you, so it wasn't like you weren't fresh in his mind."

"Huh. Do you think he really *is* just that bad at faces?" Adam stood up, shaking his head. It was stupid to get his hopes up, but at least the hurt from Corin's lack of recognition was fading. "Ah, whatever. I'm getting the beers in. Usual?"

Adam only stayed for a couple of pints. Like Corin had said, it was a work day tomorrow, and jabbing needles into someone's skin was best not done on too little sleep and with a hangover.

It was an easy walk of less than a mile back to Mum's house: past the abbey and along mainly residential streets. Correction: back *home*. It was his house now. Mum had wanted him to have it.

Adam's key turned more easily in the lock this time, as if the house was getting used to him. It still felt odd, coming back to a home that was empty and silent. Let alone one with all kinds of emotional baggage attached.

Was he crazy, moving in here? Okay, so he'd be saving on rent once the month was up, but houses came with responsibilities, didn't they? Council tax, and water rates, and fixing stuff that went wrong.

He'd have to do the garden. Paint the window frames. Get the boiler serviced so he didn't die of carbon monoxide poisoning.

And all of that was nothing compared to the memories that lived here, crowding him out of the kitchen and hiding under the single bed in his childhood room. He hadn't slept well since he'd moved back in. The bed was too narrow and the room too small—even with the window open, there hadn't been enough air.

That was one thing he could fix. Adam grabbed the T-shirt and boxers he slept in and carried them across the landing to the front bedroom, where his mum had slept. Where his dad had slept too, once upon a time that he barely remembered. Evie had stripped the bed, but there were clean sheets in the drawers in what had been her old room. About to go get them, Adam noticed a faint whiff of lavender that took him back to his childhood. It'd been Mum's favourite perfume.

He flung open the windows, and a chill breeze blew in, painting over the floral scent with the smell of damp earth, grass, and petrol fumes. That was better.

Adam made up the bed with sheets worn thin with years of washing, and the old-fashioned wool blankets Mum had preferred. He drew the line at the candlewick bedspread, though. As far as he was concerned it could die in a fire. He'd have to make it back to the shared house soon to pick up his duvet—there was only so much he'd been able to carry in one trip on the Yamaha—but at least he'd brought the Celtic knot throw he'd got at a medieval festival a while back. Adam shook it out to cover up the scratchy blankets, then plugged his phone in to charge, displacing the ugly lamp on the bedside table.

That was better too. It made the room look more like it was his. What next?

Mum hadn't left many knickknacks in here, but she'd hung pictures on the walls. The one of the tor could stay. It was cool to compare it with the real thing visible from the window. The Scottish landscape, though, with its purple heather, deep green pine trees and a stag dead centre, turning as if surprised by the artist . . . Adam raised his hands to take it down, then hesitated. It showed the land of her birth; Adam's own heritage, through her. Should he leave it?

No. He lifted the painting carefully from its hooks. He wouldn't get rid of it; maybe it would go in the living room. He just didn't want to sleep with it staring at him, that was all.

He carried it downstairs and propped it against a wall in the living room. The colours in the painting seemed to lift the drabness of the room somehow. What had Mum used to tell him about the origins of the picture? She'd brought it with her when she'd moved down here to marry his dad.

As he straightened, a voice behind him said, "My father took the photograph that was painted from."

Adam whirled, and for a moment thought he saw a shadowy figure in the doorway, moving through the hall.

His breath caught. "Mum?"

But when he went out into the hall, there was nobody there.

CHAPTER EIGHT

C orin cursed himself as he strode down the street. God, he'd been an idiot. Of *course* it had been Adam who'd joined them at the pub. He and Scratch were old friends, and the Prince of Wales was probably their local. But instead of working things out logically, Corin had behaved like a complete weirdo. And he'd hurt Adam, making it seem like he hadn't cared enough to remember him.

The worst of it was, it was so far from the truth. He *liked* Adam. Okay, so he hadn't been planning to make any romantic overtures. That didn't mean he wanted to offend him.

It didn't help that he knew, inside, that some of his pain was entirely selfish. It was one thing to decide he wasn't in the market for a relationship. It was quite another to have it conclusively demonstrated to him that he'd now never be capable of one. Who'd want to be with someone who couldn't remember what they looked like?

Corin hunched his shoulders as he strode down the street. The headwind ruffled his hair and slipped chill fingers under his collar. What had he been thinking of anyway? Making *friends*? So he could upset them by never recognising them, and then finally be forced to admit he was brain-damaged and have easy banter turn to awkward concern?

That was what he'd moved here to get away from, for God's sake.

It'd been nice, though. Going for a pint with a mate. Like he'd used to do without thinking, before the accident. And Scratch was easygoing enough. Maybe he wouldn't care about Corin's injury.

He just had to be best mates with Adam, didn't he?

Corin should never have made that tattoo appointment. Well, that was easily sorted— he could ring and cancel. Tomorrow. He'd do it tomorrow.

Friday night, Corin somehow still hadn't got around to cancelling his appointment at Furious Ink. He *had* finally managed to cook his first proper meal in the new place, having shopped for groceries in his lunch hour. Afterwards, he settled down on the sofa with a book. Trying to watch TV was pointless—everyone looked the same in modern dramas, making it impossible to follow the plot.

He was getting into the story of a London bobby meeting a wizard and a ghost in Covent Garden when there was a knock on the door. Frowning, Corin went to answer it. He *had* ordered a couple of new Ethernet cables, but it was late for a delivery.

The man on the doorstep was an inch or so shorter than Corin, with mid-brown hair and wearing casual clothes. He had a small rucksack on his back.

"Hello?" Corin said politely. The man didn't answer, just stared at him. Corin's pulse rocketed. "What is it?"

The stranger shook his head slowly. "You still don't recognise me, do you? It's me, you daft tit."

The face could have been anyone. But the voice was one Corin knew better than he knew his own—had known all his life, in fact. His big brother's. Suddenly, he was furious. "Declan? Would it have killed you to say something earlier? You know I can't— What the hell do you want, anyway?" He clenched his fist to quell the urge to slam the door in Declan's stupid face.

Declan took a step back, holding up his hands. "Easy, mate. Haven't seen you for a couple of weeks, have I? Didn't know if you'd, you know—"

"What, got better? I suppose if I'd lost a leg you'd be asking if it'd grown back yet. I'm not going to get better. Ever."

"Sorry, all right? It's just taking a bit of getting used to."

"Really? I can't imagine how hard that must be for you." Sarcasm dripped from Corin's voice like day-old blood in an abattoir.

Declan stood there. Blinked. Then smiled. "So anyhow, I heard there's some good pubs in this place. Want to check out the local beer with me?"

Corin gaped. "What?"

"Come on. I'm buying. First round, anyhow. You can put your hand in your pocket after that, you tight bastard. Speaking of which . . ." Declan slung his backpack off his shoulder and pulled a bottle of vodka out of the side pocket. "Housewarming gift. We can crack it open when we get home from the pub."

"You're staying?"

"Not forking out for a hotel when you've got a perfectly good sofa, am I? And you can't expect me to drive back to Swindon half-cut." He laughed. "If I survived the trip, Lori would kill me when I got home. So where are we going, then? I passed a pub on the way over that looked all right. Isle of Avalon, you been there?"

"No. But we can give it a go." So long as it wasn't the Prince of Wales. "I don't know if they do food—have you eaten?"

Declan shrugged. "Grabbed a burger on the way down."

Corin rolled his eyes. "If you'd said you were coming, I could have cooked you a meal."

"If I'd said I was coming, you might have told me to piss off. Anyway, come on, get your arse in gear. We're wasting valuable drinking time."

"I wouldn't have told you to piss off," Corin protested, pulling on his jacket. He *wouldn't* have. At least, not in so many words.

"Course you wouldn't. Right, last one to the pub gets the beers in." Declan clattered down the metal staircase at an easy jog.

"Hang on, you said you were buying!" Corin followed at a run.

The Isle of Avalon was halfway down the high street, opposite a Tandoori. The pub turned out to be less touristy than Corin had feared from the name. Outside, there wasn't a lot to distinguish it from the centuries-old shop fronts it stood between, save for the swinging pub sign and the smaller windows. Inside it was small but welcoming, with a fire in the modest hearth and a collection of antique beer adverts on the walls. A darts board hung at one end of the broad oak bar, and there were signs pointing to *The Snug* and *The Pool Room*.

They pulled up a couple of barstools and ordered a pint of Becket's each. "Quiet in here for a Friday night, innit?" Declan murmured under his breath. There were only half a dozen people in the bar with them, although sounds of more were coming from the pool room.

"I expect everyone's at the Prince of Wales. It's live music night," Corin told him without thinking.

"Yeah? Any good?"

"How would I know? I've been here less than a week."

Declan scratched his head. "Yeah, about that . . . Everyone's been asking about you. Haven't known what to tell them."

"Who's *everyone*?"

"Your mates, remember them?"

Corin shrugged. "They've always been your mates, really." It had been like that since they were kids; Declan went out and did stuff, met people, and chivvied Corin into tagging along. He'd been more comfortable socialising online—*your imaginary friends*, Declan had teased him. Their parents' concern had been worse— highly social people themselves, they'd dragged him along for several excruciating sessions with a psychologist and hadn't seemed particularly reassured when she told them there was nothing wrong with being an introvert.

Anyway, most of the people Corin met in real life barely knew Linux existed, let alone had an opinion on the relative merits of Ubuntu versus Xubuntu. At least online it was easy to meet people who liked to talk about these things.

"They're *our* mates." Declan's tone was a familiar mix of fondness and exasperation. "Just cos I saw them first doesn't mean I planted a bloody flag."

Except in the ways that it did. "What are you doing here, anyway? Not that it isn't good to see you," Corin added hastily. He hoped Declan hadn't noticed his wince at *see you*. If he didn't look at Declan, it was almost like the way it had always been between them. "But shouldn't you be taking care of Lori?"

"Nah, she can look after herself. Her words, not mine. No, this weird thing happened in my life, so I wanted to talk to you about it."

"What weird thing?" Corin frowned. *Weird* and *Declan* didn't belong together. Declan was normality and solidity. Safety.

"See, there's me and my little brother, lived close to Swindon all our lives, then he ups and buggers off fifty miles away, and all the warning I get is a bloody text message the night before he goes." Declan cocked his head. "So what's that all about, then?"

Corin might have known he wouldn't escape that easily. "I needed a change of scene. Fifty miles isn't all that far."

"Took me the best part of two hours to get here. You're going to be bugger all use as a babysitter when the kid's born."

Corin's conscience stabbed him. "Sorry." He honestly hadn't thought about that—how selfish did that make him?

"Hey, I was joking. Think we'd trust you with a baby? If the poor kid started crying, you'd probably plug it into a USB port to recharge." He laughed. "So come on, tell me about it."

"I needed to get away," Corin repeated. How could he explain the sheer *loss* he'd felt, looking at people he'd known half his life and feeling no connection with them at all?

"You always were an independent little sod," Declan said casually. "I know you like to stand on your own two feet. But there's no shame in letting people help you out when you need it."

It felt like they were having two different conversations. Corin shook his head. "How's Lori doing?"

"Great— That reminds me." Declan pulled out his phone and showed a fuzzy monochrome picture of some disconnected white blobs inside a larger black blob. "Had her first scan yesterday. That's your nibling, right there."

Corin stared. "Its head's not attached to its body."

"That's how the photo went! Trust me, all important bits are there. *And* attached."

"Do you know what it is yet?"

"It's a baby."

Corin resisted the urge to chuck a beermat at him. "I meant, boy or girl."

"Not a clue. Hence, *nibling*."

"Ready to be a dad, then?"

"Oh, fuck me, no. But yeah. Can't wait." Declan's smile was so wide even Corin couldn't mistake it.

Corin raised his glass, and they toasted the next generation. "Have you sent the picture to Mum and Dad?"

"Nope." Declan's tone was hard. "I'm not in a hurry for another round of them going on about screening for birth defects. Just cos Lori's a few years older than me, they've got this bee in their bonnet that it's a high-risk pregnancy."

Corin winced. By his reckoning, Lori would be forty by the time the baby was born, so he could sort of understand their reasoning, but he couldn't see how it was helpful to keep pointing this out. "Maybe they want you to be prepared for the possibilities?"

"You know what happens if the tests come up positive, right? They offer you a termination, which is why Mum and Dad keep banging on about it. But there's no way we'd be going for that, so what's the point? And it's not like the tests are risk-free, either." Declan took a long draught of his pint and set the glass firmly back on the table. "It'll be our kid, no matter what wonky genes it's got, and we'll make sure it gets everything it needs. End of. If they can't deal with a grandkid with Down's or whatever, that's their loss."

"Yes." The fervent agreement came out without Corin having to think about it. More surprising, though, was the surge of emotion that came with it—but was it really that surprising? The memory of Mum's tears and Dad's embarrassment when they'd visited his newly brain-damaged self in hospital wasn't likely to fade anytime soon. He took a slow sip of his beer to try to rein it all in. "You're right," he added. "It's not up to them."

Declan clapped him on the shoulder. "Good man. So, to change the subject, you met anyone yet?"

Corin rolled his eyes. "I've been here less than a *week*. And besides, I'm not looking for a relationship."

"Did I mention relationships? Serious question: Have you met anyone? Including, but not limited to: friends, lovers, casual shags, wankers down the pub, and/or little old ladies who need their shopping carried."

"Of course I've *met* people. Just because I work at home doesn't mean I never get out of the flat. I haven't turned into a hermit."

"No? Good. Cos that's the way you were going back in Avebury. Lately." Declan took a deep swallow of his beer. "So why aren't you looking for a relationship? It's been ages since you were last seeing anyone. Serial monogamist, that's what you used to be." He frowned. "Is it the same word if it's blokes?"

"I don't know and I don't care." Corin took a deep breath. "I've spent the last six months getting over my injuries, remember? And before that . . . I was seeing someone, okay? For months. But he— It ended." He'd never told Declan about Blair. Probably because he'd known, deep down, exactly what Declan would think about Blair wanting to keep their relationship a secret at work.

Declan would have guessed the real reason for the secrecy straight off. *God, I'm an idiot.*

And Declan was looking at him sharply. "You were seeing someone? Cos I don't remember him visiting you in hospital."

"It had already ended then." *A whole thirty seconds before the accident, in fact.* Corin stifled a despairing laugh.

"So? Maybe you weren't shagging anymore, but he still could've taken half an hour to come and see you when you were lying in hospital half dead. Wanker."

"No. He couldn't." Corin's voice sounded hoarse in his own ears.

There was a sigh. "Bit of a git, was he? He still could've—"

"No, he couldn't because he's *dead*, for God's sake!" Corin took a hefty swallow of his beer, wishing it were stronger.

"Fuck, was it that bloke who was in the car with you?"

"Yes, all right?"

"You poor sod." Declan put a hand on his arm and gave a gentle squeeze.

Corin stared at his pint, unable to look into the eyes of the stranger who spoke like his brother.

"And now you're blaming yourself for whatever went wrong, because he's dead and can't forgive you, am I right? Christ." The stranger scrubbed a hand over his face. "Sometimes shit just happens. You had a thing, it didn't work out for whatever reason, and then fate kicked you both in the arse. End of. Give yourself a break, okay?"

Corin gave a jerky nod and took a gulp of his beer. Maybe he *should* give himself a break. It wasn't like he wasn't being punished for what he'd done, was it?

Declan downed the rest of his pint in one. "Fuck me, I need some chips after all that. Drink up, and we'll find another pub."

Corin nodded. He had zero appetite, but he was suddenly desperate for a change of scene.

They found a chippy before they found the next pub, which Declan took as a sign they should get his food there and take it back to Corin's flat to break open the vodka.

The smell of hot grease worked its usual sly magic, and Corin found himself stealing half of Declan's chips as they walked back through town. "You're a terrible influence," he muttered as he nabbed another. "I actually cooked a healthy meal tonight."

"Yeah? That's why you're hungry now. Gotta get your basic food groups in: starch, grease, and burnt crunchy bits."

"I regret introducing you to Terry Pratchett. And you missed out 'sugar.'"

"No, you don't. And who wants sugar on chips?"

"You, apparently, from the amount of ketchup you've drowned them in."

"What, they put sugar in ketchup? That's just wrong. Still, tastes all right."

Corin found himself rolling his eyes. "Do you ever read the label on *anything*?"

"Nope. What you don't know can't hurt you."

Bollocks to that. Corin's chest went tight, and the smell of grease, so appetising a moment ago, made him nauseous. What he hadn't known had nearly fucking *destroyed* him.

CHAPTER NINE

"Oi, Earth to Adam, are you there?"

Adam jumped at Sasha's voice and nearly dropped the tattoo machine he was cleaning. It was a bloody good thing he hadn't been working on a client or he might have been looking at a hefty discount and a cover-up job. "Sorry, what?"

Sasha was holding up the work mobile "Your two o'clock's on the phone. She can't make it."

"Right. Yeah." He hurried through the studio to grab the phone from her. "Uh . . . Crystal?"

"It's Chrissie, but close. I'm so sorry, but . . ." She launched into a tale of her elderly neighbour having a fall and needing to be taken care of.

Adam told her not to worry about the missed appointment, expressed concern about the neighbour, and suggested she ring when she was ready to rebook. When he hung up, Sasha was staring at him. "What?"

"You never forget a client's name. What's the matter with you? You've been off with the fairies for days now."

Shit. Had he really been that obvious? "Sorry, Sash. Been a bit distracted."

"Wanna talk about it?" She made a pointed gesture at the empty studio—they were both between clients.

Adam bit his lip. "You know how some people say they've, like, seen stuff? Seen people. I mean people who aren't alive any more. Do you think there could be something in it?"

Her tattooed-on eyebrows nearly hit her hairline. "You're asking me if I believe in ghosts?"

"Well, yeah." Except it sounded stupid when she put it like that. He swallowed. The last thing he needed was his boss convinced he was losing it.

Sasha cocked her head. "Why?"

Couldn't she simply answer the question? "It's since my mum died," he admitted with a rush. "I keep thinking I can see her."

Her face, unexpectedly, hardened. "Jesus. They really do fuck you up, don't they?"

"What?"

"Your mum and dad. Like in the poem. 'They fuck you up, your mum and dad. They never mean to, but they do.'" She gave him an unhappy smile. "Except maybe sometimes they do mean to."

"What the hell, Sash?"

"Scratch told me about your mum. She did a right number on you when she was alive, and she can't stop haunting you now she's dead!"

"That's not— It wasn't her fault." What the hell had Scratch been saying?

"Whose was it, then? Yours? You were just a kid, and she didn't care if you lived or died."

"That's bollocks," Adam snapped. "What do you know about it anyway?"

"Told you. Scratch told me. All the times she *forgot* to pick you up from football and left you hanging around a dark playing field on your own. How she'd never take you to the doctor even if you were crying in pain."

"Scratch needs to learn to keep his mouth shut about other people's business." Christ. First telling Corin that Adam fancied him, and now *this*.

"Oi. He told me cos he *cares*, you wanker."

"So what does he think you're going to do about it? Give me a cuddle? Be my new mum?"

Sasha glared at him. "You know what your problem is, Adam Merchant?"

"No, but I'm sure you're going to tell me!"

The shop doorbell chimed as a middle-aged woman in vintage wear and petticoats strode in. Adam and Sasha froze, mid-face-off.

The woman stared at them. "Should I come back later?"

Adam unclenched his fists as Sasha pasted on a smile and turned to the customer. "Sorry, my lover, come on in. Did you want to make an appointment?"

By the time the customer had left, Adam had cooled down. And he still had a few minutes before his twelve o'clock touch-up job. "So go on, what's my problem?" he asked in a mild tone he was pretty proud of.

Sasha gave him a searching look. "You really want to know?"

"Yeah. Not saying I'm going to agree with you, mind."

"You need to stop trying to live behind a bloody brick wall. Just cos something's personal doesn't mean it has to be private, yeah? Let your mates help you out."

Adam's temper threatened to rise again. "By having a good old gossip about me?" *Heard the latest about Adam? His mum never loved him. Oh, and now he sees dead people.*

Sasha sighed. "Look, I love Scratch, I do, but he's got the emotional intelligence of a dead badger. He's worried about you, and he doesn't know what to do. So he talks to me. Is that honestly so bad? You know I'm not one to spout off to anyone who'll listen."

Adam had to give her that. "It's difficult, that's all. Having people know about that stuff." Despite his best efforts, prickles of shame crept into his chest. *Why wasn't I good enough for you, Mum?*

"You ever been to, like, counselling or anything about it?" she asked, her tone uncharacteristically tentative.

"No. And I'm not going. There's no point raking everything up now."

"If you don't rake the leaves up come autumn, they'll rot."

"I thought that was supposed to be better for the environment anyway. I appreciate you, you know, caring, but I'm fine, okay?"

Sasha opened her mouth, but for a second time he was saved by the bell as his touch-up job arrived.

It was while he was taking payment from the client up at the front desk that a familiar face caught his eye through the window. Corin was walking past, with a man Adam didn't know. Adam was about to smile and nod at him but was put off by the way Corin simply stared at him as he passed, with no sign of recognition.

Shit. Adam guessed that night in the pub really had fucked things up. But if Corin was trying to avoid him, why not simply walk past with eyes front—nothing to see, move along now? The moment had been over in, well, a moment, but Adam couldn't shake the unsettling feeling it left him with.

He didn't have long to brood on it, though, as Scratch turned up at the shop not ten minutes later.

"All right, Adam?" he called cheerily, then went on without waiting for an answer, "Sasha, darling, you get lovelier every day."

Sasha took time from working on the wolf on her client's chest to give him the finger. "And you get hairier. Better watch out—you're in Adam's bad books."

Scratch's gaze shifted from one to the other of them. "What did I do?"

"You cared about him. Not allowed, that, is it?"

Adam could have cut the sarcasm with a knife. Okay, so maybe Sasha was still a little sore about their disagreement earlier too.

"Uh, mate? You gonna tell me what this is all about?"

"Don't mind me," Sasha's client put in helpfully.

Adam grabbed his phone and checked his jeans pocket for his wallet. "Sash can fill you in while I'm out. Right. Orders for lunch? I'm going to the Breezy Moon."

Scratch caught his arm. "Oi, hang about. What've I done?"

Adam gazed at his earnest, familiar face and couldn't be angry any longer. He lowered his voice. "It doesn't matter. But . . . don't go telling people stuff about my mum, okay?"

"Me? I'd never. Sasha's not people. I've known her years."

Yeah, but I haven't. Adam couldn't bring himself to say it. "Fine. But ask me, next time?"

"Course, mate. Uh, you want me to come along to the caff with you?"

Adam huffed a laugh. "What, to hold my hand? Tell me what you want to eat and I'll get it."

Maybe he wasn't angry anymore, but it was still a relief to get out onto the street. Alone. Although, it'd be funny if he bumped into Corin and whoever he was with, seeing as they'd been headed down this way too. *Funny* meaning *not amusing in the slightest*. Would Corin pretend he didn't know him again?

Sod it. If it happened, he'd simply have to give the bloke a big grin and a loud greeting to serve him right.

CHAPTER TEN

C orin hadn't exactly been feeling at his best when he woke up on Saturday. "I'm blaming you for the way my head feels like it's going to explode," he grumbled to his brother as he sipped on his mug of strong coffee and hoped his stomach wouldn't revolt.

Declan laughed, the bastard. "You can lead a bloke to vodka, but you can't make him drink. Not my fault you're a lightweight. So if I were to suggest a quick run up the tor . . ."

"Fratricide would be a distinct possibility, yes."

"How about we take a wander round the town, then? Not been here before, have I? You can show me the sights. At a leisurely pace, suitable for the terminally hungover. And us poor bastards with backache. Did you know your sofa sags?"

Corin raised a middle finger in reply and got laughed at again.

He felt better after he'd forced down a couple of slices of toast and marmalade, and had a shower. He peered at the stranger in the mirror. Close examination revealed bloodshot eyes and a sallow tinge to the stranger's skin, which made Corin feel a fucked-up kinship with him.

Declan poked his head in while Corin was shaving. "Hey, if you see us both in the mirror, can you tell which one's you?"

"Obviously." Corin gestured with his razor. "Bit of a giveaway, this. And I know where I'm standing. And that I haven't got an annoying smirk on my face."

Declan let that one slide. "Huh. So what about photos?"

Corin shrugged. "Probably? I mean, I'd recognise my clothes. Or remember the picture being taken. And I'm taller," he added to annoy Declan.

"By half an inch. You're not exactly looming over me, are you?"

"It's a whole inch, ta very much. And I can still look down on you." The stranger with the razor now wore a smirk that was, in fact, disconcertingly like the other man's.

The one that wasn't Corin rolled his eyes. "At least you've cheered up. Come on, finish scraping away that bum-fluff you call a beard and take me out and show me a good time."

The sun was high, and the day was bright and mild when they stepped outside the flat. More like the end of summer than autumn, although the colours in the trees that dotted the streets and flourished in churchyards confirmed the season was firmly on the turn. Buskers and other performers were out on street corners, and as Corin and Declan neared St. John's Church, what looked like a wedding procession jigged past. It was led by a woman in a medieval-style, deep red dress holding a rough-tied bouquet of red and white flowers, on the arm of an older man in a velvet waistcoat. The women who followed her wore long dresses and flowers in their hair, and were banging drums and singing a wild song. A little girl and her mother, not part of the procession, started dancing along with them.

"Blimey, it's hippie central here, innit?" Declan muttered as they, like most of the weekend shoppers, tourists, and other pedestrians, stopped to take in the sight.

Corin found he was smiling. "They seem to be having fun. Could be you and Lori, if you ever decide to tie the knot."

"Nah, we're happy as we are. Don't need a piece of paper to keep us together, and Lori's never been into the whole big-white-dress thing." Declan cocked his head. "What about you, though? Find yourself a bloke, make an honest man of him . . ."

Like that was ever going to happen now. "I look terrible in white. Come on, show's over, let's keep moving." Corin strode off down the high street without waiting to see if Declan would follow.

He did, of course. Corin's mood softened a little. When had Declan ever knowingly let him down? "It's been good to see you," he said when Declan caught up to him. "Good of you to come, especially with Lori expecting."

"What, like I'm going to neglect my little brother for the whole nine months just cos my girlfriend's up the duff? Lori's doing great, I told you." Declan gave him a gentle shoulder bump. "If I know her, she's off down the shops buying stuff for the baby, which I am *quite* happy to miss. There's only so many animal-print onesies I can get excited about, and I hit my limit a while ago."

As they wandered past Furious Ink, Corin couldn't stop himself taking a glance through the window. A dark-haired man standing at the desk stared straight back. A jolt ran through him. Was that Adam? He was the right build, the right colouring—and he'd given Corin a nod, hadn't he?

By the time Corin had worked it all out, though, they'd passed by, and it was too late for him to respond. Great. Adam must have thought he was being rude again. Did tattooists get their revenge on customers by giving them really bad ink? Or somehow making the process more painful than it need be? Of course, that would be bad business practice. Corin was probably safe. *If* he turned up to his appointment, which he hadn't been planning on doing, had he?

"Thinking of getting a tattoo?" Declan asked idly. He must have noticed Corin's interest in the studio.

Corin cursed under his breath. Did nothing pass Declan by? "Might be."

"What, seriously? You?"

"You don't have to sound so shocked." Irritated by his brother's reaction, Corin decided he bloody well *would* be getting that ink done. After all, he'd left it a little late to cancel. He wouldn't want to be impolite.

"Surprised, that's all." Declan gave him a light dig with his elbow. "Bet I can guess what it is."

"Bet you can't."

"You're on. Loser buys lunch. It's a heart with *Linus* in it."

"Linux. And no."

"Uh . . . some *Minecraft* thing?"

"I haven't played *Minecraft* in years."

"Damn. Ankh with an owl? Something with cables? Or I know, the wi-fi symbol?" Declan's voice lifted in enthusiasm.

"No."

"Huh. On/off switch?"

"No. It's nothing to do with computers."

"Well, that's just cheating, then. Go on, tell me."

"A butterfly. In Celtic knotwork."

"Didn't see that one coming. Celtic stuff I get, that's cool, but why a butterfly?"

"I liked it, that's all." He didn't want to get into the symbolism. It felt too personal, between him and Adam—and all right, he didn't want Declan ribbing him about it. "Not going to tell me it's too girly?"

"Nope. You might tell Lori I said that, and then I'd be sleeping on the sofa for six months. Anyway, who cares about all that bollocks nowadays? It's not like when we were kids. People can like what they like. Me and Lori, we've agreed we're not buying into that *pink for girls* crap. If we have a son who likes dresses, or a daughter who wants to drive a tank, or a kid who's neither, that's fine with us."

Corin's heart swelled. He darted a glance at his brother, then wished he hadn't. Still, the jolt of seeing a stranger's face didn't overcome the warmth flooding through him. "Is that an apology?" he asked before he could stop himself.

"Maybe." Declan sounded uncomfortable. "Corin, you know I was only trying to look out for you, right? Help you fit in? And I was just a kid then. I didn't know bollocks."

Still don't was the reply on the tip of Corin's tongue, born from years of brotherly back-and-forth. It was probably even the reply Declan was hoping for, to lighten the mood and banish all the heavy emotion that had settled between them. But Corin didn't want to do that—didn't want to let the moment pass without acknowledging it. "Yeah, I know you always meant well."

Declan coughed and muttered something that was lost to the noise of passing traffic.

Because he wasn't a shit brother, Corin added, "So, what if your kid wants to support Manchester City?"

"Then it's no child of mine and will be out on its ear. Obviously."

Both of them laughed a little louder than that warranted as they walked on, and Corin decided a gentle nudge was in order. "So, lunch? You're buying, remember?"

Declan heaved an exaggerated sigh. "*Fine*. But I'm choosing where we eat. I know what you're like. You'd pick somewhere because it looked *interesting* and we'd end up spending fifty quid on two leaves of lettuce and a vegetable I've never heard of."

"Isn't that all vegetables? Apart from chips and peas."

"Hey, chips are one of your five a day. And peas are even green. What about this place?" Declan stopped outside the café they'd just reached.

"This is *literally* the first place we've seen." And it was a bit too close to Furious Ink for Corin's peace of mind.

"Yeah, but it seems all right. Despite that New Age name." The shopfront proclaimed it the Breezy Moon Café, in cheerful yellow text on a sky-blue background. "I can see at least three kinds of meat on the menu."

"I hate to break it to you, but bacon, sausage, and pork chops are all technically the *same* meat."

"Next you'll be telling me eggs aren't a vegetable. C'mon, there's an all-day breakfast in there with my name on it, and one meal isn't going to kill you."

Corin rolled his eyes and pushed the sky-blue door open. Inside was the same blue and yellow colour scheme. It was busy, but luckily there was a table being vacated at the back. Corin grabbed it for them while Declan went up to the counter to order from a young woman in a sunshine yellow apron.

After the amount of alcohol he and Declan had got through the previous evening, Corin wasn't sorry to be served with a full English breakfast ten minutes later. He could feel himself becoming steadily more human as he tucked into his bacon, eggs, and sausage.

The Breezy Moon Café did takeaways too, and there was a steady stream of customers for hot sausage rolls, bacon butties, and the like. More of them were teenagers than he would have expected—wasn't there a McDonald's in town? Or was that not cool anymore?

Most came in two by two, like animals into a somewhat cannibalistic Ark, but there was one dark-haired man on his own who was either buying for his mates or had an inhumanly high metabolism.

As the man waited for the last of his order, his gaze wandered over the tables—and met Corin's.

Corin's chest went tight. Was that a jolt of recognition in the other man's eyes? He wasn't smiling. Was it . . .? Could it be Adam? The build and colouring were right, but the same could be said about half the young men in Glastonbury.

Shit. He was probably just some stranger, annoyed at Corin for staring. Corin dropped his gaze back to his plate.

"You all right?" Declan asked.

Corin's brain was still scrambled. "What?"

"Got a funny look. Seen a ghost?"

Corin couldn't help laughing, though it wasn't funny. *No, but I may have seen a man who sees ghosts.* He couldn't say it. "No. I thought maybe I'd seen someone I know. But I can't tell."

"Yeah? Who is it?" Declan twisted round in his chair to stare at the counter. "The fit bloke with all the bags?"

"You think he's fit?" Corin couldn't believe that was the first thing to come out of his mouth.

"I might not swing that way, but I've got eyes. Want to invite him over?"

"No—God, no. He could be a complete stranger! And he's leaving, anyway." Adam—if it *was* him, which it *wasn't*—had pocketed his change and was heading for the door, sparing not a glance behind him.

"Bugger. He looked just your type. Ah well, plenty more fish in the fryer."

"Your grease addiction is worrying. I hope Lori's taken out life insurance." Corin hesitated. "How would you describe him? Apart from *fit*."

"Uh, I dunno. Tall, fashionably skinny. Had a tatt on his arm—some sort of tribal stuff, maybe? Black, no colours. Couldn't see much. It only showed where he'd pushed his sleeves up." Declan frowned. "But you could see that, yeah?"

"I didn't notice it." Corin had been too busy staring at the man's face, as though if he gazed at it long enough it'd crack and give up its secrets. But ink made the man more likely to be Adam, didn't it? "What else?"

"Short dark hair? I only saw him for a mo."

"But you thought he was my type."

"Yeah. Kinda, anyway. Apart from the ink."

"Why would that make a difference?"

"Oh, right. Forgot you're into that now." Declan shrugged. "Doesn't matter anyway, does it? He's gone. You going to eat that hash brown?"

CHAPTER ELEVEN

Adam barely noticed the other pedestrians who dodged around him as he made his way back down the high street, lunch bags in his hand.

Corin had been in that café. With the bloke from the street. Which, yeah, didn't mean anything in itself—the man was allowed to have mates, for God's sake—but their body language had made it seem like they knew each other *really* well.

And then Corin had looked at him—or rather, looked *through* him. What the hell was all that about? When he'd glanced away, it'd almost been like he was ashamed, which, again, what the hell? He didn't owe Adam anything, so it couldn't have been because he'd been with another bloke.

Unless he was a closet case? But it wasn't like him and that bloke had been obviously a couple. They could have been close friends. And if it was that, then why not acknowledge Adam? Christ, a polite nod would have done. It had been so weird that Adam's plans of shaming him with a friendly greeting had gone straight out of the window.

The whole thing was doing his head in. He started wondering if he'd imagined it all. Shit, more hallucinations—that was all he needed.

No. It wasn't just him, was it? The other night in the pub, Scratch had been there too when Corin clearly hadn't had a clue who Adam was.

Lost in thought, Adam almost collided with a group of teenagers walking three abreast. "Sorry," he muttered, standing aside to let them pass.

"Should have gone to SpecSavers!" one of them called back after him, to raucous laughter.

Stepping back out on his way, Adam stopped dead, and then had to apologise again, this time to a lady who almost bumped into *him*. Could that be it? Could Corin have some problem with his vision? Adam's step faltered. That would explain it, and Jesus, that must suck, if so. Hell, it would be Adam's worst nightmare—losing his sight, and with it, his art.

And there Adam had been, making it all about *him*, while Corin was struggling with a disability—maybe, but it was starting to seem increasingly likely—and Adam had done bugger all to help. He'd have to step up. *If* Corin ever spoke to him after this.

Adam pushed open the door to Furious Ink to find Sasha and Scratch sitting on the sofa with their heads together. They glanced up with identical solemn expressions.

"Fuck, who died?" Adam blurted out.

Scratch's face creased in a worried frown. "Uh, your mum did, mate," he said slowly. Then he yelped as Sasha elbowed him in the ribs. "What?"

She glared at him. "Simon Greczik, do you *ever* think before opening your gob? Cheers for lunch, Adam. Did you remember the brown sauce?

"Yes." Adam passed over her bag, then leaned back on the front desk to give them both a searching look. "What's been going on here while I was out?"

Scratch sent a nervous glance Sasha's way. "We was only talking."

"About me." Adam checked which bag held his lunch and put it down on the desk beside him.

Scratch reached for his pasty, then let the arm fall when Adam didn't hand it over. "Not *only* about you."

"Jesus. What was I just saying, literally *seconds* before I walked out that door?"

Sasha stood. Arms folded, she fixed him in the eye. "What was *I* saying, for that matter? We're your mates. I don't give a toss what you say—we happen to care if you're haunted by visions of your dead mum."

"I heard her talking too." Fuck, why the hell had he said that?

Scratch's eyes went wide. "You heard her? Like my sister?"

"*What*?" Adam and Sasha said simultaneously.

"'Fore I knew either of you, that was. I had a sister, see. Couple of years older than me. Got mown down by a drunk driver when I was four."

Adam frowned. "Yeah, I remember you telling me." There had been pictures of her up in the Grecziks' living room, the colour faded with the years. A little girl with dark, curly hair and a cheeky grin.

Scratch shrugged. "So I used to hear her, sometimes. After she'd gone. She'd come up with games to play, tell me stories, that sort of thing. Like she used to when she was alive. Never saw her, though."

"You never told me that." Adam realised he was gaping at Scratch and shut his mouth.

"Didn't want you thinking I was barking, did I? Hadn't heard her in years, by the time you and me was mates, anyhow. Reckon she thought I was okay on my own by then."

Sasha had been quiet for a long time. "Your sister, though . . . That was good, right? It was a comfort for you, cos she wasn't completely gone?"

"Well, yeah. Course, me mum and dad didn't know what to make of it, but I was happy."

"But—" Sasha caught herself with a guilty glance Adam's way.

Adam's chest felt cold. "But you think my mum's, what, some kind of evil spirit? The *bad* kind of haunting?"

"No!" Sasha paused. "But maybe you should think about getting the house cleansed? We're not short of people round here who'd do it for you."

Adam folded his arms and glared at her. "You want to exorcise my mum."

She held her ground. "If she's hanging around, it's not healthy for you *or* her. Help her to move on. That's all I'm suggesting."

"My landlady could do you a deal on a job-lot of sage," Scratch put in helpfully.

Adam sighed and thrust a paper bag at him. "Don't you have work to go back to? Eat your pasty."

"Will you think about it?" Sasha persisted.

"Maybe." Right now, he felt like even that was a concession she didn't deserve.

It seemed to mollify her, though, as she opened up her paper bag and took out her bacon butty.

Adam finally felt safe enough to take out his own sandwich. Trouble was, he didn't seem to have much appetite anymore. Christ, things had been so much simpler when he'd only been worried he was losing his mind. Finding out his two best mates seriously thought ghosts could be real . . . It made his guts churn to think about it.

Could Mum still be around, in some way?

And did Scratch really have such a low opinion of her? He'd never said anything back when they were growing up. Although maybe there *had* been a lot of invitations round to tea at the Grecziks'. Lifts to and from football.

"So Adam, you seeing that Corin again soon?" Scratch asked in what was presumably an attempt to lighten the mood.

Adam gave a despairing laugh—thankfully, only in his head. "His appointment's in ten days." He took a bite of his sandwich, hoping that would signal the end of the subject.

It didn't, apparently. "I don't mean that. Give him a bell. Ask him out for a drink."

"I haven't got his number." *And he wouldn't welcome a call from me anyway.* Although, if it was simply that Corin had an issue with his sight, maybe he wasn't as indifferent to Adam as he seemed? Maybe that was why he claimed not to want a relationship—he was self-conscious about it or just didn't want anyone's pity?

"No? I have." Scratch swallowed a mouthful of pasty and held out his hand. "Gimme your phone."

God help him, Adam was tempted. But— "You can't go giving people's numbers out."

Sasha looked up, a smear of brown sauce on her lip. "He's right, Scratch. You really can't."

"I'll call him, then. How about next Friday? All of us, down the Prince of Wales."

It wasn't a *totally* bad idea. A new bloke in town would probably welcome the chance to get out and meet people. "I guess?" Adam couldn't help it coming out sounding like a question.

"Who's playing?" Sasha asked.

"Think it's them blokes with the guitars made out of old tin boxes. They're good, they are." Scratch took an unfeasibly large bite of his pasty.

"You mean the Baton Rouge Brothers? Yeah, they're not bad. Their stuff's a bit slow, though. Hard to dance to."

"S'posed to be slow, innit? It's, like, the genre. All right to chat a bloke up to, though." Scratch sent a meaningful glance in Adam's direction. "Slow, heavy beat . . . sounds good to me." He made some suggestive hip movements.

Adam had to laugh. "Cheers, mate. I see you're being your usual subtle self."

Sasha raised a tattooed eyebrow. "Thought you were only into thrash metal, Scratch."

"Me? I got eclectic tastes."

"What, and a dictionary for Christmas?" Adam teased.

"Nah, new comic book. *I Sing the Body Eclectic*. Had to look it up, didn't I?" Scratch grinned. "So you're in, then?"

"I'm in. Hell, even if Corin doesn't go for it. Sash?"

"I'm not busy that night. So yeah, okay."

Adam narrowed his eyes. "But remember I saw him first, you got that?"

"Course, mate!" Scratch made an expansive gesture with his pasty-holding hand, and a flake of pastry wafted through the air to land on the desk. "You know I've only got eyes for the lovely lady here, anyhow."

The lovely lady made an unimpressed face. "Get lost, Greczik. And clear up your mess."

Scratch beamed. "See? She loves me."

Adam shook his head, finished his sandwich, and prepared to get back to work.

CHAPTER TWELVE

Declan insisted on doing the tourist trail after lunch, which at least gave Corin an excuse to visit places he'd have felt daft going to on his own. So they trekked out to the Chalice Well and paid their entry fee.

There was more to the place than Corin had expected; not just the holy spring itself, but also gardens laid out with walkways. The flower beds were looking fairly bare, but he could imagine in summer they'd be a profusion of colour and scent. "It's peaceful here, isn't it?" he murmured as they gazed at the gentle flow of water over softly rounded, rust-stained stones into a manmade pool. Even the ever-present tourists were speaking in hushed tones, barely audible over the trickle of the water. "Spiritual."

"Yeah, seems like the place to come if you want to get lost inside your own head." Declan's tone wasn't approving.

Corin rolled his eyes. "You were the one who wanted to come here. What next—quick walk up the tor?"

"Nope. I can see it from here—what's the point in slogging all that way uphill?"

"To get you in shape for when you're running around after a toddler?"

"Nah, they don't start walking for around a year. I've got plenty of time. Isn't there an abbey around here somewhere? That's *not* up a bloody big hill?"

"Fine. But it's halfway across town. So no moaning to me about the walk."

It didn't, actually, take them all that long to backtrack to the abbey, which took up a sizeable area right in the middle of town. It was set in pleasant, green parkland, with ancient trees in their autumn colours making a vivid contrast to the pale stone of the ruins. Fat squirrels scampered across the grass, perhaps used to cadging treats from visitors.

Some smaller buildings on the site were more or less intact, but all that remained of the great church were a few fragments of walls and window arches, although intricate decoration could still be seen in places. Corin wasn't religious, but he caught snatches of a similar kind of peace here to that in the Chalice Well gardens.

"Old King Henry did a proper job knocking this place down, didn't he?" Declan commented as they wandered around the ruins, stopping to scoff at King Arthur's supposed burial place, a medieval marketing ploy.

"I think it was seventeenth century builders who did most of the damage, taking the stone to reuse."

Declan laughed. "You call them historical vandals; I call them early eco warriors. Wasn't there something in the news about this place a few years ago?"

Corin shrugged. "I don't remember seeing anything."

"That's cos you never read the papers. The internet can't tell you everything." Declan tapped away at his phone with a distressing lack of irony. "Yeah, here it is, in the *Sun*."

"Oh, we're calling the *Sun* a newspaper now, are we?"

"I knew we should never have let you go to uni. *Anyway*, some woman took a photo of a ghost monk. One of the ones that got their heads chopped off by Henry VIII— No, wait, they got the full hanging, drawing, and quartering. Lucky bastards, bet they felt proper special. Two monks and an abbot, it was. They've all been seen haunting these ruins. Right up your street, this, innit?"

"What?" Mention of ghosts had got Corin thinking about meeting Adam that first time, and for a moment, he thought Declan had read his mind.

"You know. Spirits and all that crap. You sounded really into it back at the Chalice Well place."

"I said I liked it there because it was *spiritual*, not because it was swarming with spirits." Corin grimaced, remembering Adam in the mist on the tor. "Don't think I'd want to meet an actual ghost."

"Yeah. A death like that, they've got to be feeling pretty vengeful, even after all these years. If I ever get bumped off in a way that's only half that gruesome, you'd better believe I'm coming back to haunt the bastard what done it."

Corin's blood chilled. If anyone was a candidate for a haunting, wouldn't it be him? "Ghosts aren't real. Come on, it's getting colder. We should get a move on." He strode off without a glance at his brother, then felt like an idiot as he stood pretending interest in a particularly crumbled bit of stonework waiting for Declan to catch up with him. Because he couldn't be certain he'd be able to pick him out of a crowd.

"You okay there?" Declan's tone was mild.

Corin huffed. "Fine." They fell into step together.

"I've been thinking. You ought to watch out," Declan said after a few moments. "Someone walks up to you in the street and acts like they know you, they could be anyone. *I* could be anyone. I could be a ghostly fifteenth-century monk—"

Corin rounded on him. "*There aren't any ghosts*. People see spirits because they *want* to see them. Because they miss the person who's died, and they want to see them again. It's a trick of the mind. And you're hardly dressed like a monk—although I see you're working on a natural tonsure—and I know what your voice sounds like," he finished in a rush.

Still smiling, Declan took a step back, holding up his hands, palms open. "Oh, vicious. I like it. Strikes me you're the one who needs to keep his hair on, though. I just want to make sure you're looking out for yourself."

Corin scrubbed his face with his hands. "Sorry," he said, not sounding any more regretful than he felt. Seriously, how could Declan joke about *dead people*? It had been barely six months since the accident—

He jumped as Declan's arm landed across his shoulders. "Come on, let's get you home, baby brother. It's about time I was making tracks. Don't want to outstay my welcome." He laughed in Corin's ear.

"What welcome?" Corin said mulishly, feeling like a child in a strop even as he said it.

"And there's a question. Don't worry, I'm used to it." Declan gave him a one-armed squeeze. Corin allowed it grudgingly, if also a little gratefully.

The sun was going down by the time they made it back to the flat.

"Want to stay for dinner?" Corin offered as they stepped inside. "I could rustle up a meal that probably won't kill you."

"Don't worry about it. I told Lori I'd be back early evening, and she said she'd leave something on the stove for me." Declan grinned. "Most likely, a note saying 'Cook your own dinner, you lazy sod,' but I'd better get back for it just in case."

He slung his rucksack on his shoulder, and Corin followed him out onto the exterior stairs, more reluctant than he'd expected to see his big brother go.

"This is it, then," Declan was saying. "You take care of yourself, all right? And keep in touch, you bastard. I don't want the next time I hear from you being a postcard from Outer bloody Mongolia."

Corin smiled. "Yeah, point taken. Repeatedly. Give Lori a hug from me, okay? And go careful on the motorway."

Declan pulled him into an awkward embrace and clapped him soundly on the back. He clattered down the stairs, gave a final wave and then was lost from view as he headed down the street to where he'd parked his car.

Corin stood there for a while at the head of the staircase, thinking. He felt better, for having seen his brother, and for the first time, wondered if moving here had been a mistake. It'd been fine between him and Declan, after the initial wobbles. They'd fallen back into old patterns easily enough.

Maybe he should have stayed with the people he knew?

But it hadn't been Declan he'd been trying to get away from, had it? It had been all the casual acquaintances. The ones who took offence when he didn't recognise them, or assumed he *did* and was deliberately ignoring them. Like his Avebury next-door neighbour, who'd clearly been in a mood with him for some unintentional slight the last time he'd spoken to her. Or the lady in the post office, who hadn't been impressed with him for asking after her sick mother, because it turned out she wasn't the lady he'd thought she was at all, but her sister-in-law helping out. Actually, that one he could understand, as she was Asian and old enough to remember when "jokes" about people from ethnic minorities all looking the same had been distressingly common. It hadn't made him feel any less mortified about it, though.

Even worse were the ones like the guy who ran the Avebury coffee shop, who'd obviously heard Corin had a brain injury, if not the full details. He'd gone from unsubtle flirting to taking exaggerated care to speak to Corin kindly and clearly, as if he were a child or a dementia patient. If that hadn't drummed into Corin that he was no longer seen as relationship material, nothing would.

Dark was falling now in earnest, and lights in windows shone brightly. There were fewer people passing by—and one man standing by a wall, gazing up at Corin. Had Declan forgotten something? No, this man was dressed differently. The colour of his jacket was black, not khaki, and he wasn't wearing jeans. Apart from that, there was little to distinguish him—he had white skin and darkish hair, although it was hard to tell the colour in the fading light. He was dressed more smartly than the average Glastonbury weekender, and with a wrench, Corin was reminded of Blair, who'd always liked to look his best—

No. It couldn't be.

Could it?

Ghosts aren't real.

But if Adam had really seen his mum on the tor, did that mean . . .?

Chilled to the bone, Corin scrambled back into his flat and locked the door. He leaned against it, his heart racing.

Had Blair come back to haunt him?

CHAPTER THIRTEEN

Corin got up late on Sunday, after an uneasy night plagued with dreams of Blair that he was grateful to only faintly remember. He shovelled down a half-hearted breakfast of toast and no marmalade, because Declan had finished the jar, and then flopped into the sofa with a heavy sigh. He didn't know what to do with himself. Or rather, he *did*—he needed to buy another lamp and an extension lead, and it would make sense to do a proper food shop for the week ahead—but he was having a hard time summoning up motivation.

After Declan's whirlwind visit, the flat seemed depressingly quiet and empty. Had he made a mistake, cutting himself off from everyone to move here?

No, he told himself firmly. He liked Glastonbury, with all its quirks. What he was missing was the way life had been before the accident, and he was never going to get that back. Better to start afresh, in a new town, with people who wouldn't have to get used to the change in him. Who wouldn't expect anything of him.

Except that wasn't true, was it? They'd expect him to act like, well, a normal person would. To recognise people he knew. To give them a friendly greeting when he saw them on the street. Restless, Corin jumped to his feet and strode over to the window.

The sun had peeked out from behind heavy clouds and was shining on the high street rooftops and the tor beyond. Corin felt a sudden urge to get out to the tor. He could buy a sandwich on the way and eat it on the hilltop. Take a spare, in case the homeless person was still there on the pathway—if not, it'd keep for tomorrow. Getting some fresh air had to be better than mooching around in his flat on his own.

Maybe he was doing this wrong. Should he be upfront with people about his disability? People like Scratch, who'd been so friendly. And Adam, who'd . . . been hurt, mostly. Queasy guilt filled Corin's insides. If he'd simply told them at the studio that he was face blind, Adam would never have assumed he was being snubbed or that he was too boring to remember.

But, despite himself, hot shame flooded through Corin at the thought of explaining to Adam he had brain damage. He could imagine the awkwardness and the pity in Adam's voice afterwards. It would be like the guy in the Avebury coffee shop all over again. And it was stupid the way that prospect was like a knife twisting in his gut, because he *knew* his liking for Adam wasn't going to lead to anything.

He'd just prefer that fact not to be rubbed in his face, that was all.

The hospital nurses had been kind. They'd told Corin—and his parents, when they'd flown back for a brief visit—that he shouldn't feel ashamed of his condition. Unfortunately, a large proportion of the rest of the world didn't seem to have got the memo. It might be frowned on these days to joke about the mentally impaired, but that didn't mean nobody did it anymore. They were simply more selective of their audience. And while Corin hoped fervently that he'd never think any less of someone else for having a disability, somehow he couldn't see himself in the same light. Which was probably all kinds of prejudiced and wrong, but that didn't stop him feeling that way, did it?

But brooding on it all wasn't going to make it better. Corin jammed his feet into his trainers and threw on a jacket. Keys, phone, wallet . . . Right. He was going out.

As he stepped out of his flat onto the external staircase, Corin found himself scanning the surroundings for the figure he'd seen last night. There was no one there, of course. Or rather, there were a fair number of people passing by on the street, but no lone man staring up at him. He clattered down the steps and out towards the street at a purposely brisk pace, but couldn't stop himself coming to a halt at the corner where he'd seen the man and turning to look up at his building.

There was nothing to see. No posters in windows, no loose tiles on the roof. Not even an antique satellite dish. Nothing to explain a passerby's interest in the property. And his flat was the only one with an entrance this side of the building. Which meant it had to have been Corin he was interested in . . .

No. That was crazy. And egotistical. Why would a stranger have been so interested in Corin? Unless it wasn't a stranger—unless it was someone who knew Corin?

Then why not wave or call out to him? Make himself known? Unless for some reason he couldn't? Corin shook his head. He refused to believe in ghosts. Maybe he hadn't seen the man at all. It must have been a trick of the twilight—a conjunction of shadows that had made him think he'd seen a person. There was a word for—pareidolia, that was it. The human tendency to see faces everywhere.

Except pareidolia didn't account for Corin's clear memory of what the man had been wearing. A black jacket and dark trousers. Smart casual clothes, not the worn-in jeans, dark goth fashion or bright hippie wear more usually seen around town.

Corin cursed under his breath and spun to head out into the street. He was making too much of this. Some random man on his way to pick up his date had stood for a few minutes gazing up at the flat. So what? Maybe he'd considered renting it himself, but Corin had got in first. It meant nothing.

Less than an hour later, Corin was sitting on only slightly damp grass on top of the tor, feeling ridiculously proud of himself for having managed to navigate there on foot with only minimal help from the GPS on his phone. The fresh—almost too fresh—air up here had blown away his worries, for now at least. Here he was, out in the world, among people. Granted, he wasn't exactly interacting with them, but they were there.

It was clear and sunny now, and the view from the tor was glorious. Somerset spread out before him, its patchwork fields liberally dotted with trees clad in autumn golds, reds, and browns. Plenty of others were taking advantage of the good weather too. A middle-aged couple with an over-excited golden retriever were making their way up the path, the dog walking three times as far as his humans in his joyfully meandering route. Laughing voices behind Corin alerted him to a family with two tiny children playing hide-and-seek around St. Michael's tower. A lean, ponytailed runner in Lycra jogged past, panting, earbuds in her ears and her gaze not deviating from her path.

Corin unwrapped his carrot and hummus sandwich and took a bite. It actually wasn't bad. He'd bought an all-day-breakfast sandwich too, but the rough sleeper on the path, whose name was Kai and who used they/them pronouns, had chosen that one. Corin had even managed to tell Kai he might not recognise them again if he saw them elsewhere. Because he was face blind. He'd said the words.

Kai hadn't seemed too bothered by the news. They'd simply thanked him for the sandwich. Of course, they were probably used to people looking past them. But anyway, it was a start. Maybe he'd be able to tell other people now. Like Scratch. And Adam.

Well. Maybe.

Corin didn't linger once he'd finished his lunch. The wind was getting up, clouds had gathered, and the damp was soaking through his jeans. Much longer up here and he'd be shivering, so he shoved the sandwich packet in a pocket and stood.

He'd barely taken a step when his phone rang. Corin pulled it out and stared at it. Who the hell was *Si*? There was a Simon at the office, but they didn't work together and there was no reason for his number to be in Corin's phone. He hesitated, then accepted the call. "Hello?"

"All right, mate? Listen, you busy Friday night?" The warm, locally accented voice seemed vaguely familiar.

Corin was thrown by the friendliness. "I, uh— Sorry, who is this?"

"Didn't I put me name in? It's Si. Simon. Scratch."

A wave of almost-relief washed over Corin as the pieces clicked into place. And now he came to think about it, didn't he have a faint memory of Sasha calling Scratch *Simon*? "Oh, sorry. Your voice sounds different on the phone. How are you?" he hurried on, trying to make up for his earlier coldness.

"Me? I'm good. So you're on for it, then?"

"On for what?" Great, now he was confused again.

"Friday night. Prince of Wales. Me and a couple of mates are going to see the band. It's a good'un, mind. Baton Rouge Brothers. Dark swamp blues."

Corin had absolutely no idea what that meant. But the thought of having something more than his own company to look forward to at the end of the working week was suddenly irresistible. "Okay," he said recklessly.

"Yeah? Good on you, mate. We'll be there from around half past eight, that okay?"

"That's fine." Corin took a deep breath. "Who else is going? Anyone I know?"

There was a pause. "You remember Sasha? From the tattoo studio? With the hair?"

"Yes, I remember her." Thank God. He'd have a fair chance of recognising their group with Scratch and her in it.

"And Adam, of course."

Corin swallowed. "Right. Well, I'll see you on Friday."

It would be fine. Wouldn't it?

It would have to be.

Corin drew his jacket closer around his body against the growing chill, and set off towards home.

Halfway down the path, a persistent drizzle set in, its mist-like effect turning the landscape and its inhabitants to grey. Shoulders hunched against the rain, Corin reached Kai's gate and found they'd vanished to who-knew-where. Melted away like the spirit of Adam's mum, the first time Corin had come here.

Would there be another ghost waiting for Corin when he reached his flat?

Corin shook his head. *Think about real things. Like the social event you just let yourself in for.*

Not the terrifying possibility that Blair was haunting him.

CHAPTER FOURTEEN

A lone in Mum's house—*his* house—on Sunday morning, Adam mooched about reorganising the kitchen. Half the time he ended up putting the crocks and pans back where he'd found them.

He still couldn't quite get his head round how seriously both Sasha *and* Scratch had taken his maybe-ghost stories. Growing up in Glastonbury, he remembered him and his mates thinking it was hilarious, all the stuff the New Age visitors seemed to believe in—spirits, fairies, and the like.

Of course, when he'd been a little kid, Adam had *wanted* to believe in fairies. He'd spent hours staring out of his bedroom window in the dark, hoping to catch a glimpse of Gwyn ap Nudd and his fae hordes flying past on the wild hunt. Maybe he'd be one of the lucky few mortals who, the stories said, were taken along for the ride?

But around when he'd hit his teens, he'd faced the facts: the stories weren't real, there was no wild hunt, and a horned god didn't hold court under the hill. No one was coming to take him away from his cold, silent house with a mum who didn't seem to want him. He'd thought that was what growing up was about. Giving up your childish dreams.

Later he'd felt more sympathy for that lonely kid. He'd gone so far as to get himself inked with the images from those dreams, remembering how those stories had been something to cling to when he'd needed them. But at the time, he'd joined his mates, laughing at the tourists and daytrippers who hadn't seemed to get the memo that fairies and spirits weren't real. Hadn't Scratch used to laugh along with the rest of them? And yet all the while he'd had his own haunting.

If ghosts were actually a thing. Which Adam wasn't ready to concede yet. Even if he didn't have any other explanation for what he'd seen and heard.

Except for the possibility he was losing his mind . . .

Should he try what Sasha had suggested? Cleanse the house? Go down one of the magic shops and buy a shedload of sage, incense, crystals, and fuck knew what else? He'd feel like a total dickhead. And anyway, it wouldn't be right, trying to cleanse the house of his mum's spirit. As if Mum—if she really was still here in some form—was a stain on the carpet or a patch of mould on the wall.

His gut revolted at the thought. No. He wasn't going to do it. End of.

Maybe he should try talking to her? Ghosts were supposed to hang around because of unfinished business, weren't they? And if it was him she was appearing to, that meant it had to be something to do with him, didn't it?

There was one bit of unfinished business he was only too keen to get cleared up. Hell, maybe that was *why* she hadn't . . . crossed over, or whatever was supposed to happen when someone died. Because she must have known he'd want to ask her about it.

And she wanted to tell him. After all these years. Which meant she really did care about him, right? Adam stared out of the kitchen window, the view a little blurry. Maybe she'd just been bad at showing it.

How was he supposed to talk to a ghost, though? Did he need, like, a Ouija board? He hadn't been using one when he'd heard her a few days ago. Maybe simply speaking aloud would be enough? He drew in a breath—then paused. He'd heard her when he was in the living room, looking at the Scottish painting.

Adam put down the saucepan he'd been half-heartedly trying to find a home for, and strode into the living room. It was a bright morning, and the sun shining through the living room windows somehow made the place appear even more drab. He should hurry up and get new curtains. Maybe some throw cushions too. Red, maybe. Those would brighten the place up—

And he was procrastinating again. Adam wiped his palms on his jeans and went to crouch in front of the painting still propped against the wall. The stag gave him a wide-eyed look, as if surprised to see him. He should really hang that properly.

"Mum?" Adam swallowed. "If you're here and you can hear me—" He stopped, suddenly unsure of how to continue.

There was no answer. But then, he hadn't exactly finished his sentence, had he?

"I'm sorry," Adam said in the end, his throat unaccountably congested. "I was going to come to see you. Soon. We just ran out of time, okay?"

The house was silent, except for the distant sound of an upstairs window rattling in the breeze. Unless it wasn't the breeze . . . ?

"If there's something you want to tell me, I'm listening, yeah?" Adam waited, but there was no reply. Disappointment crashed through him, followed by annoyance at himself. Had he honestly thought it would be as easy as making a phone call? "You can tell me anytime about . . . about my dad. I'm not mad at you or anything. I just want to know."

There was no answer. Not so much as an encouraging rattle from the window. Was he being selfish, here? Making it all about him, all about his needs?

"But if not, you should be at peace, Mum. You don't need to worry about me. And I, well, I love you, okay?" Adam had to clear his throat to continue. "You're my mum, and you always will be. Even though we didn't always get on. You're still my mum. You can . . . You can rest now."

Adam felt hot and uncomfortable, but also lighter inside.

He straightened. A whole day off work. He should use it. Make the house look better. Get those cushions, some throws, and the curtains. Not red, though, now he came to think about it. Deep green would be better. Or purple, like the heather in the painting. Or both. Yeah, both would be good.

Course, it'd be a bugger getting that sort of stuff home on the Yamaha. Adam wondered how Evie would feel about being asked to come shopping with him and bring her car. She'd most likely tell him to sod off and get a more sensible means of transport for himself. That would be the adult, responsible thing to do, wouldn't it? Put practicality over fun.

Yeah, right. Grow up, be sensible, stop believing in fairies. Because that'd made him so much happier when he'd tried it the first time.

Hang about though—Mum must have had a car, mustn't she? She'd always had one when he was a kid. And with no mortgage to pay off, and the money Dad sent her every month, there was no reason she'd have had to give it up.

Adam grabbed his phone and called Evie.

"Oh, hi, Adam."

In the background, he could hear people talking. "Sorry, is this a bad time?"

"No, no. We're only out to brunch."

Adam laughed. "*Brunch*? People actually do that?"

"Yes, Adam, people do that. Did you have a reason for calling, or did you simply want to mock my lifestyle?"

"Yeah, actually. Uh, a reason. Not the mocking thing. Did Mum have a car? And if she did, what happened to it?"

There was a pause. "Of course she did. I put it in the garage." The unspoken *obviously* was pretty clear.

"I'm an idiot." Adam hadn't even *looked* in the garage out the front. He'd assumed it would be full of junk, like the one at his old house share.

"Far be it from me to argue." She huffed and went on briskly, "You'll have to send the V5 form in to the DVLA to register the change of ownership. And get insurance, if you're planning to drive it. It can't be on the road until you've done that."

"Right. Where will I find all that stuff?"

"All the documents should be in her files. I thought you'd have gone through those already."

Adam cast a guilty glance over at the dining table with its neat stack of cardboard folders, exactly as Evie had left them.

"I've been busy. Sorting stuff out. Moving in." Trying to pass a message beyond the veil. "Uh, listen, can we meet up sometime? To, uh, talk?" He couldn't ask her about death and spirits over the phone. Especially not when she was in the middle of *brunch*.

There was a pause. "Fine. We're busy today, but maybe one evening this week or next? You could come round for dinner."

"Couldn't you come round here?" Her husband Paul was a financial advisor in his midforties who liked opera and shared Evie's disapproval of her and Adam's Dad. To date, Adam had only met Paul the once, which had been plenty. They had *literally* nothing in common apart from Evie, and no way was Adam going to talk about Mum's possible ghost in front of him. "I'll cook," he added belatedly.

"*Can* you?"

"*Yes*. I cooked all the time for me and Dad." It had been that or survive on a diet of microwaved frozen dinners.

"Okay. I'm sorry, but I have to go. Would Wednesday suit you? Oh, no, sorry—we've got something on that night. Look, I really do have to go. Can we sort out a date another time?"

"I guess." Adam tried not to sound too disappointed. "Enjoy the rest of your *brunch*."

"Thanks."

They hung up, and Adam headed for the kitchen, where Mum had kept her keys in a drawer jumbled with assorted batteries, elastic bands, candles, and other oddments. Sure enough, there was a bunch with a car key and what might be the key to the garage. Adam couldn't believe he hadn't noticed them before. Then again, he'd mostly been interested in cutlery and cooking utensils.

Adam jogged down to the garage, unlocked the double doors, and swung them open.

Inside, hidden in the gloom, was a little black Ford Ka, ten years old by the number plate. Mum had had a Fiat when he'd left home, so she couldn't have got this one new, but it looked in good condition, with no dents or spots of rust. Inside, it was clean and smelled of pine air freshener, with noticeably more wear on the mats on the driver's side. When he switched on the engine, it started fine despite weeks of inactivity, and the mileage was low. Adam was tempted to take it out for a spin, but with no insurance, even a short run around the block would be a stupid risk. Not worth losing his licence over—or getting an ear-bashing from Evie, for that matter. Reluctantly, he locked it up again and walked back to the house to start on the paperwork.

When his phone rang, he jumped a flipping mile. He fumbled to accept the call. "Scratch? Hi, mate. How's it going?"

"He's up for it." Whatever he was talking about, Scratch sounded pleased.

"Uh, what? Who?"

"That Corin. He's coming on Friday."

"He is?" Adam's spirits leapt—only to crash as a thought struck him. "Does he know I'm going too, or does he think it's just you and him?"

"Course I told him you'd be there. And Sasha."

"And he was still okay with it?"

"Course he was. I told you he fancies you."

"Maybe. Guess we'll find out Friday." Adam said goodbye and ended the call in an optimistic mood.

Things were looking up.

CHAPTER FIFTEEN

Corin's week went by slowly, up until Thursday night, when whoever was in charge of time apparently decided a massive amount of overclocking was in order. He sat on his sofa, picking at the remains of his dinner—an attempt at an internet recipe for tortilla española that ended up stuck to the pan and that probably tasted nothing like an authentic Spanish dish—and all he could think of was, *Tomorrow's Friday*.

He'd been looking forward to a night out with a group of... well, maybe it was too early to call them *friends*, but people he knew to talk to, at any rate. Right up until it was almost upon him, and the doubts set back in with a vengeance.

The problem was, the more he thought about Adam, the more certain he was he didn't want to stop at being friends. There was something about the warmth in Adam's voice, those intense eyes of his, and the way he held himself—almost with a wariness, as if he'd been let down by people in the past and was half-expecting it to happen again. It intrigued Corin. Made him feel oddly protective.

Which was a sick joke in itself. Corin jabbed viciously at the last few slices of potato on his plate. He couldn't even recognise Adam when he saw him—how the hell could he protect him from anything?

At least there hadn't been any further mysterious figures lurking in the shadows, so he definitely wasn't being haunted by Blair. Which was a ridiculous idea, anyway. If ghosts actually existed—and that was a *big* if—then why would Blair have waited months to start haunting him? It didn't make sense. No, Corin had seen some random man hanging around and, his imagination fuelled by Declan's talk of ghosts and the circumstances in which he'd first met Adam on the tor, had read too much into it.

Right. Blame it all on Declan and Adam. Because it couldn't possibly be Corin's own guilty conscience that had him seeing spectres.

Corin stood and took his plate out to the kitchen. He scraped off the remnants of his dinner, wishing he could get rid of his worries so easily. A workout tonight might be a good idea. Maybe he'd be able to banish the sick feeling in his chest by sheer physical effort.

But he couldn't banish the knowledge that if it hadn't been for him, Blair would still be alive.

By the time he finished work on Friday, not helped by his lack of sleep the night before, Corin had decided to text Scratch that he wouldn't be coming. And then switch his phone off. What had he been thinking, anyway, arranging to meet them at the pub? He already knew he wouldn't be able to recognise Adam. He'd managed okay with Scratch so far, but if Scratch was interested in the band playing, the chances were plenty of other biker types would be too. All it would take would be another young woman with similar hair to Sasha's, and he'd have zero hope of working out who he was supposed to be joining. It was a recipe for disaster.

He'd just picked up his phone to text, when it rang, startling him.

It was Declan—thankfully, because if it had been Scratch, Corin might have had to start believing in telepathy as well as unquiet spirits, and he wasn't sure his sanity could take that. "Hello?"

Declan's voice was loud and cheery. "All right then? Thought I'd give you a bell to see how it's going."

"Fine. It's going fine." Corin hoped he didn't sound too defensive. "How's Lori?"

"She's great, ta. She's waving at you."

"Tell her I'm waving back. Been busy this week?"

"Not so bad. Got a full weekend coming up, though. It's Rob's thirtieth—you remember Rob? So we're all spending the day at the paintballing range on Saturday. Then down the pub in the evening."

Declan paused. "He said to invite you along if you can make it at this short notice."

Reading between the lines, Declan had asked if he could bring Corin. To save him from his friendless existence all alone in Glastonbury. But seriously, paintballing? Declan had to know it wasn't exactly Corin's favourite activity. And how the hell would he be able to tell friend from foe?

Corin was suddenly thankful he hadn't sent that text to Scratch. "I, uh, I think I'll have to give it a miss. Going out tonight, so I doubt I'll be up for an early start."

"Oh, yeah? Where are you off to?"

"Pub. There's a band playing that's supposed to be good." Hopefully Declan wouldn't ask for details. All Corin could remember was something about swamps.

"Yeah? Glad to hear it." There was a bit more sincerity in Declan's voice than Corin was entirely happy hearing. "You, uh, going with someone?"

"Meeting some people there. I've been out for a drink with them before." It was sixty-seven percent true. Thirty-three percent, at least.

"That's great! Good to hear you're making friends. So your mates, are they computer nerds too?"

"Uh, not so much." Corin didn't want to admit how little he actually knew about any of them. "Listen, sorry to cut this short, but I need to get ready. Talk to you another day?"

"Yeah, yeah, that's cool. I'll give Rob your best."

"Cheers, Declan." They hung up, and Corin wiped his hands on his jogging bottoms. He'd have to go to the pub now. Declan would be bound to ask about the evening the next time they spoke, and Corin wasn't going to lie to him outright.

Oddly, though, instead of feeling trapped, he felt as though a weight had lifted off him. It was all out of his hands. He whipped up a quick dish of rice, chorizo, and kidney beans for his dinner, which tasted a lot better than yesterday's effort had—*Note to self: find some authentic recipes*—and relaxed afterwards with a beer. He could do this. If he didn't see Scratch or Sasha, he'd just have to hang around at the bar until one of them spotted him. If all else failed, at least he'd get to see a band.

He set off soon after eight. The Prince of Wales was less than a ten-minute walk away, but Corin didn't go anywhere these days without allowing time for wrong turns. And if he arrived early, hopefully the pub would be less busy so he'd see the group he was meeting more easily. He'd put on dark jeans, a plain T-shirt, and his leather jacket, so he'd hopefully fit in well enough with whatever crowd turned up.

It was full dark, and a chill breeze followed him down the high street, wafting the scents of half a dozen different cuisines his way. Plenty of people were out, but unsurprisingly it was a younger demographic than in daytime. Hardly anyone was alone, like him. Fresh-faced lads and dolled-up young women were in their own swaggering groups, and couples walked hand in hand. Girls with boys, and girls with girls, which was good to see. If there were any male-male couples around, they weren't letting on, but Corin was used to that. It was part of the price of living in a small town.

Would Adam be one for holding hands in public? Corin couldn't see it. He seemed to have an ingrained caution that would likely leave him wary of public displays of affection.

Not that Corin was likely to find out first—hah—hand. Although Adam *had* seemed interested. Scratch had said he was too. Maybe he wouldn't care about Corin's issues?

Brain damage. Call it what it is. Corin's hands tightened into fists. He forced them to relax. *Would you go off Adam if you found out he had some kind of disability?* This time, the internal voice sounded a lot like Declan. And no, the idea was crazy. Maybe he should try trusting Adam?

That would mean trusting Scratch and Sasha too, of course. He didn't think Scratch would treat him any differently—he seemed pretty easygoing—but Sasha was an unknown quantity. *If they don't accept you as you are, you're better off without mates like that,* Declan's voice said flatly. "Easy for you to say, with friends coming out of your ears," Corin muttered aloud, then winced. Nobody on the street was giving him strange looks, though—thank God for Bluetooth.

Corin passed the Market Cross and turned right down what he hoped was the correct street.

It was a reassuringly short walk before he saw the familiar pub sign of the Prince of Wales. A few people were standing outside despite the chill in the air, drinks in hand. Almost immediately, Corin spotted a woman with bright red hair next to a bearded biker—and another man, who was waving at him. "Corin, glad you could make it," he called out.

It was Adam's voice. Corin grinned back, relief flooding through him. And something more—something he couldn't quite identify or maybe wasn't ready to. "Good to see you again," he said sincerely.

Adam's smile was blinding. "Come on inside, we'll get you a drink."

Scratch knocked back the rest of his pint and belched. "All right, mate? Good to see you too, and not just cos we've been freezing our arses off out here—cheers for that, Adam."

"Anytime, mate," Adam said blithely. He'd insisted they wait outside for Corin? The warmth in Corin's chest grew.

"At least you lot are dressed for it." Sasha had a point, clad as she was in old-school punk gear, a black leather miniskirt and fishnets. She turned away from Scratch pointedly as she strode towards the door. "How you doing, Corin? Settled in all right?"

Corin hurried to keep up with her. "Yes, thanks. Um, sorry about the wait in the cold."

Scratch gave him a shoulder bump. "Don't be daft. Right on time, weren't you?"

"Thanks for inviting me. It's been a while since I've seen a band." Even before the accident, there hadn't been a lot of live music in Corin's life. It hadn't been Blair's thing at all.

"Yeah? You ought to come along to Download next year," Scratch said easily as they stepped inside the pub, which was busy but not yet crowded.

"I wouldn't," Adam chipped in, as they found a table near the back. He pulled out a chair next to Corin and turned his way. "Unless you actually *like* wading through a sea of mud to queue for a blocked Portaloo. And everything you own getting soaked through and staying that way. He dragged me along one year, and my trainers were growing mould by the end of the weekend."

Scratch laughed. "'S all part of the fun, ain't it? Sometimes it's sunny. You ought to give it another try."

"Yeah, don't hold your breath for that, mate."

Sasha remained standing, arms folded—either she was impatient or still cold. "Right, who's drinking what, my lovers?"

They gave her their orders—pints all round. "Do you want a hand?" Corin asked awkwardly. As the new guy, should he have been the one to get the first round in?

Sasha raised an eyebrow. "At least one of you bastards knows how to treat a lady. No, thanks, I can manage." She strode off, her high-heeled Dr. Martens and that tight miniskirt giving her hips a wiggle.

"Is she on the pull tonight?" Adam asked, watching her go.

"Who knows?" Scratch answered. "Ours not to reason why."

He sounded a little wistful. Corin wondered again about him and Sasha. "What's Glastonbury festival like?" he asked, to break the silence. "I've never been."

"Too big, too commercial, and too full of rich kids on drugs," was Scratch's verdict.

Adam laughed. "Showing your age there, mate."

"Like you weren't five minutes ago, eh? You and your *Too posh for a Portaloo*."

"Nothing to do with being *posh*. Just cos I don't wanna get dysentery—"

"You're an artist. Ain't you supposed to suffer for your art?"

"That's suffering for someone else's art. You can count me out, ta very much."

"Bit divisive round here, the festival," Scratch went on. "Sasha does all right, but some of the local shops see footfall halved while it's on. All the folk avoiding town cos they think it's gonna be rammed, see? And you can forget trying to drive a car within five miles of Pilton."

Corin made a mental note not to drive *anywhere* local at festival time if he could possibly avoid it.

"Bikes, man. They're the way to go," Adam put in, and Scratch nodded his head sagely.

The pub was filling up quickly as Sasha returned with a tray of drinks, carrying them like a pro through the milling crowd. She'd even bought bags of crisps.

As Adam leaned forward and grabbed a bag of salt 'n' vinegar, his thigh pressed against Corin's—and when he relaxed back again, somehow the contact was still there.

Corin's heart sped up.

CHAPTER SIXTEEN

Adam found it hard to keep his mind on the casual banter around the table. Corin hadn't moved away, so for the last twenty minutes, their legs had been pressed together, thigh to thigh. It was impossible not to hope that Corin was into him.

If he didn't watch out, other things would be getting up and all. Adam downed the last of his beer and set his glass down with a flourish. "Right, my round."

He made to stand up, but Corin forestalled him with a hand on his arm. "I'll get this one."

"You haven't finished your drink," Adam protested half-heartedly, distracted by the casual contact that was all too brief.

"Don't want to get drunk tonight." Corin was already on his feet. "Same again, everyone?"

When he'd gone, Sasha leaned in with a raised eyebrow. "Think he's worried we'd draw dicks on his face if he passed out?"

Scratch laughed. "If you drew it, Sasha my love, that dick would be a work of art. Just like mine, as it happens," he added with a wink.

She lifted a delicate middle finger in his direction. "You mention your dick in my hearing again, Simon Greczik, I'm going to cut it off, pickle it, and give it to your mum for her mantelpiece."

Adam laughed. "That's a weirdly specific threat. Do I want to know?"

Scratch shook his head. "Best not to ask. And if you ever have a daughter, don't send her to an all-girls school. They teach 'em terrible things in those places."

"Taught me not to take any of your bollocks, anyhow." Sasha put down her drink, glanced up, and beamed over Adam's shoulder. "I don't believe it. Chelle's here. See you losers later."

She grabbed her drink and took it with her. Adam twisted in his seat in time to see her giving a massive hug to a young woman with jet-black hair and almost as many piercings as her. He turned back to Scratch. "Old mate of hers?"

"Ex. Least, I think so. Never was sure how together them two were. Thought she'd moved over to Bristol."

He didn't seem bothered about it, but . . . "Worried they're going to get back together?"

"No. Well, maybe. Not cos I'm jealous, mind. Chelle's a laugh, and God knows she's a looker, but she's too fond of the old amateur dramatics, that girl."

Adam raised his eyebrows. "I'm guessing you don't mean she's a theatre buff."

"Too bloody right. But Sasha ain't daft. She knows when to leave well alone." Despite his words, Scratch shot a concerned glance her way.

"So, you're not . . ." Adam wasn't sure how to put it. "You're always flirting with Sash. I thought maybe you wanted to be more than friends."

"What, me and her?" Scratch shuddered theatrically. "No, thanks. I prefer my gonads still attached to my body, thank you very much. Nah, it's just a bit of fun, that's all. She knows I don't mean nothing by it."

Adam felt weirdly disappointed. Sasha hadn't been with anyone, as far as he knew, for as long as he'd known her. And Scratch had been single for longer than that. Call him a romantic, but it would have been nice if they'd been able to make each other happy. "Is there anyone you've got your eye on, then?"

"Who, me? I left my heart in that there London, you know that." While Adam was still trying to process the bombshell Scratch had just dropped—Christ, it'd been *years* since Scratch left London, and no, he definitely *hadn't* known that—Scratch stood. "Gotta go see a man about a dog. Possibly a racehorse. You look after that Corin when he comes back, all right? Don't go letting that grass grow."

Scratch took himself off in the direction of the gents', leaving Adam sitting alone and trying to sort out his scrambled thoughts. It was nice of Scratch to leave him to speak to Corin alone, but it was flippin' hard to concentrate on how to chat someone up when he'd just found out his best mate had been nursing a broken heart for the last half-dozen years. And why was it only coming up now, when Adam had been back in town for weeks already? Was it something to do with Corin appearing on the scene?

Adam glanced over at the bar to see how Corin was getting on. He'd got the drinks and was holding all three of them, but instead of making a move to bring them over, he was standing still, scanning the crowd.

Adam frowned. He was doing it again—looking right past Adam as if he didn't see him. But he'd found their group okay earlier. Course, all three of them had been together then. Bigger target, easier to see? It *must* be some kind of vision thing. Adam stood up and waved a hand to help the poor guy out.

Corin stared, shot a glance over his shoulder, then visibly steeled himself to walk over with the drinks.

"Sorry, mate," Adam said as soon as Corin was in earshot. "I should have come and helped you out there."

"It's fine, thanks." Corin didn't seem to have any issues putting the drinks on the table without spilling them. Or finding his chair and sitting down. "What happened to the others?"

"Sasha saw a mate and Scratch had to pee." Adam hesitated but went ahead anyway. "Listen, I've got to ask. Are you partially sighted?"

Corin froze. "I— No." He stared at the table, his shoulders slumping.

Adam felt like shit. *Way to ruin a good night out.* "Sorry, mate. None of my business anyway. Shouldn't go round asking personal—"

"It's brain damage," Corin cut him off.

For a moment, Adam wasn't sure he'd heard right. Was this a wind-up? But Corin's face was as serious as he'd ever seen it. "Uh . . ."

Corin carried on, his words oddly inflected, as if he had to force them out. "I was in an accident—a car crash—and now I can't recognise faces anymore."

"Fuck me, that sucks," Adam blurted out.

It seemed, crazily, to be the right thing to say. Corin actually laughed—although it sounded a bit stressed—and met his eye. "You've no idea." At least his tone was more natural now.

"Guess not." God, imagine living with a condition like that. "So, uh, when you look at me, do you just see a blur? Is it like those faceless portraits by Coco Dávez?"

Corin shook his head. "I don't think so? Sorry. Not that up on art. It's hard to explain, but I can see individual features. I know you've got brown hair and eyes, and I could describe the shape of your face. But you look like someone I've never met. My brain can't fit the pieces together."

And now Adam was picturing faces as a cubist jumble of features, like a messed-up jigsaw. He couldn't wrap his head around the idea of seeing someone but not recognising them. "Is it still like that for people you know? Family and close friends, I mean?"

"Everyone." Corin sat back and closed his eyes for a long moment. "If my own brother walked in here now, I wouldn't know him from, well, Adam."

Despite the brave attempt at humour, Corin's mouth was a thin, miserable line. What the hell did you say to someone who told you something like that? "Here was me thinking you were just trying to pretend you hadn't seen me all the time," he quipped weakly.

Corin hunched in on himself. "Sorry."

"No, hey—you shouldn't apologise for it. It's not your fault." Adam gave what he hoped was a reassuring smile and decided to go for it, his heart speeding up like that one time he'd taken a pill from a mate in London. "Bit of a relief to hear it's nothing personal, to be honest. Cos I like you. Was hoping maybe you liked me."

Corin stared at him—and now he was alert to it, Adam could see how his gaze moved, tracking Adam's features and returning to rest a little lower than eye level. Looking at his mouth, maybe. Was that a good sign? That had to be a good sign, right?

Then Corin sighed and turned his gaze away again. "Still, after what I've told you?"

"Doesn't change who you are, does it? And if it did, I've only known you since it happened anyway, so I don't see what it's got to do with anything," Feeling fiercely protective, Adam put a hand on Corin's arm. "I mean, come on, you didn't run screaming when I started babbling about seeing ghosts, did you?"

Corin stared at the hand on his arm. His other arm twitched, as if maybe—Adam's breath caught—he wanted to cover Adam's hand with his own. But he let it fall back to the table. "I'll never recognise you," he said in a low voice. "Even if we hooked up, I'd walk past you in the street five minutes later."

"But you can recognise Scratch and Sasha," Adam couldn't help himself from saying, some tiny part of him still hurt about that.

"Scratch: beard, biker clothes, and spiderweb tattoo. Sasha: red hair, partly shaven, and those eyebrow tattoos and the piercings. It's called finding an identifier. Something I can recognise people by. If you gave Scratch a shave and put him in a suit, I wouldn't know him."

"Give Scratch a shave and put him in a suit and his own mum wouldn't know him. But yeah, I see what you mean. So, like, I haven't got an identifier?" *Isn't there* anything *memorable about m*e? his inner child whined. He slapped it down.

"No. Sorry." Corin sent him a wry glance. "If it helps, good-looking people are the hardest to recognise. Regular features, nothing weird that stands out."

"Huh." Yeah, his inner child could put *that* in its nappy and smoke it. Or crap on it. Whatever. "Okay, I'll take that compliment."

Corin gave a weak smile and visibly relaxed, and Christ, Adam was an idiot. How hard must it have been for the guy to tell him all this? He was obviously a pretty private person. And here Adam had been, making it all about *him*. He squeezed Corin's arm. "Thanks for telling me, and I'm sorry if I've been a dick about it."

Corin glanced up at him. "What? No, you haven't. I know it's hard for people to deal with."

Adam huffed a laugh. "Yeah, gotta be a lot harder for you, mate. So, is there anything I can do to help? Should I, like, start wearing a name tag? Or—I know—wear a red bobble hat at all times?"

Corin's smile seemed more genuine this time. "You don't have to go that far. Just speak to me, when you see me. I'll know your voice."

It was weird to feel so affected by a simple statement, wasn't it? After all, there were dozens of people, maybe hundreds, who knew Adam's voice. But the way Corin said it made it seem intimate, somehow. Like he'd made a special study of the way Adam spoke. Like he'd done all he could to try to know him, even if he couldn't recognise his face. "I will," he said, and squeezed Corin's arm again.

This time, Corin's free hand did come up to cover his, and Adam's heart leapt.

Then Scratch sauntered back, munching on a packet of pork scratchings. "Oi, none of that now. Band's about to play. C'mon, you wanna be near the front, don't you?"

Adam wanted to yell at him, because seriously, timing? But then he glanced at Corin. The shy smile directed his way lightened his whole being. He smiled back.

He could wait.

CHAPTER SEVENTEEN

Corin's heart pounded as he followed Scratch and Adam over to where the band had set up. He felt like he'd stepped off a cliff and instead of meeting a messy death on the rocks below, had landed in a bouncy castle. Could this really be working out okay?

To be honest, he wasn't sorry for the interruption. Things had been intense there, for a moment, and it was good to be able to catch his breath.

After a few minutes, the lights dimmed, and the band introduced themselves in strong West Country accents that shifted several thousand miles further west when they started to sing.

Googling *dark swamp blues* had taken Corin to a YouTube video of a skinny young man in a cowboy hat playing an oddly hypnotic guitar solo, all ominous chords and slides. It had sounded like it belonged in a Western movie soundtrack, accompanying a band of outlaws as they rode slowly into town to face death or redemption or, more likely, both.

The Baton Rouge Brothers were actually quite a lot like that. There were two of them, both tall and thin, wearing skinny jeans, Western boots, and cowboy hats—black ones, obviously. They had a pedal-operated drum kit, as well as the oddest-looking guitars Corin had ever seen—they seemed to have been constructed from old boxes they'd found lying around in their garage. Their music was good, with a heavy, slow beat and a creepy edge.

As if to prove his point, they launched into a song with the refrain, "This is Hell." Corin found himself smiling.

Adam nudged him and leaned in close. "Not bad, are they?"

Corin raised his voice to compete with the music. "Pretty good. You've seen them before?"

"Few times," Adam half yelled back.

They gave up talking after that to enjoy the performance. No one was dancing, but there were a lot of heads nodding and toes tapping to the beat. Corin and Adam stood close enough in the crowd that they were constantly touching without even meaning to, as people shifted position to get a better view or pushed through the throng to reach the bar. Corin felt drunk on a single pint. As if he'd won the lottery without so much as buying a ticket. High on proximity and unexpected hope.

Space got tighter as a faster number got a few of the women pushing their way to the front to dance. Sasha, with her scarlet hair, stood out as one of them. She was dancing with a black-haired woman—a friend? Girlfriend? Or just someone she'd met on the dance floor? Jostled out of position, Corin felt a hand take his own and glanced over, startled.

"Don't worry. It's me," the smiling man next to him said in Adam's voice. "Adam," he added, as if to make absolutely sure Corin could be confident in his identity.

There was a world of difference in Adam's matter-of-fact assertion of who he was, and Peter's awkward, patronising manner in their Zoom calls. Corin squeezed his hand, and Adam's smile broadened.

When the set finished, they were still holding hands. Corin let Adam lead him over to where Scratch was propping up one end of the bar. They must have lost their table while the band was playing. Corin didn't care. He was too restless to sit down anyhow.

"Got the beers in already," Scratch greeted them, and smirked in the direction of their joined hands. "You don't have to thank me."

Adam gave Corin's hand a last squeeze and let it go. "All right, then, we won't. Hand 'em over."

Corin took delivery of his own pint of beer with a nod and a smile. He hadn't meant to drink any more tonight, but he didn't have to worry now about revealing his attraction to Adam. The thought made his heart swell.

"Good, them lads, aren't they?" Scratch said proudly, as if he'd personally mentored the musicians.

Sasha appeared suddenly and slung her arm through Scratch's, her face flushed. "Where's my drink?"

Her tone was short. Had something upset her?

"Here you go, Sasha my love." Scratch handed her a tall glass.

She gave the dark liquid in it a suspicious sniff and then smiled. "Simon Greczik, you're a fucking treasure."

"Been telling you that for years. Now drink your Jägerbomb before it goes off."

Corin gave Adam a questioning glance.

Adam shrugged and turned to Sasha. "What happened to your mate, Sash? Chelle, was it?"

She glared at him over the top of her glass. "Don't fucking ask." Then she turned to Corin with a smile so quick and broad it had to be fake. "You two been getting on all right?"

"Uh, yes. Thanks. Good band," Corin added to take the focus off him and Adam.

"Think I'll be heading off soon," Adam said. "Work tomorrow."

"God, don't remind me," Sasha replied, as Corin was still trying to process the unwelcome surprise. Was Adam going to leave him like that?

"Thought maybe I could walk you home," Adam murmured in Corin's ear, and his heart leapt.

"That'd be great."

"Cool. Hey, Scratch, you okay seeing Sasha home?"

Sasha slammed her empty glass down on the bar. "Fuck you. I can see myself home."

Scratch slid his arm around her. "Ah, but who's gonna make sure I get back safe? You get all sorts out on the streets late at night. I might wake up in a bath with no kidneys if I don't have you to watch out for me."

"Is there really nothing going on between those two?" Corin couldn't help asking as he and Adam made their way down the street a few minutes later. Not holding hands—but close enough together that their shoulders brushed.

Adam laughed. "Don't ask me. Scratch swears not, though. I think they're just good mates, you know? He met her when he moved back here a few years ago, and I guess maybe he needed someone to be there for him?"

"He was having a bad time?"

"Ah...Not mine to tell. But yeah, I reckon he was. Not that he let on back then, the bastard." Adam fell silent for a few paces. "Wish I'd been around for him. I should have been. Should have known."

Corin grasped his hand and gave it a quick squeeze, then let it go regretfully. "You shouldn't blame yourself. I don't think anyone can know what's inside someone else's head. No matter how well you think you know them." He hoped Adam hadn't picked up on the note of bitterness there.

No such luck. "Voice of experience?" Adam's tone was blessedly light.

"You could say that. My ex," Corin explained awkwardly.

"Ah. We don't want to talk about him, do we?"

God, no. Blair was the last person Corin wanted to talk about. Now or ever.

"Or her or them, of course," Adam said before Corin could muster a reply.

"Him. I'm not into other genders. Not in that way."

"No? Me neither. Hey, look, we've got something in common already." Adam smiled, and tangled their fingers together once more for an all-too-brief moment. "So I was thinking, we should, like, go out, yeah? Just the two of us. I'm working tomorrow, but if you fancied getting together on Sunday?"

"Sunday's good," Corin said quickly, then kicked himself mentally. *Was that too eager?*

Judging by Adam's grin, it had been exactly the right amount of eager. "Great! Uh, how are you on a bike?"

"What kind of bike?" Corin asked cautiously. Was Adam another pedal enthusiast? "I haven't had a bicycle since I was a kid—"

"Oh, no, Yamaha. I know some people aren't that keen on riding pillion, but if you wanted, I could pick you up? We could head out of town? Or, if you'd rather, I expect you've got a car? I mean, I've *got* one, but I can't actually drive it until I get the paperwork sorted out." Adam ducked his head. "So, yeah. Bike?"

Was he nervous too? Corin warmed to him even further. Then he considered the question, and a chill shot through him. *Would* he be okay on the back of a motorbike? At least in a car, passengers were protected by crumple zones and airbags. Motorbike riders were horrifyingly vulnerable. And what if Adam was a speed freak?

"Shit—sorry." Adam's hand on Corin's arm made him jump. "That was so fucking thoughtless of me. Course you don't want to go on the back of a bike after you nearly died in a fucking RTA."

He sounded stricken, and Corin wanted nothing more than to reassure him. "No, it's fine. I can't expect you to keep my accident in mind every time you speak. I'd rather you didn't, to be honest. And the short answer is, I don't know if I'd be okay. I do drive, when I have to, and I've been a car passenger since it happened. I get a bit nervous, though." Corin's face was burning. He hated sounding weak. "But we could try?"

"We don't have to. We could stay in town, no problem."

"How about we make that plan B? If the bike ride doesn't work out?"

"You sure? I don't want to push you into doing stuff you're not comfortable with."

"You're not." Corin grimaced. Staying in his comfort zone was tempting, no doubt about it—but if he'd done that all evening, he wouldn't be here with Adam now, would he? "It might not work out. But I'd like to try."

"That's cool. And don't worry. I'm a careful rider. Learnt in London—you can't afford to go around being an idiot on those roads."

"That's reassuring." They'd somehow reached Corin's flat already, and he waved at the external staircase. "This is me."

"Up there? Cool. You must get some good views."

Was he angling for an invite up? Corin had been wondering if he should extend one—but much as he liked Adam, his chest went tight at the thought of moving so fast. This time last week he'd resigned himself to lifelong celibacy. What if Adam expected Corin to recognise him, once they'd been intimate?

"Hey." Once again, a hand on his arm interrupted Corin's frantic thoughts. "You okay? Cos I'd better be off home now—work tomorrow for some of us, yeah?—but it's been great getting to know you. I'm looking forward to Sunday. Pick you up around two?"

Relief flooded through Corin—carrying with it the faintest whiff of contrary disappointment. He'd been overthinking it again. "Two works for me. Have a good day tomorrow."

"You too. And, uh, slap me if I'm being cheeky, but—" Moving slowly enough that Corin could have easily ducked out of the way if he'd wanted to, Adam leaned forward and gave him a gentle kiss on the lips. The heat and the pressure, with the faint taste of beer, were there one moment and gone the next, and left Corin yearning for more.

Adam drew back, smiling broadly. "Nice. See you Sunday."

His lips still tingling from the kiss and his heart singing, Corin watched Adam walk away until he turned into the street and was lost.

Corin was still riding the high as he made his way up the metal staircase to his flat. He most likely wouldn't sleep a wink tonight, with excitement—and yes, happiness—fizzing in his veins.

What the hell. Sleep was overrated, anyway.

CHAPTER EIGHTEEN

Adam slept better than he had since Mum's death and woke up still buzzed from the night before. That had gone well. *Really* well. He wasn't sure what was going on in Corin's head, but the skittishness from their first few meetings had seemed to disappear, as if he'd decided Adam was someone he could trust. All Adam had to do now was live up to that. And yeah, he could do that. He could do that in *spades*. He walked to work in the brisk autumn sunshine with a smile on his face. Despite the early hour—for the weekend, anyhow—quite a few people smiled back.

When he reached the studio, Adam sauntered inside and drew in a deep breath. "Mmm, I love the smell of disinfectant first thing in the morning."

Sasha glanced up from the transfer she was preparing, her expression sour. "I see someone got his end away last night."

Adam rolled his eyes. Affectionately. "Nah, we're taking it slow. Seeing him tomorrow. What's up with you? Hangover?"

Her eyes narrowed. "No, just obnoxiously cheerful wankers talking too loud."

"Hangover it is, then." Adam sent her a winning smile. "Sit tight and I'll get you a coffee. Proper one, from the caff. I'll even throw in an almond croissant."

Sasha grumbled something that sounded like, "Must be paying you too much," as he strolled out the door.

Adam was in luck and didn't have to queue at the Breezy Moon. No doubt it'd be rammed by lunchtime, but for now there were only life's natural early risers: a gaggle of mums with tiny babies and an elderly couple bundled up against the nonexistent cold inside.

He made it back to the studio in short order and handed Sasha her cup and a paper bag with a flourish. "Want some headache pills with that? Forgot to ask earlier, but I could nip out to the chemist's if you want."

Sasha glared at him again, but the fire had gone out of it. "I'll live." She softened further after her first bite of croissant and sip of coffee (black, like her soul). "So, you and that Corin, then?" Her tone was more cautious than congratulatory. She put her coffee carefully on the desk. "You're a thing now?"

Adam raised an eyebrow. "Like I said, I'm seeing him tomorrow."

"And he's coming in for his ink, what, next week?"

"What about it?" The warm glow that had surrounded him since he'd woken up took a dousing.

She gave a lopsided shrug, her mouth turned down. "Be careful, okay?"

"Careful of what?" Adam's temper sparked. "You've got an issue with him because—" He stopped himself just in time from saying, *he's got a brain injury*. Sasha didn't know that, did she? "Uh, what's your issue with him?" he finished weakly.

Sasha's eyes narrowed. "The issue is you dating a client."

"Since when is that an issue? All this time, you knew I fancied him. And you never said anything about it being a problem."

"It's not a problem, okay?" Sasha picked a sliced almond off her croissant and waved it as she spoke. "Not unless it is."

Adam sipped his latte, suddenly wishing he'd got himself something sweet at the café too. "You've lost me."

"Seeing Chelle last night made me think. You know me and her were together for a while? And I still like her, but I always felt . . ." Sasha pulled her half-eaten croissant out of its bag, then crumpled the bag in her fist. "Fuck, this is hard. I broke up with her cos I wasn't sure it was me she really cared about. Not me inside. More like, you know, Sasha Fury, who's got her own tattoo studio. Like, if I'd been Sarah who worked in Sainsbury's, she wouldn't have given a shit about me."

Adam blinked, confused. "Who's Sarah?"

Sasha gave a despairing laugh. "I am, you twat. That's what my mum and dad called me. Changed it, didn't I? And that's not the point. All I'm saying is, be careful your Corin isn't just after you because you're a tattoo artist. Because he thinks it's cool, or he wants to shock his family, or something like that. And it strokes your ego, yeah? Them coming in and looking at us like we're the high priests of alternative culture. But they're not seeing the real you, and when they finally do, they'll piss off, cos you haven't lived up to their fucking stupid expectations."

"Is this about me or you?" Adam asked drily. "Corin's not like that, okay?"

"Yeah, well, you wouldn't be the first to think that." Sasha folded her arms. "So what have you two got in common, then? Apart from an appointment next week?"

"I'll find out, won't I? When I see him tomorrow." Adam found *his* arms were folded now too, and unfolded them quickly because the last thing this conversation needed was both of them getting all passive-aggressive. "I get you're trying to be a mate, but you don't need to worry. I'm a big lad, okay? I can take care of myself."

"Uh-huh? So what have you done about cleansing your mum's house?"

"That's not—" The shop door jangled, and Adam's first appointment walked in. Talk about saved by the fucking bell. "Morning, mate. Come and sit down and we'll get started on your shoulder."

Thankfully, by the time Adam was finished with the shoulder, Sasha was busy with her own client. Good. He wasn't interested in carrying on that conversation. Corin wasn't, like, a groupie or whatever.

Kind of weird, though, how he'd told Scratch he wasn't on the hunt for a bloke. What had changed his mind?

The amazingness of Adam himself, clearly. He glanced in the mirror specifically to give himself an eye roll.

Then he noticed Sasha giving him the side-eye over her client's shoulder and hurried back to work cleaning his tattoo machine.

By the time he knocked off for the day and headed home, Adam had got his good mood back. Fancying a fry-up, he made a short detour to Morrisons to pick up bacon, eggs, and mushrooms, which turned into more of a proper shop when it struck him he might end up cooking for Corin tomorrow.

His arms felt like they'd stretched several inches as he hauled his shopping bags into Mum's house. Adam dumped them on the kitchen floor and straightened cramped hands. "Next time I fancy doing something like that, remind me to fetch my bike and my rucksack first," he told the empty room.

Feeling a bit of a tit but doing it anyway, he waited, just a minute, in case an answer came. Then he shook his head at himself and started putting his shopping away.

As he fried the eggs and mushrooms for his dinner, Adam's thoughts turned to Corin. Not that they'd been far from him all day. How had Corin spent his Saturday? Was he cooking a meal now too?

Come to that, why the hell hadn't Adam suggested they meet for dinner this evening, instead of leaving it to Sunday to see him again? Adam had half a mind to give him a call and ask him over—

An egg spat loudly. *Right. Pay attention to the frying pan before everything goes up in smoke. Speaking of which . . .* Adam took a hurried glance at the bacon under the grill and yep, that was well on the way from crispy to charcoal. He turned off the gas and plated up quickly, then carried his meal out to the dining room to eat in front of Netflix on his laptop. Mum's TV was so old it barely got Freeview.

Adam started watching some new American show Scratch had raved about, but his mind kept wandering and he had trouble keeping track of what was going on. Was that conventionally pretty, dark-haired young woman the main character's ex or was that the *other* conventionally pretty, dark-haired young woman— Adam froze, his fork halfway to his mouth. Was this how Corin felt *all the time*? Like he'd lost the plot and was searching for clues as to what he'd missed?

Shit. That had to really suck. And Corin couldn't rewind real life or look up the cast members online. Or maybe he could? That was what social media was for, wasn't it? And what about those facial recognition algorithms? Adam frowned. There had to be something software could do, right?

Then again, if anyone would know about that sort of thing, it'd be Corin.

Adam shovelled down the rest of his meal, which was now only lukewarm. He still couldn't get his head around it. People's faces were their identity, weren't they? Passports, driving licences, ID cards . . . At the heart of them all was a photo of their owner's face. Faces were who a person *was*. They showed where you came from. Who you were related to—and who you weren't.

Adam sighed as he stood up to take his plate into the kitchen. It was past time he started looking through Mum's letters. Or, to be more accurate, looking *for* Mum's letters. He'd been putting it off for too long. Which was crazy, because it wasn't like he didn't already know the worst, was it?

He washed up—Mum had been ideologically opposed to dishwashers—and dried his hands thoughtfully. He and Evie had checked all the drawers in the house, and there were no unexplored boxes under any of the beds. The only place any old letters were likely to be was up in the loft. He should check there sooner rather than later—after all, there might be any amount of other stuff up there too. Not to mention things that, as a homeowner (and how weird was that?) he ought to keep an eye on. Water tanks that might leak. Felting that could come loose and let the rain in. Wasps' nests. Rats' nests. Faceless old women—huh. What would Corin make of someone with no face at all? Anyway, back to the attic.

Adam had vague memories of Dad fetching Christmas decorations down from the loft when he was little. Mum had never let Adam go up there—especially after he'd broken his arm, when she'd become paranoid about him getting hurt and ending up in hospital again. And yeah, it'd definitely been the last part she'd been most worried about. At least, that was how Adam remembered it. Come to think of it, he wasn't sure Mum had gone up there after that either. By the time he was in his teens, she'd got fed up with Christmas. They'd only had a tree because he'd pestered, and that had been decorated with baubles she'd kept in a box under Evie's bed.

Strange how it was all coming back to him now. Although maybe it wasn't so strange, at that. Here he was in the house where it'd happened. It was bound to jog a few memories. Adam climbed the stairs and gazed at the opening to the loft. Dad had always used a stepladder, hadn't he? Adam couldn't remember there being a pull-down loft ladder. Shit, where the hell was a ladder likely to be? Maybe in the garage? He hadn't exactly done an exhaustive search of the place. All he'd noticed was the car.

Which reminded him—he hadn't sent in the paperwork for that yet. Best get it done while he was thinking of it.

Nodding to himself, Adam made his way back downstairs.

CHAPTER NINETEEN

Corin's Saturday had seemed to take place in an odd pocket of time that somehow both crawled and sped past. He'd spent most of it trying to get the flat looking less just-moved-into—after all, if things went well, Adam would see it tomorrow. His first proper visitor. Family didn't count, not that Declan would let him get away with saying that out loud. If he was here, which he wasn't, and should Corin give him a call? Casually mention he'd got a date?

Corin frowned, doubt stabbing him in the gut. *Was* it a date?

Yes, it had to be. They'd held hands and kissed. Adam had said he liked him. It was a date. They might not have *said* it was a date, but it was definitely a date.

Corin slumped on the sofa, which slumped underneath him in a companiable fashion. He'd be quite happy never to hear the word *date* again, after all that agonising over its definition. He glanced at the time, only to realise there was a reason for his low energy levels. Where the hell had the day gone? Into all those boxes he'd stacked for recycling, no doubt. But at least the place was looking lived-in, with its shelves full of books, games, and Marvel figures.

It looked lived-in, yes. It looked lived-in by a geek. Corin sighed. It was probably all for the best. Adam was bound to find out sooner or later in any case, if the title of *software engineer* hadn't given it away already. Anyway, time for dinner. He threw himself to his feet and went to check out the fridge.

Thirty minutes later, Corin was reflecting that (a) sliced ham was not an adequate substitute for shellfish in paella, and (b) on no account should he offer to cook for Adam tomorrow.

Tomorrow. He swallowed. Was he crazy, going on a date with Adam? Could it possibly end well?

Corin still hadn't got an answer to that question next morning. He woke up late, mostly because he'd had trouble sleeping and had spent most of the night watching *Witcher* playthroughs on YouTube. Still, that meant he didn't have too much time to kill before two o'clock rolled around.

On the other hand, it meant that when he panicked over having nothing edible to offer Adam and dashed out to the nearest supermarket to stock up, he had less than ten minutes to spare as he ran back to the flat. Thank God, Adam didn't arrive early enough to witness his frantic dash.

Corin had put away the shopping and was *almost* sure the flush had faded from his cheeks when the knock came. He ran a hand through his hair, winced as he realised he'd ruined a good fifteen minutes' careful styling, and opened the door.

The man on the doorstep smiled. "Hi, it's me. Adam. You all right?" His tone was easy, relaxed.

Warmth spread through Corin's chest. "Come in. Would you like a coffee? Uh, have you had lunch?"

The smile broadened. "Thanks, no thanks, and yeah, I'm good. Have you eaten? Wouldn't want you falling off the bike from lack of food."

Corin was struggling to remember which order he'd asked his questions in. "I'm fine, thanks. Uh, did you want to go straight out?" That flush was definitely back. He could feel it.

"Hey, no way I'm leaving here without taking a peek at the views. You're well high up here, aren't you?" Adam strode to the nearest window. "Cool. Weird how different the shops look like from above. And wicked, you can see the tor from here." He spun to beam at Corin. "I can see it from my place too. It's closer, but not so high up. Did I tell you I've got a house on the Roman Way? Used to be my mum's. I've only been living there a couple of weeks."

That made sense. "It must be hard with all the memories in the place."

Adam's face changed in a manner Corin couldn't interpret. "It is, and it isn't. It's like, in a way I feel closer to Mum now than when she was alive? Uh, sorry. That must sound weird."

"No, not at all," Corin said quickly and not entirely honestly. "You're an only child, then?"

"No, I've got a sister. Evie. She's older than me." Another expression Corin couldn't decipher. "Mum left everything to me. I tried to get Evie to go halves, but she . . ." He shrugged. "You've got a brother, right?"

Corin blinked. Had he mentioned that? "Yes. Declan. My big brother."

"So we're both the baby of the family, then." Adam's tone was oddly flat.

"I suppose. Declan's always looked out for me." Corin tried for a wry smile. "Our parents were busy with their own lives."

Adam's expression softened. "Parents, eh? Who'd have 'em? Though I won't hear a word said against my dad."

"Your parents were separated?"

"Divorced, yeah. Since I was nine or so. I stayed with my mum, but when I was sixteen I went to live with my dad in London."

Corin tried to imagine what that must have been like. His mum and dad might not have been terribly involved in his life, but at least they'd always been a unit. "Were they okay when you came out as gay?" he blurted, then winced. "Sorry. That was rather a personal question."

"No worries. And yeah, Dad was fine." Adam frowned. "Don't think I ever actually came out to Mum. How about you?"

"They weren't bothered by it." He'd been eighteen when he'd made the big announcement, and about to go off to uni. They'd reacted with mild surprise—whether at the revelation or at the fact that he'd chosen to tell them, he'd never been sure—and then gone with the discussion about their next barbecue. As he'd left the room, Mum had called out, "Remember to always use a condom." It'd made him feel hot and squirmy, and although strangely touched by her concern, he'd avoided eye contact with her afterwards. She hadn't seemed to notice.

"Now," Adam was saying, "are you sure you're going to be okay on the bike? Cos we can totally hang around town if you'd rather."

"No— I mean, yes. I'll be fine." Corin mentally crossed his fingers. "Want to get going?"

"Yeah, why not?"

Corin grabbed his jacket, and they made their way down the metal stairs.

"Here she is." Adam waved a hand at the motorbike parked at the foot of the staircase.

Corin blinked at the old-fashioned dials above the handlebars. "Is that bike older than you are?" he blurted, then cursed himself. *How to charm your date, by Corin Ferriman.*

Adam grimaced. "No, but, uh, close. Hey, she's a good little runner. And she was all I could afford." His tone was defensive.

Oh God. Corin scrambled to recover the situation. "She? Does she have a name?"

". . . No?" Adam's smile restored his confidence.

"Come on. Confess. I promise not to laugh. Much."

"Well . . . she's Japanese, yeah?"

"I do know where Yamahas come from."

"So I call her Miku."

"Miku?"

"From Hatsune Miku. The anime popstar? You've heard of her, right?"

Corin laughed. "Of course I've heard of her. I'm a computer programmer. Can't say I've ever listened to her music, though. How come you're a bigger nerd than I am?"

"Aw. Feeling inadequate? Don't worry. Come back to mine and I'll soon have you singing along to all her greatest hits."

Corin's throat seized up as his mind oh-so-helpfully flashed up images of how Adam might be intending to achieve that.

". . . Or not, you know," Adam said, sounding awkward. "We can hang around town, that's cool."

"No, no, I'd like to." Corin's cheeks felt hot.

Adam smiled. "We'll see where we get to, yeah?" He handed Corin a helmet.

Corin took it with a sinking feeling. He should have foreseen he'd be spending the rest of this date with helmet hair. With a silent apology to the styling gods, he put it on as Adam settled himself on the bike seat, then climbed on behind him. Adam started the engine, and they pulled slowly out onto the road.

Adam rode with far more consideration than Corin had expected, based on teenage dates with boys on bikes. Most of them had treated speed limits as a suggested minimum and corners as opportunities for grandstanding, but riding with Adam was smooth and reassuring. Corin found himself relaxing more and more as they rode on. And holding on to Adam's waist, their bodies pressed close together, was a pleasure in itself.

He'd forgotten to ask where they were going, Corin realised with a jolt as they reached the edge of town and carried on into the Somerset Levels. Adam was heading north. Where did this road lead to?

The next sign they passed told him the city of Wells was this way. Of course. Not that it was necessarily their destination. He'd have to wait and see.

The countryside sped past, farmers' fields now spread out like a patchwork tablecloth as far as the eye could see, and now obscured by roadside trees or hedges. Corin had almost forgotten how much countryside there was around Glastonbury—clearly he needed to get out more. But then, he hadn't been keen on using the car, had he?

It was odd how safe he felt in Adam's hands. Logically, a passenger on a motorbike was far more vulnerable than one in a car, yet he didn't feel a sickening jolt of dread at junctions and roundabouts. He wasn't counting the minutes until he could get off the road.

They passed through small villages without stopping, keeping rigidly to the speed limit, and were into Wells before Corin even twigged that they were close. Adam drove a winding route through town to a car park off the high street, where he parked the bike and pulled off his helmet with a grin. "Sorry, mate, I realised halfway here I forgot to say where we were going. Have you been here before?"

"No, never." Corin made a most likely doomed attempt to ruffle up his flattened hair. "All I know about Wells is that it shares a bishop with Bath. And I got that from watching old *Blackadder* shows."

"Yeah? What's your favourite season? Mine's the fourth one. That ending, when they go over the top of the trenches to get mown down by machine-gun fire..." Adam shook his head.

"Poignant. You don't expect that from a comedy show." Corin gave a wry smile and handed over his helmet at Adam's gesture. "Is it shallow if I say I preferred season two because Rowan Atkinson was weirdly fanciable in Tudor getup?"

Adam glanced up from locking the helmets to the bike and laughed. "Yep. Shallow as fuck. You've given yourself away now. Although I'll admit there was something disturbingly hot about him with a beard and earring."

Adam would look pretty hot with a beard and earring, Corin couldn't help musing. Actually, now he came to think of it—"How come you don't have any piercings? Um, sorry, that came out sounding weird. I just mean, it seems to go with the job. Like Sasha. And the ink, of course. You're the least tattooed tattooist I've ever met."

"Met a lot of us, have you?" Adam's tone was teasing. "But yeah, I know—not exactly a great advert for my trade, am I? I do have ink, on my chest, back, and shoulders. But nowhere you'd see while I've got my kit on. My dad made a deal with me. He'd support me changing career, as long as I didn't get any ink done where it'd show. In case I changed my mind and wanted to go back into graphic design. Some clients are funny about that kind of stuff."

"So how long have you got to keep to that?"

"Until I'm making a living out of it, so— Huh. I guess I don't, anymore." He grinned. "Wicked. What do you reckon I should get done first?"

"I'm not the best person to ask. I'd be tempted to tell you to go for a really eye-catching and unusual design."

Adam darted him a sharp glance. "So you could use it to recognise me by? A— What was it? An identifier?"

Corin nodded, his heart sinking. He shouldn't have brought that up. Who wanted to be reminded that their date couldn't pick them out of a line-up? "Like I said, you shouldn't listen to me."

"No, that'd be cool. Something unique." Adam frowned, then his brow cleared. "Gonna have to think about that. So anyway, want to take a wander? There's some really old bits in town, if you're into that kind of thing."

The bands around Corin's chest eased. "I moved from Avebury to Glastonbury. So clearly I hate all old stuff with a passion. Modern tower blocks are way more to my liking."

Adam laughed. "It'd serve you right if I took you on a tour of 1960s council housing on our next date."

"I'll look forward to it," Corin said straight-faced, while hot little butterflies invaded his insides. *Planning another date already?*

"'Fraid you're gonna have to make do with the cathedral and the bishop's palace today. Ready?"

Corin nodded, and they set off down the high street, which gave way to the cobblestones and open expanse of Market Place.

"Do they still have a market here?" Corin asked as he glanced around.

"Wednesdays and Saturdays. Course, some of the stalls are the same ones you see in Glastonbury on a Tuesday. You been to that yet?"

"Not yet." Corin frowned. Unusually for him, he was getting a sense of recognition—unless it was simply a quirk of his damaged brain. "This place seems weirdly familiar, but I know I've never been here before."

Adam laughed. "Maybe you've seen *Hot Fuzz*, then? It was filmed here. A lot of other stuff has been too. Wait till you see the Bishop's Palace. Perfect backdrop for a bloke in armour to sit on a horse exuding knightliness."

The far side of Market Place was impressive enough, with a turreted gateway and battlemented buildings that appeared more like the entrance to a medieval castle. If a medieval castle housed a local solicitor's firm and a women's clothing store, that was.

When they walked through the gateway, Corin realised he'd been right about the castle. The Bishop's Palace could have been conjured from the tales of King Arthur, with its crenelated ramparts, turrets, and an actual moat. "Those medieval bishops didn't exactly go in for vows of poverty, did they?"

"Not so much, no. And back in those days, if you had it, you flaunted it. Money, that was. Come on, there's loads to see."

Adam paid for their entry, and Corin followed his infectious smile around the complex. There were gardens, ruins, and the wells, which were actually springs, for which the city was named. They took a walk on the ramparts and gazed at the views of Wells Cathedral, which easily rivalled Notre Dame in its Gothic splendour, and the distant Mendip Hills. Glastonbury Tor was visible too, its tower once again shrouded in mist. Adam gave a wry chuckle. "Bet you, when you met that weirdo up on the tor, you never thought you'd end up here with him."

Corin leaned on the wall beside him, their forearms touching. "Not a weirdo. Losing a parent can't be an easy thing to go through."

"Yeah. Messes with your head. Although—" Adam seemed to catch himself. "Hey, fancy a coffee? There's a café in here, or if you've had enough God-bothering grandeur, we can find a place in town."

What had Adam been about to say? And why stop himself? But it would be prying to push. "Either's fine with me."

They ended up in the café on site because it was handy and the cakes were enticing. "Wanna grab a table, and I'll order?" Adam suggested as they walked in.

"No, I'll order. You paid for entry."

Adam hesitated. "Okay. I'll watch out for you coming back and wave so you know where I am."

Corin's heart swelled again with that strange mixture of pleasure and pain. He didn't *want* to be someone his date had to make special allowances for, but it was nice that Adam did, and that he thought about it without having to be reminded.

There was nothing worse than having to continually ask for help— Corin shook his head at himself. All right, there were any number of things worse than that, but it never seemed like it at the time.

He managed to order them coffee and cakes, experiencing only minimal confusion when the two women behind the counter turned out to have similar colouring. Then he turned, tray in hand, to look for Adam.

A smile had him setting off in the right direction even before he saw the promised wave. There was a certain curve to Adam's mouth he was beginning to recognise, a hint of lopsidedness that belied the otherwise perfect symmetry of his features.

Either that, or he was about to make a new friend. "I hope you're Adam," he said as he put the tray on the table. "Otherwise my date is probably not going to ask me out again."

"He'd have to be an idiot, then," Adam's voice said. "Yep, it's me. I can prove it. Ask me anything."

Corin pulled out the chair and sat. "Who won Eurovision in 1987?"

Adam laughed. "Buggered if I know. I wasn't even born then."

"Correct answer." Corin grinned and handed Adam his slice of carrot cake.

"Cheers, mate." Adam dug in, then paused with the forkful halfway to his lips. "Listen, I was thinking—couldn't you do something with facial recognition software? I thought that was a big thing in policing these days. Anti-terrorism and all that shit. Could you build yourself some glasses that look people up for you?" He popped the cake into his mouth.

Corin put down his coffee cup and gave a rueful smile. "Sorry to disappoint, but the title *software engineer* means just that. I don't build stuff. I only write code. It's not like in the movies where the genius hacker is also a dab hand with a soldering iron and can knock up complex robotics from stuff he finds lying around the house."

"Okay, have someone else build them for you?"

"There's the small detail I'd have to rob a bank first for the funding." Corin took a bite of his fruit cake. It was good—rich and moist with a strong hint of brandy in the flavour.

"That sucks. They should make it available on the NHS."

Corin shrugged. "I'm not sure I'd use it even so. I might be a computer nerd, but that doesn't mean I fancy lugging one around everywhere I go. Not one much larger than my phone, at any rate. And to be honest, I wouldn't want to get dependent on it. You remember I told you about coping strategies, like looking for an identifier? It takes practice. I'm still getting better at it. At least, I hope I am."

Adam nodded slowly and gestured with his fork. "So, you're saying you'd get rusty if you had a computer doing it for you half the time?"

"Exactly." Should he tell Adam he was starting to know his smile? But the last thing Corin wanted was to make him self-conscious about it. He might start doing it differently. Corin took another bite of his cake instead.

"How's the fruit cake?"

"Not bad. Want to try some?"

"Go on, then."

Corin chopped off a generous amount from the end he hadn't bitten into and held it out to Adam on his unused fork. Instead of taking the fork from his hand, Adam bent his head, eyes twinkling, to take it in his mouth. "Mmm," he mumbled around the large mouthful. "'S goo.'"

Corin's jeans began to feel a little tight, and he hoped his face wasn't as flushed as it felt. There was something so intimate about feeding someone, and it had been a long time. Blair had found that sort of behaviour childish—

That doused the mood like a stone-cold shower. God, Blair was only six months dead. No matter how things had ended between them, should Corin be here, enjoying himself with another man?

Adam swallowed. "Uh, so, that was supposed to be sexy, but I'm guessing from your face it didn't exactly work for you. Sorry about the awful table manners."

"No, I— " Corin flung himself back in his chair. "I'm sorry. It's me. You made me think of my ex, and . . . Oh God. Way to ruin a date. I'm really sorry."

Oddly, instead of stomping off and leaving him like any sane person would, Adam gave a soft smile, and patted the hand Corin still had resting on the table. "Hey. It's okay. Bad breakup?"

Corin gave a despairing chuckle. "The absolute worst."

"Is that why you moved across country?"

"Kind of. Only not in the way you think." Corin sighed. "It's complicated. It happened six months ago," he added, so that Adam wouldn't think he was on the rebound. Even if he was, in a way.

"Was that about when you had your accident?" Adam's voice was sharp.

"Yes." Now Adam would assume Blair was a bastard who'd dumped Corin while he was lying in hospital with brain damage. He probably ought to feel ashamed of the bitter part of himself that was pleased at that thought.

Adam rubbed his fingers over Corin's hand. "If you wanna talk about it, I'm here. But if you don't, that's okay too." He flashed a sudden, bright smile. "And it's your turn to try my cake. If you don't mind sharing a fork."

Corin smiled. "Well, we've kissed already, so I expect I'll survive it."

"Sure? Could be one of those double-exposure things. Like the pillar of fire in that Rider Haggard book. Second time's fatal."

"If your kisses also confer immortality, I think we should have discussed that in advance."

Adam's eyes lit up. "I can't believe you actually got that reference. Did you grow up in a library too?"

"Are you going to be really disappointed if I admit I've only seen the film?"

"Gutted. In fact, that's it. Sorry, we're just not compatible."

"I guess I'm not getting that cake, then?"

Adam grinned and held out a forkful. "Which movie was it?" he asked, as Corin closed his lips around the cake.

Corin rolled his eyes and gestured at his full mouth. The carrot cake was light and sweet, with a robustly flavoured cream cheese icing. "I think it was 1960s?" he said when he'd swallowed the mouthful. "*Hammer House of Horror*? It had one of their main actors in it, I know that. Peter Cushing or Christopher Lee. Not sure which. And . . . Ursula Andress, was it? With an amazing gold headdress on." His smile faltered. "Not that I'd know any of them if I saw the film again now."

Adam reached across the table and grasped his hand. "I could tell you who's who if you like. If we watch it together. Or, you know, any movies you like."

"I'd like that," Corin managed, his heart full.

"Anytime." Adam squeezed his hand, then let it go.

Corin tried not to feel too disappointed. They were in public, after all. "So what are the tattoos you've got? You never said."

"Oh, right." Adam seemed a little distracted. "The one on my chest is Gwyn ap Nudd leading the Wild Hunt."

"I thought the Wild Hunt was supposed to be led by Odin? Or the Hogfather." *Great. That's the way to impress the cool tattooist: hit him with the nerd jokes.*

To Corin's surprise, Adam beamed. "You're a Pratchett fan? I love the Discworld. Read those books so many times. Which one's your favourite?"

"Is that a trick question?" It would be like choosing a favourite child. "The wizard books, I think."

"Yeah? I like the ones about the witches. *Lords and Ladies*, best book ever. It's got, like, everything in it. Shakespeare and fairies." Adam cocked his head. "You know Gwyn ap Nudd is the king of the fairies, right? At least, that's what they say. He rules over the underworld in the heart of Avalon."

"Which . . . is Glastonbury Tor?"

"Yep. Dig deep enough on the tor and it's fairies all the way down." Adam's tone was redolent with mischief. "Except when they ride out on the Wild Hunt, coursing through the air after a bloody big mystic stag. Or reaping men's souls, depending on what you believe."

"So what do you believe?"

Adam laughed. "I like to keep an open mind, but my ink shows a bloody big stag. With enormous antlers. Not that I'm compensating for anything, I'll have you know."

Corin was suddenly absurdly conscious of every part of his body and in particular those parts in closest proximity to Adam. He took a sip of his coffee, but it'd gone cold. "Ugh. Do you want another drink?"

"No, I'm good. Unless you . . .?"

"No. No, I'm fine." Corin gave him a smile, feeling oddly shy. "We should probably make a move, then."

Adam stood up with easy grace. "Yep. No more slacking. I'm on a mission to seduce you with sightseeing."

It's working. His heart light, Corin stood and followed Adam out of the café.

CHAPTER TWENTY

It was the best afternoon Corin had spent in, well, *ever*. His chest grew tight as the sun dipped toward the horizon. "So, um, I guess we should head back?" he said to get it over with. "Unless you want to eat somewhere here?" Corin tried not to sound too reluctant, telling himself he'd be fine on the back of the bike in the dark, with Adam driving.

It hadn't been the darkness that'd made Blair crash the car, had it?

"Actually, I was hoping you'd come back to mine? Uh, for a meal?" Adam gave a crooked grin. "Not making any assumptions here."

"I'd love that," Corin said, his heart soaring.

"Cool. You like Italian? It's kinda my go-to. Or I can do omelettes—pretty much anything you like with eggs, in fact—or, yeah, I think I've got the ingredients for a chili. Meat or veggie, whichever you like."

Corin blinked. "Do you live in a restaurant? Or did you buy out Tesco this morning?"

Adam laughed. "I like cooking, so sue me. Come on, car park's this way. I'm hungry."

The bike ride back to Glastonbury, the sun setting on their right, was every bit as smooth as the trip out had been. Adam skirted the edge of town, bringing the Yamaha to a halt midway along a long, straight road at the southernmost end.

"This is it," Adam said as he led the way up a flight of stone steps. "The house I grew up in until I was sixteen."

He opened the front door and switched on the light, gesturing Corin ahead of him. "Living room's on the left."

Corin stepped inside. It had the feel of an old person's house. A specific type of old person. Not the sort with myriad family photos lovingly displayed and a plethora of knickknacks crowding the shelves—although perhaps Adam had cleared some away? There were no obvious empty spaces, though. This, with its drab brown curtains and sparse furnishings was the house of an old person waiting to die. *God, that's morbid.*

But hadn't Adam said his mum was only sixty? "It must have been a shock for you when she died," he said, then realised it was a total non sequitur.

Adam didn't seem fazed, though. "Yeah. It was her heart, you know? Me and Evie—that's my sister—we didn't have a clue." He shook his head slowly. "I hadn't even seen her since I moved back to Glastonbury. Thought I had loads of time. Just shows you, doesn't it? You never know what's round the corner."

Corin winced. *Sometimes literally.* He struggled for something to say. Platitudes about how he was sure she knew Adam loved her didn't seem right—hadn't Scratch said they were anything but close? He blurted out, "Were you hoping for . . ." and then didn't know how to finish.

Adam seemed to fill in the ending all by himself. He nodded. "Yeah. Thought it was about time we cleared stuff up. And Evie's here too. Blood's thicker than water, and all that?" It ended with a questioning tone, as though Corin might doubt . . . What? Adam's motives? His intentions?

In Corin's opinion, blood could be overrated. "At least you have your sister here," he said in the end, hating how banal it sounded even to him.

Apparently Adam didn't think so, because he brightened. "Yeah. And maybe Mum wouldn't have wanted to see me anyway? It's so weird, though. Like, the way she left everything to me? I mean seriously, what's that all about? I couldn't look Evie in the eye after we found out what was in the will."

"It must have been hard," Corin said. Great. Now he was repeating himself.

"Evie was good about it, though. And I guess it's like a rite of passage? Clearing out a house after someone's passed on. All part of growing up." Adam hesitated. "So, uh, your mum and dad—are they still around?"

"Define *around*," Corin said drily, then wondered if it had come out bitter instead. "They're still alive," he added quickly. "In good health too. They moved to Spain when Dad took early retirement. Just before Brexit, which they weren't too pleased about."

"Must've been tough when you had your accident, having them so far away. But they must have visited? Did they come back to stay for a while? Look after you while you were recovering?" Adam's tone was curiously intent.

Or maybe there was nothing curious about it at all. "They visited while I was in hospital," Corin said. "But they're very involved with local life, so it was hard for them to get away for long. And I didn't like putting them out." *And upsetting them with constant reminders of my damaged status.* "We're not that close anyway," he added in a rush, his face heating. "They've always had busy social lives, and I never fitted in. Not loud enough. Not sporty enough." He gave a twisted smile.

Adam put a hand on his arm. "I know what it's like, yeah? Me and Mum—it was complicated. And then there's my dad . . ." He half laughed and shook his head. "That's *beyond* complicated."

Corin's heart clenched even as warmth flooded through him, and he drew Adam into a hug. Curious how a moment ago, he'd felt *he* was the one in need of comfort. Now he felt stronger, with a fierce urge to protect Adam from all the *complications* of this world. "Like you told me: if you want to talk about it, I'm here. And if you don't, that's okay too."

Adam hugged him back, then drew away slightly, looking him straight in the eye. "You mean that? It's a fair old story."

There was the usual dissonance between the known voice and the unmappable features, but Corin smiled anyway. "I haven't got anywhere else I'd rather be."

"Okay, but I'm not telling this on an empty stomach. Did you make up your mind what you want to eat?"

"Anything," Corin said. "All of the things you mentioned sounded great. Whatever's easiest."

"Pasta, then? I've been meaning to try out a proper puttanesca sauce."

What on earth is that? "Sounds good," he said, and crossed his fingers. At least Adam had turned out to be a man after his own heart where experimental cookery was concerned.

Adam, Corin realised half an hour later, was *not* a man after his own heart. Adam's experiments *worked*. The tomato and olive sauce with garlic and capers was the best Corin had ever tasted. "This is amazing," he said, trying to twirl his spaghetti around his fork in the effortless way Adam seemed to manage.

"Didn't turn out too bad, did it? I might try it with tuna next time. Never been so keen on anchovies."

"How did you learn to cook? Was it your mum or your dad who taught you?"

"Mostly the TV and recipe books, to be honest." Adam shrugged. "Mum was always the meat-and-boiled-veg sort, and Dad could burn water. How about you?"

"Still picking things up as I go along. Although not very quickly."

Adam laughed. Apparently he thought Corin was joking.

After they'd eaten and washed up the pans together, there was an odd moment when Corin wasn't quite sure what was coming next.

Adam hung up the tea towel and took a deep breath. "So . . . my dad."

Corin grasped his hand. "You don't have to tell me about him. I'd like to hear it, but not if you've changed your mind."

Adam pulled him in for a kiss. "You're perfect, you know that?"

Speechless, Corin could only stare at him.

"And yeah, I want to tell you," Adam went on, as though he hadn't just rocked Corin's world. "I'll put the kettle on first, though. Coffee? I've got decaff. Or tea, if you're a heathen."

"Either." Corin would have drunk ditchwater if it'd meant Adam opening up to him about a matter that was clearly of huge import in his life.

Please God he'd find the right thing to say afterwards.

CHAPTER TWENTY-ONE

Adam cupped his hands around his mug of coffee. It was good to have something warm and solid to hold on to. Speaking of which, why the hell had he suggested they return to the dining table when he could have been sitting on the sofa right now holding on to Corin?

Right. This wasn't a sofa-cuddle type of conversation. He steeled himself and began. "When I was sixteen, I more or less ran away from home. Went to my dad's. Didn't tell anyone I was going, not even Scratch. Just packed a bag and got on a train to London."

"Because you weren't getting on with your mum?" Corin asked.

Adam huffed, exasperated. "Has Scratch been talking to you too?"

There was a pause. Possibly a guilty one. "What do you mean?"

"He went on to Sasha about how my mum basically neglected me, which isn't—" Adam caught himself at Corin's shocked expression. "He didn't? Tell you, I mean?"

"No. All he said was that you weren't close. Sorry. I assumed—it's the usual thing, isn't it? But I shouldn't have."

"No, it's okay." Adam scrubbed his face with his hands. "Sorry. Bit sensitive. You probably noticed."

"Don't worry about it. And I didn't mean to interrupt."

"Right." Adam struggled to regather the thread of his thoughts. "So, I turn up on Dad's doorstep, around seven o'clock at night cos I didn't know what I was doing on the Tube, and he opens the door and stares at me like I beamed in from another planet."

He'd tried not to let it show, how small he felt faced with the broad-shouldered man in the doorway. On the way down, he'd told himself Dad wouldn't seem like the gruff giant of his childhood memories, not now he was all grown up himself. He'd been wrong.

It wasn't only that the bloke towered over his five-foot-ten frame. Dad was built like a rugby player, with shoulders that could fill a doorway and more muscle on him than Adam had seen outside of the World's Strongest Man competition.

"Are you going to let me in?" Adam had demanded, all bravado on the outside, while inside, he was bricking it. If Dad didn't want Adam in his house, he wouldn't get in. End of. "I've come all the way from Somerset. I'm bloody starving, and I'm busting for a pee."

Dad stared at him so long Adam almost lost his nerve and legged it back to the Tube. "Does your mum have any idea where you are?"

"Maybe," Adam said, meaning *no*. "Can I come in? It's freezing out here." He shifted on his feet. The sun had gone down, and Adam really did need to pee.

Dad stepped back. "Loo's on the left," he said shortly.

Thank God. Adam hopped inside quick, dumping his backpack on the floor, and headed for the door with a plaque reading *This is it*.

He peed, washed his hands, and glanced in the mirror. *Shit. Looking a bit pale there.* Adam had taken a deep breath and squared his shoulders before stepping back out into the hall.

Dad was waiting for him, arms folded. "First things first. You're going to ring your mum and tell her where you are."

"Like she'll care."

Dad frowned. "She's probably out of her mind with worry. Where does she think you've gone?"

"Told her I was going round to a mate's."

"Took a wrong turn, did you? Ended up a hundred and fifty miles off course in North London by accident?"

"Yeah, well, like father like son."

Dad's face did something weird, and he turned away. Adam tensed. *Jesus Christ, shut your fucking mouth before you really piss him off.* But nothing happened, so Adam pulled out his phone and dialled Mum's number.

As she didn't answer, he left a message on the answerphone: "It's me. Adam. I'm at Dad's." He turned back to Dad and demanded, "Happy now?"

Dad gave him a long look, then sighed. "You're hungry, you said? Come on into the kitchen."

It was a big kitchen, with a proper table to sit at. Dad made Adam a cup of tea and a cheese sandwich, and they grabbed a chair each. Adam bolted the sandwich gratefully but couldn't help screwing his face up when he tried to wash it down with a gulp of tea.

"You want sugar in that?" Dad asked.

Adam ducked his head. "Nah—don't really like tea."

Dad grunted. Then he just sat there, staring at Adam.

It got Adam's back up. This was his dad, right? And he'd buggered off and left him when he was barely nine years old. Would it be too bloody much to expect an apology? He wanted to ask why Dad had never visited, but he'd have come off sounding like a whiny kid. "So what's it like living in London?" he asked instead.

Dad startled. "It's okay," he said slowly. "Plenty of things to do. Plenty of opportunities. How's it been back in Glastonbury?"

Adam shrugged. "Boring. Fuck all to do, and it's full of bloody hippies."

"Do you swear like that in front of your mother?"

"What's it to you if I do?"

Dad scrubbed his face with his hands. "Nothing, I suppose. Christ."

Adam laughed, the nerves getting to him.

"School going okay?"

"No. That's boring as fuck too."

"Look, can we take it as read you're a big, hard lad and lay off the f-words?" Dad sighed. "As a favour to me. Last time I saw you, you didn't even know what it meant."

"Whose fault is that?" *And why should I do you any favours?* Adam didn't ask, because it wouldn't exactly help his case.

Dad stared at him for a moment, then stood up abruptly.

Shit. Adam's chest went cold, and he struggled to swallow his mouthful of sandwich. He was fucking this right up, wasn't he? And now Dad was going to chuck him out, maybe with a clip round the ear to send him on his way, and it'd hurt because he was so much bigger—

Dad turned away and opened the fridge. "Do you drink? Because I, for one, could do with a beer."

Adam slumped in relief and tried to get his head in gear. "Uh. Yeah. A bit." Mostly cider, if he was honest, but beer was just cider made out of some other stuff than apples, wasn't it?

"Here you go, then." Dad set a can of Guinness on the table in front of him. "That'll put hairs on your chest."

He sat back down, pulled open his own can, and took a long swig. Adam tried to look confident as he followed suit.

It didn't taste anything like cider. It didn't even taste much like the lager his mate Archie's dad sometimes shared with them, if he was in a good mood and Archie's mum wasn't home. Adam swallowed, hoping his face didn't give him away. Shit. It was a bloody big can too.

"I expect you felt I abandoned you," Dad said.

Adam snorted. There was no *felt* about it.

"Okay." Dad paused to take another swig. "But things were complicated. I'm sorry, though. It wasn't your fault and you shouldn't have had to suffer."

Adam's insides felt hot and strange, and he wasn't sure how much was the beer. He'd thought, when he'd imagined his dad apologising for leaving him, he'd feel . . . bigger, somehow. He'd pictured himself grandly forgiving his dad and telling him what to do to make it up to him. But now that he was here, with this bloke out of his memories who wasn't familiar at all, his throat had closed up. He took a gulp of Guinness to ease it and barely managed not to choke.

Dad gave a soft laugh. "Go easy on the booze, okay? I'm not giving you another. How much do you even weigh? Eight stone?"

"Ten," Adam said indignantly, although to be honest he didn't have a clue. They didn't have any bathroom scales at home. But he'd heard the phrase *eight-stone weakling* and he bloody well wasn't one of those.

"Soaking wet with a pack on your back, maybe," Dad muttered, shaking his head. "Why did you come here, Adam? To give me a bollocking for leaving? Because if that's what you want, have at it; although trust me, I'm feeling guilty enough already."

"I want to come and live with you," Adam blurted out.

Dad stared at him again, eyes wide, for a long moment. Then his face fell. "I'm sorry. That's not possible."

"Why the hell not?" His chest tight and that *fucking* lump back in his throat, Adam stood up. "If you're trying to tell me you haven't got room, that's a fucking joke. In this house? You could put up half my class in here."

"It's not a question of room."

"Then what?" Adam felt sick. "Did Mum tell— Is it because I'm gay?"

Dad's eyes went wide again. "What? No. *No.* I didn't even know. That doesn't make any difference to me. It's complicated, that's all."

"What's complicated? You're my dad. You're supposed to look after me." And, fuck, there he was, the whiny little kid. Adam's eyes stung, and he blinked furiously. There was no *way* he was going to cry.

"Adam, sit down. Please. It's just . . . What about your education? You're what, fifteen?"

That stung. In more ways than one. "Sixteen. Did my GCSEs this year."

"Right. But you'll want A levels, won't you? To go to uni?"

Adam shrugged. "I don't want to stay at school."

"Then what do you want to do?"

"You've got this building company. I checked it out. I thought I could come and work for you."

Dad sighed. "Adam, the people I employ are skilled tradesmen. There's no place for a teenager with no experience and no qualifications."

"Then I'll go to tech college. Do whatever."

"It's not that simple. You're a minor. You can't just up and leave your mum. Not before you're eighteen."

"But you're my dad! What difference does it make if I'm with you or with her?"

"It's not—" Dad took a breath. "The difference is your mum has custody of you under the divorce settlement. If I took you in, I'd be breaking the law."

"But what if she says it's okay?"

Dad smiled, although he seemed sad. "She's not very likely to do that, is she?"

"Why not? It's not like she wants me around."

"Adam, I don't want to patronise you, but most teenagers feel that way."

"She never talks to me unless she has to. She barely even looks at me. If I say I'm going out, she never asks where I'm going, and she never says anything whatever time I get home. And she never remembers to pick me up from after-school stuff. I always have to walk home. In the dark." Adam's voice broke on the last couple of words, and he told himself it was on purpose. He was going for the sympathy angle, right?

Dad was staring again. "Is this true?"

"*Yes*. I wouldn't have said it if it wasn't."

Maybe it wasn't *totally* true—there were odd days when she'd change, be all over him so much it twisted his gut with a sick sadness he was desperate to escape—but it was mostly true. Nine times out of ten. If you got ninety percent in an exam, it was like you'd got everything perfect, because nobody ever got one hundred percent, did they?

Dad took a deep breath. "We'll give her another call. I expect she's frantic, you coming all the way to London . . ." He trailed off, most likely due to the *yeah, right* expression Adam was sure he was wearing. "We'll call her, and you'll stay tonight, and we'll talk about things tomorrow."

"You can call her," Adam had muttered.

"Fine." Dad pulled out his phone—a brand-new iPhone, Adam noted with envy—and paused to glance at Adam, his expression uncertain. "Same land line number?"

Adam nodded, then since it probably wasn't in his best interests to be a dick, reeled it off. Dad looked relieved as he dialled.

When Mum picked up, he didn't mess about with *Hello* or even *It's Joe*. "Adam's here. He's fine."

Adam couldn't hear what Mum said in reply, but a crease appeared between Dad's eyebrows and his voice got louder. Harder, too. "We both know that's not true." There was a longer pause. "I'm not having this argument with you again. You should have told him."

Told him? Told him what?

"He seems like a good lad, but legally speaking—" Dad paced as Mum clearly talked over him. "And what about the moral question, then? You *lied* to both of us—" The hand not holding the phone clenched into a fist.

Adam's heart raced. *Not* because he was afraid of this tall, built stranger who was his dad. He just wanted to know what was going on, that was all.

"Oh, for— I can't talk to you." Dad hung up the call, shoved his phone back into his pocket, and sat down heavily at the kitchen table, his head in his hands. "Shit. I should've taken that in private."

"What didn't she tell me? What's she lied about?" Adam asked, his voice small.

"I need another beer." Dad didn't move to get one out, though. "I don't suppose you'd agree to leave this till tomorrow?"

Adam stared at him. "*No.* Dad, what is it?"

"Fair enough." Dad huffed a bitter laugh, shaking his head. "Except all this has been anything but fair, hasn't it?"

"*Dad.* Tell me."

"All right. But I want you to know how sorry I am. Adam, I wish things were different—always have, ever since I found out—but I'm not your real dad."

CHAPTER TWENTY-TWO

"*I'm not your real dad.*" Corin couldn't imagine hearing those words directed at him—and God, Adam had been only sixteen and a runaway from an uncaring mother. "I'm sorry," he said, knowing how inadequate it was. "That must have been a terrible thing to hear."

Adam's mouth twisted. "Yeah, not going to lie, that was a harsh one."

"So, he said he found out. Does that mean your mum had an affair?"

"That's what Dad reckons. He never suspected, though—not at the time. Didn't find out until I had an accident when I was a kid and had to go to hospital. He worked out my blood type meant I couldn't be his. Mum always denied it. Insisted he was my dad." Adam gave an awkward shrug. "We did DNA tests in the end, me and Dad. He said, otherwise, it was just his word against hers, you know? It proved she was lying."

God. "I'm sorry."

"It's okay. Was a few years ago now. And Dad was great about it, once he got over the shock of having me turn up on his doorstep out of the blue."

"I can't help noticing you still call him Dad."

"He is my dad. In all the ways that matter. Okay, we had a bit of a blip when I didn't see him for years, and maybe I had a few issues with that, but he—" Adam's voice cracked a little, and Corin felt a fierce urge to hold him. But they were sitting on opposite sides of the dining table, almost formally, and it was by Adam's choice. Corin got that—sometimes it was easier to hold yourself together if there was nobody offering to do it for you.

The impulse to comfort won out, however, and he reached across the table to grasp Adam's arm. Adam drew in a shaky breath but didn't pull away. "He really stepped up to the plate, you know? Said I could stay for a week, and we'd take it from there. And we talked a lot, about how he'd been totally screwed up by finding out the truth, and he realised now that he hadn't been fair on me and Evie."

"So you stayed in touch?"

"*Way* more than that." Adam looked up, smiling, and Corin's heart skipped. "So, over the next few days, there were a lot of phone calls to Mum. Most of which didn't end well. I thought I'd be sent back anyway, but at the end of the week, Dad tells me he's been looking into sixth-form colleges locally, and did I want to stay and do my A levels in London? All that, for a kid he hadn't seen in years, and who wasn't his."

"That's amazing." An odd, hollow sensation made its home in Corin's chest.

"Yeah. It was the first time . . ." Adam shook his head, still smiling. "First time I ever felt like someone actually wanted me around, you know? Cos he didn't have to do anything for me, but he still did it."

Corin knew what the odd sensation was now. It was envy. "Your dad must be someone special."

"Yeah. Yeah, he is," Adam said with evident feeling.

There was a silence. Corin wasn't sure how to break it—but then his phone pinged with a message. Declan had sent him a picture of Lori showing off her bump, with him next to it sticking his gut out and the caption, *Don't wanna brag, but I reckon mine's bigger.*

Corin laughed and showed it to Adam. "My brother. And his girlfriend."

"Hey, yeah, I recognise him. Last weekend, right? You walked by the studio with him." Adam stretched and yawned, glancing at Corin's phone again. "Shit, is that really the time?"

Corin hadn't realised how late it was, either. The skies outside were pitch-black. He'd wondered, when Adam had brought him here, if they'd end up spending the night together, but after everything Adam had told him, the mood didn't feel right. Corin felt close to him, but also, if he was honest, a little overwhelmed. "I should get going," he said reluctantly. "Work tomorrow."

"Yeah?" Adam paused. "You could stay if you want. I've got a couple of spare rooms upstairs if you don't want to share. Or I can run you back if you'd rather. No pressure."

"Thanks, but I'd better go. But there's no need to take me on the bike. I can get an Uber. Or walk—it can't be that far." And he probably wouldn't get too badly lost if he used his phone's GPS.

"Hey, it's no trouble. And I bet you'll be starting work earlier than I will."

Corin couldn't argue with that. As he recalled, the tattoo studio didn't open until eleven at the earliest. "Thanks, then. I'll get my coat."

Far from a nerve-wracking experience, the ride back to Corin's flat seemed too short, although admittedly, it was along brightly lit streets at low speed. For a moment, when they got off the bike at the foot of his staircase, Corin considered asking Adam to come inside. To spend the night with him. But no. It would seem weird, having declined to stay at Adam's, and anyway, he really did need some time to process everything. "Thanks for the ride," he said as he handed his helmet back to Adam. "And thanks for the day. It was great."

"No worries. And yeah, it was good." Adam smiled and hung Corin's helmet on the handlebar of his bike. His own helmet, already doffed, was on the seat. "We should do something like that again. Soon."

Adam stepped closer and put his arms around Corin's waist, drawing him in. Corin went eagerly and pressed his lips to Adam's. They fitted together with ease, and the kiss was soft and sweet, lasting for a long moment until Adam drew back with a smile.

"Are you busy evenings this week?" Corin asked. "I should offer to cook dinner for you, but honestly it might be safer to get a takeaway."

Adam laughed. "Hey, no worries. I've got adventurous tastes. Either would be good. I'll have to get back to you on the day, though—promised my sister I'd see her a night this week, and she often has stuff going on. But definitely, we'll do that. And if all else fails, I'll be seeing you on Wednesday anyway."

The tattoo appointment. Corin had almost forgotten about that. It didn't seem so important, now. Telling Adam that was unlikely to go down well, though. "Absolutely."

Adam let go of him and stepped back. "Now come on, up you go. I've gotta see you to your door, right?"

Mourning the loss of Adam's embrace, Corin roused himself to jog up the metal staircase to his door. He lingered at the top of the stairs to watch Adam straddle the bike, turn it, wave, and ride slowly out to the street.

Despite the chill night breeze, Corin was warm inside. Today had been the best day since . . . Well, since long before his accident. It seemed he *could* have good things in his life again.

Even if you don't deserve them— Corin silenced that inner jab as best he could and cast a last glance over the surroundings while he dug his key out of his pocket.

Then he froze.

There was someone standing at the corner once more, gazing up at him.

For a moment, Corin thought it might be Adam coming back, perhaps in the hope of being invited up. But no, he'd heard the bike roar away down the street. And, besides, the figure was all wrong: the posture too straight for Adam's easy slouch and the outline of the clothes was different too—a longer jacket and tailored trousers, not tight jeans. Smart clothes, like last time. It had to be the same man. It *had* to be.

Where had he come from? He could have just wandered in off the street—but at *exactly* the time Corin had come home? If he'd been waiting somewhere, perhaps in a parked car, why get out now and show himself?

Because he wants to be seen. It had to be that. He wanted Corin to see him, because, oh, God, it was Blair, wasn't it? A wave of nausea washed over Corin. Blair—no, Blair's ghost—had been watching him with Adam. Had seen he'd moved on, found someone else, when Blair would never be able to.

All because of him.

CHAPTER TWENTY-THREE

Adam had ridden back on cloud nine after seeing Corin home, and he was still smiling when he woke up the next morning. At work, Sasha's pointed comments only made him . . . fuck, *giddier*, like he was a kid who'd had his first proper drink.

Ah, what the hell. Life was good, and he didn't give a shit who knew it.

He called Evie at lunchtime to pin down a date for dinner this week. That'd give him an excellent excuse to get back in touch with Corin and arrange to meet with him too. And yeah, maybe Adam was feeling a little guilty that he'd told Corin about Dad and not her yet. Best to get that over with. He couldn't keep it a secret from her any longer. It wasn't fair.

It turned out Monday was a good night for her this week, so Adam found himself cooking for company for the second night in a row. He smiled as he served Evie a plateful of chili and rice, then got one for himself. It was a lot less pressure when it was only his big sister rather than the really hot bloke he wanted to impress.

Had he impressed him? Adam was pretty sure he had—or at least, he hadn't disappointed him. Not with the food, anyhow.

A finger of doubt poked him in the ribs. Had telling him about his dad been a bit of an overshare? Corin hadn't hung around long after that—but then, it *had* been late, and Corin started work a lot earlier than Adam did.

And they'd kissed, after, and it'd been great. Better than great. It'd been—

"Adam, are you listening?" Evie tutted. "You're zoning out again."

"Have I? Uh, sorry. Go on. You were talking about . . ." Shit, he didn't have a clue what she'd been talking about.

She gave him a flat look. "Is there something I should know?"

Busted. "I've met this bloke." Adam hoped it sounded more casual than he felt.

Evie gave him a tentative smile. "Oh? Is he from round here? Or is it one of those app things?"

"Not on an app. Real life, in the flesh. He's a customer. I'm doing his first tattoo."

"Is he quite young, then?"

"No, couple of years older than me. I think. We haven't exactly exchanged birth certificates. He's a computer programmer. Just moved to Glastonbury from Avebury. But he's not a hippie." Adam shut up, hoping he wasn't blushing.

"You really like him?" Evie's smile was broader now.

"Yeah. Yeah, I do. I, uh, met him on the tor first . . ." Adam took a deep breath. *Full disclosure.* "I've been meaning to tell you. I've seen Mum. Heard her too. First time was on the tor when I met Corin—and he was great about it, didn't write me off as some loony seeing ghosts—and the second time was in the house . . ."

He trailed off. Evie was gazing at him with a troubled look. "You've seen Mum?"

"Uh, yeah. That's what I said."

"Adam, you can't have. She's gone."

"I know that. But you hear all kinds of stories about spirits hanging around—"

"They're just stories!" Tight-lipped, Evie folded her arms. "Even if it were true, which it *isn't*, why would Mum want to *hang around*, anyway?"

"Unfinished business." Adam's throat was dry.

"You mean because you didn't get to see her? She didn't know you were here! Adam, you've got to see—"

Shit. Telling her wasn't going to make her happy. But it wasn't fair not to. "Dad's not my dad," he blurted out.

"What?" Evie's eyes were wide.

"Mum must have had an affair. It's— We did a DNA test. Me and Dad aren't related."

"That's not— It was Dad who left her!"

"Well, yeah." Adam's shoulders hunched. "That was why."

She was shaking her head, her face white. "No. That doesn't add up. He left years before you went off to see him."

"He already knew. I told you—that's why he left. Cos he knew I wasn't his, but Mum kept denying it. He did the test to prove it to me."

"How? How did he know?" she asked fiercely.

"Remember when I broke my arm? They did blood tests, and I'm the wrong group to be his kid."

"But you lived with him all those years."

Adam nodded. "Yeah. He's a better bloke than you give him credit for."

"Is he." Her tone was flat. "Is he claiming not to be my father too?"

"What? *No*." Adam tried to smile. "You know you take after him."

Evie turned away and took in a deep, shuddering breath.

Christ, Adam was a self-centred idiot. Why hadn't he thought what this would mean to her? *No, it's fine, you're biologically Dad's. Didn't stop him abandoning you in your teens, though.*

"I'm sorry." Adam wanted to put an arm around her, but he wasn't sure she'd let him.

She didn't answer, and she didn't look back at him, either.

"So, um, that's the unfinished business. Mum never told anyone who my biological dad was. So maybe she's not able to rest until she tells me?"

Evie turned slowly, and her eyes were red. "Mum's *dead*, Adam. She's gone. She's not hanging around, and she's never coming back. If you think you've seen her . . . you need to talk to someone. Ghosts aren't real." She took in another deep, shaky breath. "I have to go. But you need to talk to someone."

"Evie—" Adam grabbed her arm as she made to leave. "I'm sorry, okay? At least wait until you're in a fit state to drive."

She pulled away angrily. "I'm *fine*—it's not me who's seeing things!"

"Please? Humour the man with the delusions," he added with a weak attempt at a laugh. "You shouldn't drive when you're this upset. Have a cup of tea before you go, okay? I'll put the kettle on."

Adam crossed his fingers and hurried into the kitchen.

It was a waste of effort. As he picked up the kettle, he heard the front door slam.

That went bloody brilliant, didn't it?

He wasn't in the right headspace to call Corin after that, but he couldn't settle to watching TV, and digging out the book he was halfway through wasn't any better. After the third time he'd scanned the page he was on without a single word sinking in, Adam stood up. He needed to be doing something—but what?

Haven't checked out the attic yet.

Halfway up the stairs, Adam remembered the ladder issue. He paused, about to turn and head down to the garage to look for one. Then again, he might as well see if there was a pull-down ladder, now he was almost there, mightn't he? He'd feel a right idiot if he slogged all the way down to the garage and back up here with a stepladder unnecessarily.

He dumped the clothes from the chair in his bedroom on the bed and carried the chair out to the landing. Stepping on top of it, he lifted the loft lid—what the hell was the proper name for one of those?—and slid it to one side.

There was, in fact, a ladder. After a couple of false starts, Adam figured out how to pull it down into place. Dad's house had a loft conversion with a proper staircase, so it wasn't an issue he'd been faced with before. The ladder was dingy grey metal and let out ear-splitting screeches as it reluctantly slid into position, ending with a final *clang*. Adam stood there, arrested by a flash of memory. He'd been in bed, and he'd heard these sounds. They'd seemed exciting.

He'd crept out of bed, to see Dad climbing up the ladder. Then Mum had told him to go back to his room and go to sleep. That was all he could remember. Adam wondered what had been happening. Had Dad been fetching his birthday present from hiding? Christmas decorations, or maybe gifts?

Weird, though. Two minutes ago he'd been almost certain there hadn't been a loft ladder here. Now he had a clear memory of it. Adam shook his head and started to climb.

After rooting around in the dark, he found a light switch by the hatch. It lit up a smaller space than he'd expected—after all, Dad had got a whole room out of his attic. That wasn't gonna happen here, though. Roof joists criss-crossed the place and would make it hard to walk around in. What space there was, was taken up by suitcases and cardboard boxes, with a couple of large bags thrown in for variety. Nothing appeared to be labelled. And everything was dusty, as Adam found out after taking a few cautious steps, making sure he kept to where nails in the boards marked the beams. He'd heard enough stories from his Dad's workers of idiots putting their feet through the ceiling, and these boards were old and probably brittle.

The first box he came to was like a punch in the gut.

Mum hadn't chucked his things out when he'd left or given them to a charity shop. Not all of them, at any rate. His books were here—battered, dog-eared paperbacks he'd got second- or more likely, umpteenth-hand, when the library had run out of variety. Faded covers showed lurid fantasy images, not all of them backed up by what was actually inside the pages, as he recalled. He delved deeper and uncovered his first art books—hell, his first sketch books. Adam flicked through one, cringing at the quality of the drawings. He'd tried to draw characters from his favourite books, but the proportions were all wrong. He put that one down and reached for the next. This one was better—much better, in fact. Not surprising, as a study of Scratch proved he'd been in his early teens when he'd drawn it. He'd forgotten what Scratch looked like without the beard he'd worn since the end of their London days. Finer-featured than Adam remembered, with a pointed chin and good cheekbones. He'd been kind of pretty, in fact. *Huh.*

"And I never had a crush on you?" Adam said out loud. "I *really* should have had a crush on you." He'd just always been a mate, with that daft schoolboy nickname that everyone seemed to use for him now. Course, he was *Simon* to his mum and dad, and he'd gone by *Si* in London all those years ago, hadn't he?

Adam shifted the box over by the hatch so he could take it down and look through the books in comfort. And then, probably, do what Mum should have done and donate the paperbacks that weren't too battered to a charity shop and recycle the rest.

Maybe not that sketch of Scratch, though. That had to be good for a laugh at the pub.

He moved on, half-expecting the next box to hold all his old Lego or maybe his school uniform. Instead, there were photo albums. Back from the days when people printed out photos instead of sharing them on social media.

Would there be any photos of him? Adam couldn't remember Mum taking any. She'd never bought the pictures the school photographer had taken every year, saying they were a waste of money—in fact, had he even sat for them? Hadn't there been notes he'd had to give to his teacher, saying she didn't want any done?

Adam almost didn't want to look inside the albums. But that was stupid, so he picked up the top one and opened it.

Evie, younger than he'd ever known her, stared out at him with a gap-toothed smile. There were photos of her throughout the album, playing with Dad, or eating ice cream with Mum. Normal family photos. Everyone smiling. Towards the end of the album, Mum was visibly pregnant. She looked happy, in a bright red dress that suited her colouring.

Adam swallowed and picked up the next album. Frustratingly, it turned out to be an older one, filled with a chubby-cheeked Evie, often with her finger up her nose. He put it down and reached for another.

There he was. A tiny baby, stared at in awe by his big sister, who was crouching by his cot. More pictures, some showing him held by a proudly beaming Dad. Adam's heart ached for him. How could Mum have betrayed Dad like that? She didn't look guilty in the pictures that followed. She seemed happy, still.

Maybe she was, with a husband who loved her and a bloke on the side. Adam shut the album with a snap. "Why, Mum? Why did you do it?" he asked aloud.

No one answered. And this wasn't making him feel any better. Adam shut up the box of photos and manoeuvred his box of books awkwardly down the ladder. Then he left it there on the landing.

He'd had enough trips along memory lane for one night.

CHAPTER TWENTY-FOUR

C orin slept through his alarm on Monday morning and barely made it to his first online meeting on time and fully dressed. Both his colleagues had commented on his appearance, with differing levels of tact.

After bolting his door against whatever shade of Blair might lurk outside, he'd spent a terrible night, waking up in the early hours from dreams of his furious ex. He'd been able to recognise him in his dreams, of course.

Blair had blamed Corin for his death. What was worse, Corin had known he deserved it.

After the meeting dragged to a halt and Corin was finally able to get his first cup of coffee, rational thought tried to impose itself.

The man he'd seen watching him last night and the night Declan had left—could it *really* have been Blair or whatever remained of him in this world? Or was Corin's mind playing tricks, as he was half-convinced Adam's had been? It was supposed to be fairly common, wasn't it, that the bereaved saw, or thought they saw, the loved ones who'd passed on? That didn't mean ghosts were real. It could just be neurons firing oddly. Corin knew only too well that the brain was a complicated thing.

Leaving aside all questions of *what* it was Corin had seen, did it even make sense that it was happening *now*? He hadn't seen Blair, whether as spirit or hallucination, in the months after the accident. Was it the power of suggestion, after Adam's confession that he'd seen his mum since her death? Was it Corin's guilt over starting a new relationship? Over surviving to start one?

Or could there truly be something mystical about Glastonbury? What was it the neopagans liked to talk about? A thinning of the veil between worlds? Something that allowed those who'd crossed over to cross back? Could that be true?

No, that was crazy. There was no evidence, *none*, that spirits of the dead were real. Corin tried to focus on his coding.

It didn't work. After half an hour's monumental lack of achievement, Corin gave up and took a break. He could work late that evening to make up the time.

Corin didn't have many pictures of Blair. It wasn't like he'd been allowed to post snaps of the two of them on social media. But he'd taken at least one or two, and he hadn't deleted any from his phone. He scrolled through laboriously until he found what was clearly a selfie with two men in the shot. Both, like the figure Corin thought he'd seen, had light brown hair and a slim build. But only one of them was wearing Corin's jacket, so that meant the other one had to be Blair.

Unless he'd lent Blair his jacket? The other man was in a nondescript blue shirt, so it was possible, and he'd definitely done that once or twice. Blair had always gone out underdressed for the weather and then complained of feeling cold. A stab of grief hit Corin right in the gut, and damn it, it wasn't *fair*. Not after what Blair had done—

But Blair had *died*. Corin had lived. What right did he have to say what was fair?

Corin tried looking in the mirror, to compare his reflection with the men in the photo, feature by feature. It was slow going, but suddenly he realised that only one man in the images had a droop to his left eyebrow. Yes! Corin felt like punching the air. That one had to be Blair, and he wasn't wearing the jacket.

That meant he could search for that eyebrow if he saw maybe-Blair's-ghost again. Except he'd only seen him in the dark, shadows masking his face. Did ghosts ever come out in broad daylight? Adam had seen his mum during the day, but only in the mist, as far as Corin knew.

And all this was ridiculous. *Ghosts don't exist.*

Corin grabbed his wallet and went out to get an early lunch.

Because it was late October, but also because apparently life existed to mock him, the supermarket was full of Halloween decorations.

Plastic skeletons of all kinds of animals, including several that were invertebrates. Vampire fangs and capes. Pumpkin lights. Pumpkin ornaments. Pumpkin buckets for collecting sweets. Actual pumpkins, with pumpkin-carving kits helpfully placed nearby.

And ghosts. Ghost signs. Ghost costumes. Toy ghosts on a string that lit up and gibbered when you flicked a switch. Corin fled the store, his appetite gone.

Adam texted him Tuesday morning: *Hi, how's it going? Hope you're not regretting our date on Sunday.*

Corin wasn't sure what to answer to that. Why would Adam think he might be regretting their date? Corin had been under the impression it'd gone really well. Had Adam thought differently? It wasn't like Adam knew about him seeing Blair—

No. Not Blair. Simply some man who, for whatever reason, liked to hang around on the corner late at night. And stare up at Corin's flat . . . Anxiety, fuelled by a terrible night's sleep, bubbled in Corin's stomach. If only he knew if it had been the same man each time.

If only he could tell who the man *was*.

And yes, okay, maybe he was regretting their date a little. Because either ghosts were real and Blair's spirit really was angry with him, or Corin was hallucinating as well as brain-damaged, and who the hell would want to date someone like that? If it wasn't going to work out between him and Adam, Corin would just as soon have not had that perfect date to show him what he was going to be missing.

Of course, Adam had seen his own ghost, hadn't he? Maybe he was some kind of a spirit magnet and being with him was the reason Corin had seen Blair?

Except Adam had been nowhere near that first time, after Declan's visit. *And God, Corin, make it all about you, why don't you?*

Corin threw himself into his work and managed to ignore the text. But when he glanced at his phone again at half-past five, there was another text from Adam: *Everything okay?*

Damn it. He couldn't leave the man hanging like this. It wasn't fair to Adam—and, oh God, somehow Corin had managed to forget he'd be seeing him tomorrow. The tattoo appointment. That was going to be incredibly awkward if he didn't answer Adam's texts.

He tapped in a quick, *I'm fine. Sorry. Busy.*

Almost immediately, there came a reply: *Still okay for tomorrow?*

For a moment, Corin was tempted to take the out Adam was offering him. He could cancel his appointment. Blame it on work. But that would be cowardly. What good would it do in any case? If Adam was going to tell him he didn't see things going any further between them, they might as well get it over with.

And if Corin was worrying over nothing where Adam was concerned . . . was he really going to let the possibly-hallucinated spirit of his ex run his life? He wanted to see Adam again. Wanted to do a lot more than just see him, in fact.

Before he could lose his nerve, he tapped out, *Yes. See you then* and hit Send.

CHAPTER TWENTY-FIVE

Nerves were buzzing in Adam's stomach all through Wednesday morning. Corin was booked in for two o'clock, and they hadn't seen each other since Sunday. They'd texted, yeah, but something had seemed off, somehow. Was Corin getting cold feet? Every time Adam had tried to flirt or joke, it'd fallen flatter than a run-over cowpat.

Messages had gone unanswered for hours—and, okay, Corin had a life and it didn't revolve around Adam, but still. When the answers had come, they'd been of the conversation-killing variety. Maybe Corin had a lot of work stress during the week? Adam clung to the hope the bloke hadn't decided he'd made a mistake.

Had *Adam* made the mistake? Should he have kept quiet about his dad? Shit, Adam had gone way too far with the whole emotional outpouring bollocks on their first date, and now Corin was running scared.

"Worried he's going to blow you off, are you?" Sasha's voice cut through Adam's spiralling thoughts. "And not in a good way?"

He glanced up from the piece he was designing to see that she'd finished inking her client, settled up, and said goodbye all without him noticing. "What? No. Maybe." He sighed. "It all went great on Sunday, but since then he's been . . ."

"Ghosting you?"

"No, he's messaged me, but I dunno. There's no spark."

"Maybe he's just shit at sexting?"

"We haven't *been* sexting."

"So that's the issue?"

"Not for me. I like him, Sash. I really like him." Adam pulled his phone out of his pocket and showed her a photo he'd snapped on Sunday of Corin gazing out from the walls of the Bishop's Palace, lost in thought. "I mean, come on. Look at that."

She snorted. "He's got the brooding expression down pat. Heathcliff in hair gel."

"Shut up. He's funny too. We got on great. We even like the same stuff." Adam narrowed his eyes. "So yeah, we've got plenty in common."

Sasha threw up her hands. "All right, all right. Jeez. 'Scuse me for wanting to look out for you."

Adam hesitated. "Seen anything of Chelle since last week?"

"Nope." She popped the *p*.

"You okay with that?"

"Yep." Her face fell, though, for a moment. Then she brightened. "Know what'd make the time go faster till lover-boy gets here? You could nip up the road and get me a bacon butty."

Adam rolled his eyes. But he fetched her the bacon butty anyway, and another for himself, although he wasn't all that hungry. The walk in the brisk air cleared his head a little, not that he'd tell Sasha that. There was no point in worrying about how Corin felt until he got here. And if he didn't, that'd answer that question, wouldn't it?

But Corin turned up dead on two o'clock. Adam took one look at the dark circles under his eyes, and any thoughts of keeping the conversation light flew straight out the window. Adam strode over to him. "Corin! It's Adam. Are you okay?" he asked in a lower voice once he was near.

"Is it that obvious?" Corin gave a nervous laugh. "Been a little stressed the last couple of days. Sorry if I've been . . ." He made an inarticulate gesture.

"Hey, no worries," Adam said quickly. "Work can be a bastard. You okay to get inked today? If you're neck deep in deadlines, we can always book you in for another day."

"No, it's fine." Corin managed a weak smile, then cast a glance to Sasha, who was ostentatiously ignoring them while cleaning up at the other end of the studio. He went softly, "I wanted to see you."

Adam's heart lifted. *Promising.* Unless he'd wanted to see Adam to tell him it was over— *Nope. Don't think like that.* "Okay, then. Walk this way." He showed Corin to his chair. "So, I'm first going to apply a transfer of the design to your skin, and then I'll ink it in permanently. Shouldn't take long. No second thoughts on the art, the placement, or anything?"

Corin shook his head firmly.

"Right then, I'm, uh, going to need you to undo your shirt." Adam cleared his throat. *Keep it professional, you wanker.*

Corin unbuttoned his shirt and bared his chest. Adam's heart beat faster. The sight was every bit as good as he'd imagined: defined pecs, smooth and hairless, and a flat, muscular stomach. Definitely not a stereotypical computer nerd.

"You didn't say, but I thought you'd want me to shave," Corin said uncertainly.

Adam swallowed, his mouth dry. "Good move. Sorry. Should have said. You use weights? Because whatever you're doing, it's working."

"Thanks." Corin reddened faintly. "Is this the first time you've tattooed someone you're, uh . . ."

"Going out with?" Adam blurted, a moment before self-doubt crashed into him like a meteor strike. Yeah, they'd been on a date; they'd kissed—but neither of them had said anything about what it all meant. They hadn't even slept together.

Corin's relieved grin sent a heady rush of warmth through Adam's chest.

Then he remembered he'd been asked a question. "Uh, no, actually. There's been one or two." He stopped there, because Corin probably didn't want to hear a rundown of all the ex-boyfriends Adam had left his mark on.

"Do you get people asking you for mates' rates? That's not me asking for a discount, by the way," Corin added quickly. "My brother's an electrician, and he says he's lost count of the number of people who think buying him a drink at the pub entitles them to get their wiring checked for nothing."

Adam laughed, tension broken. Yeah, Sasha had been totally off-track about Corin only being into him because he was a tattoo artist. "One drink? Cheap bastards. I had a bloke once who expected me to ink him for free because we were shagging. So I stopped shagging him. Nah, I'm not saying I've never done anyone a favour, but it boils my piss when people expect it. No one wants to be taken for granted, you know?" Adam reached behind him. "Okay, I'm gonna apply the stencil now. Nice and relaxed?"

"I'm fine." Corin's shoulders stiffened up immediately.

"Seriously, I need you to relax, or it won't look so good. And I'm not having you going around being a bad advert for my work."

Corin took a deep breath and settled back in the chair, letting his shoulders drop to their natural position. "Okay."

"That's good. You're doing great. Lots of people are nervous their first time."

Corin's lips twitched. "Is that an innuendo?"

Adam grinned. "Do you want it to be?"

"Well, you are about to do something invasive to my body."

"Don't forget there's fluids involved. But I'll try to keep the pain to a minimum." Adam lowered his voice. "You know, when the endorphins kick in, it can actually feel good."

God, he loved the way Corin's eyes sparkled at that.

Then Sasha gave a loud fake cough like a bastard. "Want me to shut the blinds and leave you two alone for a while?"

Corin froze. "Sorry."

Adam glared at her. "Oi, do I interfere while you're putting your clients at ease? No, I do not."

"Put him any more at ease and I'll have to apply for a licence as a massage parlour." She glanced at Corin, and her expression softened. "I'm only teasing. It's good to see you again. Gonna come along this Friday too? And there's the Samhain celebrations on Saturday."

Corin glanced at Adam. "I, uh . . . Maybe? If we haven't got other plans?"

Adam turned away so Sasha wouldn't see the soppy smile he was one hundred percent certain he was wearing. "Let's see what we feel like, hey? Okay, I do have a client coming in after you, so we should probably get on with this."

The transfer went on without issue, and then Adam got out his tattoo machine. "This'll feel like it's scratching you, and that's normal, but let me know if it's too bad or if you need a break for any reason.

Everyone has a different pain threshold, and there's no shame in taking a break."

"Got it. No macho posturing." Corin gave a lopsided smile.

"Nope. Save it for when you're showing off your ink afterwards." Adam paused. "Okay, I'm going to start now."

It should have been business as usual. It wasn't a complicated design; Adam could have inked it with his eyes closed and one hand tied behind his back, although Sasha would have had his bollocks if he'd tried anything that daft. But somehow, working on Corin, touching his bare skin and leaving his mark . . .

Adam realised to his horror he'd almost gone off line and made a hasty correction. Christ, he needed to focus. *Don't cock this up.*

It was a lot different from inking someone he'd already slept with. It felt like foreplay.

And he really needed to stop thinking like that, because in all likelihood, to Corin it felt more like a mildly unpleasant experience he was hoping would end soon. Which it would, far too soon for Adam's liking. Was that fucked up?

"Nearly done," he said, and his voice came out hoarser than it should have.

"Already?" Corin asked, his tone relaxed.

"Just a little longer . . . There we go." Adam sat back and looked at his handiwork. "You okay?"

Corin laughed. "That was *way* less painful than I expected."

Adam grinned at him. Yeah, those endorphins were a rush. "You'll be in for your next one before you know it." He wiped off the tattoo and covered it, maybe lingering over the process a little longer than for the average client, because hey, he was only human. Then he ran through the usual after-care instructions. "But you can always call me if you're worried about anything," he added, as Corin was doing his shirt back up.

"Thanks. That all seems quite clear, though." Fully covered once again—*shame*—Corin stood up, and they made their way to the front desk. "Uh, sorry. That sounded like I don't want to call you. Which I do. Actually, do you want to get dinner tonight?"

Adam sighed. "I can't." He hated how Corin's face fell, and hurried on. "Wish I could, but I need to see my sister. We had a bit of a— I told her about Dad the other night, and she didn't take it too well. Stormed out, in fact. But she's agreed to see me tonight, and I don't reckon it'd be a good idea to cancel on her. I need to make sure she's okay."

Corin nodded. "That's totally understandable. I hope it goes okay. Ring me if you need to talk afterwards?"

That was hope in his eyes, wasn't it? Adam smiled. "Yeah. Cheers. I will. And we're seeing each other Friday night, yeah?"

"Definitely." Corin's tone was as fervent as Adam could have wished for, and his smile made something flutter in Adam's chest.

Friday couldn't come soon enough.

CHAPTER TWENTY-SIX

Adam had been to Evie's a few times now, but he never really felt comfortable there. It was too neat, too *designed* looking, like a show home. According to Evie, Paul had a really good eye for colour and stuff. So the first time Adam had met the bloke, he'd joked, "Hey, are you sure you're not the gay guy, not me?" It had got him a frown and a comment of "I would have thought you'd want to overturn stereotypes, not reinforce them."

Apparently they had very different senses of humour. If Paul even *had* a sense of humour, which Adam was still on the fence about. That first meeting had pretty much set the bar for their relationship.

Tonight, Paul let him into the house and then disappeared upstairs, leaving Adam on his own with Evie.

Adam had brought her a Halloween-themed floral thing as a peace offering—some kind of orange flowering plant in a pot painted like a pumpkin. It'd seemed like a good idea when he'd spotted it in the supermarket, and she smiled as she thanked him, but as he handed it over, it looked tacky and cheap. Which, to be fair, it had been.

"Sorry about the other night," he said as he sat down on her cream leather sofa.

"Me too." Evie put the pumpkin pot on a side table, where it stood out like a turd on a dinner table against her tasteful living room décor, and perched on the edge of an armchair. "It was a lot to take in, everything you said about Mum and Dad."

"Yeah. Sorry. I kinda forgot it was all new to you? What with me knowing about it for years."

Her mouth tightened, and fuck it all, that hadn't been the most tactful thing to say, had it?

Adam winced. "Are you mad I didn't tell you before?"

"I can understand why you didn't," she said carefully. "We were out of touch for a long time. Although—" She cut herself off, standing abruptly. "Tea? Coffee, I mean."

"Er, yeah, please."

"I'll put the kettle on. We've got decaff, but only in instant, so if you want filter coffee, it'll have to be with caffeine." She was already walking out of the living room, and the last few words came faintly, with an echoey sound, from the kitchen.

"Instant's fine, ta," Adam called after her. Should he follow her? Bit late now, though, and he didn't want her to feel like he was crowding her. She seemed nervy enough already. He picked up a book from the side table where she'd left the pumpkin, wondered why on earth anyone would want to read about brutalist architecture, then put it down again. The last thing he needed was Paul coming in—because it *had* to be his book—seeing him with it, and engaging him in conversation on the subject.

Evie was soon back with two steaming mugs. No biscuits, mind, which confirmed Adam's view that he wasn't out of the shit by a long way yet.

"Cheers," he said, taking the mug she offered him and placing it on a coaster.

She nodded and sat down with her own mug. Then she took a deep breath. "I get why you didn't tell me about Dad before. But I wish you had. And those things you said about Mum, about her having unfinished business . . . It was upsetting." She raised her mug to her lips with both hands and took a sip.

"I'm sorry," Adam said yet again. "But don't you think it's reassuring, in a way? To know that she's still there in spirit? That she still cares?"

"You said she's a *restless spirit*." Evie plonked her mug on a coaster, apparently not noticing the small amount of tea that slopped over the side. "That's the *opposite* of reassuring. Why would anyone want to think that about their mum?"

Adam frowned. "You're twisting my words."

"Because of course throwing around accusations like that is going to help." Evie glared at him. "Is this man you've met the one who put all these ideas in your head about seeing Mum?"

What the hell? "No! I told you, I met him *after* seeing her the first time."

Her face hardened. "And he encouraged you to believe it. That's what you said."

"It wasn't like that." Adam's temper rose. "You can get off Corin's case right now. He's a great guy. You should meet him."

"Maybe I should." Evie folded her arms.

"Oi, you're not going all big sister on him. He's had a rough time."

"How?"

Shit. Corin was sensitive about having a brain injury, wasn't he? He wouldn't thank Adam for going around telling everyone about it. "That's not important."

Her lips thinned. "So unimportant you have to keep it a secret. This is *not* making me feel any better about him."

Adam stood up explosively. "Oh, for fuck's sake! I'm a grown man, and you're not my mum. I've had boyfriends since I was sixteen, and you never gave a fuck about any of them before." And one or two of them had been right tossers, not that he was ever going to tell her that.

"Because you weren't here to give a fuck about!" Evie's voice was shrill, and her face was red and blotchy. "You just left, the same as Dad did."

It was like a slap in the face. "Evie, I'm sorry, okay? I was sixteen. Everyone's a self-centred wanker at sixteen. Look, come here." He held out an arm.

Evie ignored it, although a tear was making a slow track down her cheek. "I want you to go now. Go on. You're good at that."

"Evie . . ."

"*Go.*" Still sitting uncomfortably on the armchair, she turned her face away from him.

Footsteps sounded on the stairs. "Is everything all right?" Paul's voice called.

"Adam's going now," Evie said loudly, but with a clear shake in her voice.

The footsteps quickened. "I'll see him out."

Fuck it. "I can find the door by myself, ta," Adam called up to him, and strode out of the house, leaving Paul standing on the bottom stair.

Outside, Adam jammed on his helmet and started up the Yamaha. Resisting a petty urge to roar away and scatter the gravel on their neat driveway, he set off down the street.

He couldn't face going back to an empty house, though. Almost before he'd made the decision, he turned the Yamaha in the direction of Corin's flat.

Corin opened the door a few inches. He was less buttoned-up than Adam had ever seen him, barefoot in slouchy jogging bottoms and a well-loved T-shirt. There was a faint sheen of sweat on his face and neck—had he been working out? It was a good look on him, although it was spoilt by a wary frown. Who was he expecting? Debt collectors? Jehovah's Witnesses?

"Yes?" Corin said cautiously through the gap.

Adam gave a hopeful smile. "It's Adam. And I know I should have called you or texted first, but is it okay if I come in? You said if I needed to talk . . ."

Corin's posture relaxed, and he was already moving back to let him in. "Of course. Come in. Sorry about the mess."

Adam stepped over the free weights on the living room floor, which presumably was what Corin meant by *mess* seeing as the rest of the place was in perfect order. "Hey, no worries. And I'm sorry I interrupted your workout."

"It's fine. I was pretty much done. Drink? There's coffee or tea, or if you want something stronger, I've got vodka or red wine." Corin frowned. "Not totally sure I've got mixers for the vodka, though."

"I'm on the bike, so coffee would be great." It wasn't like he'd got to drink the one Evie had made him. Adam had been briefly tempted to ask for alcohol, both because he could have used a drink and because it would have provided a perfect excuse to stay the night, but he was damned if he was going to rush Corin into things with a cheap trick like that.

And anyway, simply being here with Corin was easing the knot between his shoulder blades.

"Did it go okay with your sister?" Corin asked, moving into the kitchen.

Adam followed and watched as Corin filled the kettle and put it on to boil. "Not exactly. She's— Fuck it. You know how you said you'd be there if I wanted to talk about it? How would you feel about me *not* talking about it? I can't face rehashing the whole shit show right now."

"Whatever helps you the most." Corin's gaze was sincere.

Christ, could the guy get any more perfect? Adam leaned back against the kitchen counter and smiled. "Thanks. You're . . . Thanks."

Corin got out a mug and a jar of instant coffee. "This okay? Sorry I haven't got any proper stuff. I have to be careful with caffeine."

"No, that's perfect. You're not joining me?"

"I'll stick with water for now." Corin spooned coffee into the mug, then fetched himself a pint glass of water from the tap and took a long drink. The kettle boiled.

It was all so fucking domestic. Easy. Adam loved it. "So tell me, how was your day?"

"You mean the six or seven hours since you saw me last?"

Adam laughed. "Smart-arse. Yeah. How's it been?"

Corin stirred Adam's coffee and handed it over. "Milk?"

"Please."

"And it's been . . . average. Maybe a little more looking in the mirror than usual, to remind myself I actually have a tattoo now." Corin gave a sheepish grin as he fetched the milk from the fridge. "I know, I know. Baby's first tattoo."

"Hey, we've all got to start somewhere. It's healing okay, right?" Adam put his mug down, his heart pounding. He didn't want to rush Corin into anything. But maybe—just maybe—Corin was as ready as he was to move their relationship on a step? "Could check it out for you, if you like." He tried to keep his tone light. Let Corin read it as a come-on if he wanted to—or not.

Adam held his breath.

CHAPTER TWENTY-SEVEN

Corin was glad for his glass of water—it gave him a way to occupy his hands. The air in the kitchen seemed suddenly charged. That had definitely been an invitation, hadn't it? How much healing could Adam expect to see in a few hours? But although the thought of taking things further with Adam scared him, it was something he desperately wanted, now Adam was here in front of him, standing only inches away.

Was it the right time, though, with Adam fresh from an emotional scene with his sister? "You should drink your coffee first." Corin ducked his head and mentally cursed his conscience.

"Right. Get it while it's hot." Adam's tone seemed off as he stepped back and picked up his mug again.

Oh, God—he'd cocked it up, hadn't he? Corin swallowed. "We can go and sit down," he suggested, and led the way into the living room.

Adam startled him with a hand on his arm. "Hey, sorry. Was I coming on too strong?"

Corin turned to him, and "No, it's me. I was worried . . . Are you sure you're okay after your fight with Evie?"

"You're a good guy, you know that? I'll be fine. I *am* fine. Honest."

Corin relaxed as he saw the familiar quirk to Adam's smile. "I, uh, have a tendency to overthink. Sorry. Didn't mean to ruin the mood."

"Nothing to be sorry for," Adam said firmly. "Hey, nice sofa." He sat on it, right in the saggy middle part, and his eyes widened comically as it sank beneath him. "Uh, I especially like the way it's so low to the ground. Did you recently lose half your body weight? Or used to flat-share with the Incredible Hulk?"

Corin had to laugh. "I'm renting furnished, so your guess is as good as mine as to what happened to the sofa."

Adam grinned. "It was used as a trampoline by the world's heaviest toddler? Or, I know, energetic sex between a couple of body-builders. Or the previous tenant had a chubby kink and some world-class chat-up lines?"

"I take that back. Your guesses are *way* better than mine."

"I'm an artist. We have good imaginations." Adam paused. "So, to be safe, we should sit at one end each?"

That didn't sound like much fun. "Or we could surrender to the inevitable and cuddle up in the middle?" Corin suggested with a flirtatious tone and a small but significant attack of nerves.

From Adam's broad smile, one corner of his mouth a little higher than the other, Corin's attempt to recapture the atmosphere had hit its mark. "Could be right, there." Adam put his mug on the floor.

"Although that might sound the final death knoll for the poor thing." Corin hesitated. "So maybe we should lie down? Distribute the load over the largest possible area?"

Now Adam's grin was wicked, and Corin's heart soared. Maybe he hadn't cocked things up after all. He watched as Adam kicked off his shoes and stretched out languorously over the sofa, his head on one armrest and his feet on the other. Then winced. "Ow. Bugger. This was supposed to be seductive, but it's killing my back."

Corin laughed and offered Adam a hand, pulling him up to standing. "I promise my bed's much more comfortable. And"—he flushed—"for the record, that was totally seductive."

Adam's smile, only inches away, broadened in a slow, incredulous way that had Corin's heart racing. "You're sure? I mean, I probably looked a right prat lying there with my bum two feet lower than my head."

Corin gave a half shrug, light-headed from Adam's proximity and the certainty of what was about to happen. "I can be versatile as to positions."

"You—" Adam shook his head. "Did I, like, hallucinate you? Because you're just perfect."

If a chill had run through Corin's chest at the mention of hallucinations, it vaporised when Adam said the word *perfect*. "Come to bed," he said, not feeling up to anything more eloquent.

Adam pulled him in close by the hips. "You don't have to ask twice."

"I think technically I—" Corin's words were lost as Adam claimed his lips. He tasted of coffee and promise, and Corin returned his kiss eagerly. Why the hell had they waited so long? They could have been doing this since Sunday. Corin could have stayed over at Adam's, and it would have been wonderful. And if he hadn't come home, he'd never have seen Blair's ghost . . .

No. Not Blair's ghost. Just a man, and nothing to worry about—

"Hey, you okay?" Adam's voice was rough, but soft at the same time. "Sure you're into this?"

"Totally," Corin said firmly, and pulled Adam back in for another kiss. If he could still think of spirits, then he wasn't giving Adam the attention he deserved. Corin concentrated on the taste of Adam's mouth, lightly flavoured with coffee, on the heat of his body pressed close, and all his anxieties melted away. He could feel Adam getting hard, and the sensation went straight to his own cock. God, he'd been an idiot. This was right, this was perfect. How could he have doubted?

Corin broke the kiss, breathing hard. "Bed."

"Mm, sounds good." Adam was kissing his neck now, and it took all Corin had to gently break his hold so he could lead the way to the bedroom.

Moments later, Corin found himself baring his chest in front of Adam for the second time that day. The minute his T-shirt was off and heading for the floor, Adam pulled him close. "Have you got any idea what it did to me, you coming in for your ink?"

Corin laughed. "You were perfectly professional." He'd thought he was the only one who'd been affected by the strange intimacy of it all.

"Fuck professional. I wanted to lick every inch of you and then suck you off in the chair. In front of Sasha, even, which let me tell you is not actually a kink of mine. I mean seriously, have you *looked* at this chest?" Adam ran a hand over Corin's pecs, his touch almost reverent.

Corin fought to keep his composure as excited nerve endings sent an ecstatic signal straight to his dick. "Uh, yes? I had to shave it, and—" He hissed in a breath as Adam tweaked a nipple.

"And let me tell you, I appreciate it. Although hairy's good too. Fuck it." Adam bent to put his lips to a pec.

There was no other word but *worship* to describe the way Adam kissed across Corin's chest, carefully avoiding the cling-film-covered tattoo. Corin had to fight back the embarrassing moans that tried to force through his lips. "Not fair," he managed to choke out. "I want to see you too."

"Happy to oblige." Adam stripped off his T-shirt in one fluid motion, and Corin gazed, entranced, at the skin and ink revealed.

"Wow, that's beautiful," he breathed.

"Cheers. I designed it, and my old boss inked it." Adam grinned. "Told you those antlers were big, didn't I?"

The whole piece was a play on perspective with the stag at the centre, its antlers impossibly huge, while the wild huntsmen swirled around the great beast in a riot of chaos.

"Do they ever catch it? The stag, I mean," Corin wondered aloud, caressing the image as he spoke.

"Not in my book." Adam's voice was throaty and low. "Let me do a twirl for you."

He stepped back and did a graceful one-eighty. Above one shoulder blade was a raven in flight, half-living and half-dead, with its spine clearly visible. On the other shoulder glowered a dark-eyed man, his chest bare. He wore antlers to rival the stag's.

The horned god, Gwynn ap Nudd.

"Like them?" Adam asked, his back still turned to Corin.

In answer, Corin slipped his arms around Adam's waist and pressed a kiss to the nape of his neck. Adam shivered. Then he flashed Corin an impish grin over one shoulder and threw himself onto the bed. "Oh, fuck me, this is way better than your sofa. You've got condoms, right? Please tell me you've got condoms."

"I— Yes. Bedside drawer." Thank God he'd checked they weren't out of date. "Uh, ignore the, uh . . ." Corin winced as Adam delved into the drawer and emerged, triumphant, with his favourite dildo.

"This? Oh, I'm pretty sure me and this little fella are gonna be best friends. But maybe not tonight." Adam tossed the dildo back into the drawer and brought out condoms and lube. "I love a man who's prepared. Were you a Boy Scout?"

"Only briefly." Corin hadn't enjoyed the noisy, boisterous games and the general laddishness of his local troop, although getting him to admit that out loud would require the kind of treatment the Geneva Convention tended to frown on. He climbed onto the bed and wrapped his arms around Adam. "You?"

"Oh, I was never one for uniforms. Not on me, anyhow." Adam rolled over so suddenly that he was on top of Corin before he had time to react. "Speaking of clothes I'm not a fan of, how about we get you out of those jogging bottoms?"

"Want to lead by example?" Corin challenged, breathless.

"Oh, I'll do better than that." Adam pushed himself up to kneeling, his legs astride Corin's, and unbuttoned his jeans and shoved them down his hips. They were too tight to go far, but Corin could clearly see the outline of Adam's erection straining at his briefs. A wet patch at the tip grew larger even as he gazed at it, and it was an effort of will not to lick his lips.

"Take them off," he said hoarsely. "Everything. Take it all off."

"Everything?" There was a wicked glint in Adam's eye. "So, you want me to take these off?" He rolled over to sit beside Corin on the bed, and in a mockery of seduction, slowly started to strip off one sock. "Sure you're ready for this?" he purred.

Corin groaned and closed his eyes. "Do all the people you've been to bed with get the urge to smother you with a pillow, or is it only me?"

"Mm, breathplay is also not one of my kinks, but for you . . ."

Corin grabbed a pillow and hit him with it. Gently, because he was far too conscientious for his own good.

Adam burst out laughing. "Now I'm imagining you in scout camp, having pillow fights with the other chaps in your tent as a way to siphon off those adolescent energies."

"*Chaps*?" Corin scoffed. "It was the scouts, not boarding school." And he'd never made it to camp, although he was regretting that slightly now. "Are you going to stop teasing me and get those jeans off? Just asking for information."

Adam fixed him in the eye, and when he spoke, his tone was oddly serious. "Stop teasing you? Never. But I will get these jeans off."

As good as his word, he stripped off his jeans and his briefs in one fell swoop.

Corin's mouth went dry. Adam was big. Not porn-star huge, but against that slender figure . . . "You really aren't compensating for anything, are you?"

"Hey, I did tell you. Still, it's not the size, it's what you do with it that counts." His tone was verging on smug, but Corin could forgive him for that.

"So what do you want me to do with that?" Corin asked.

"I want you to get your kit off and get over here," Adam said, running his fingers teasingly over his erection.

Corin swallowed, feeling the feather-light touch on his own dick. His jogging bottoms hit the floor, quickly followed by his boxer briefs, damp from his leaking cock. "Sorry I haven't got any socks on to strip off seductively," he managed to riposte.

Adam hadn't stopped staring at him. "Consider me seduced." His voice was hoarse as he scooted back on the bed. "C'mere."

Corin eagerly climbed on top of him, straddling his lean hips and then pressing their bodies together so that every inch of his skin tingled at the contact. Their dicks met, and he couldn't have stopped himself rutting against that lithe figure if he'd wanted to. Adam was all heat and smooth skin, not a spare inch on him. *Well, maybe in one particular area.* God, he'd missed this. Missed feeling another hard body against his own—except no, it'd never been this good before.

It had never been *Adam* before. He hadn't known what he was missing. Corin buried his face in Adam's neck, leaving little nips and kisses, high on Adam's scent, all musk and clean male sweat.

"What do you want?" Adam was asking.

"You." Corin cleared his throat and tried to clear his mind, which was fogged with the ecstatic signals his body was sending to his brain. "Do you top?"

"Mm, I'm easy. If you know what I mean. Want me in you?"

Yes, please, Corin almost piped up like a kid being offered a biscuit. "God, yes," he managed in slightly more adult fashion.

"Then we'd better get you ready," Adam growled, his low tone bypassing Corin's ears and going straight to his dick.

Corin had expected to be impatient with all the necessary stretching and lubrication, but he hadn't reckoned on Adam. He used an absurd amount of lube, and it got all over the sheets and made loud squelches that had Corin laughing even while hopelessly aroused. God, Corin had forgotten how much sheer, ridiculous *fun* sex could be. And when Adam finally stopped teasing and pushed in oh-so-slowly from behind, Corin could feel every inch of him, stretching his body to its limits but no further. It was heaven.

"Y'okay?" Adam grunted, his voice tight with effort and his fingers digging into Corin's hips as he held still.

"'S good," Corin gasped into the pillow. "More."

Adam gave a slow, experimental thrust that had Corin moaning. "Still okay?"

"'M not made of glass," Corin griped.

Adam chuckled. "Nah. Marble. Like a fucking sculpture, you are. Perfect."

He pulled out a little before thrusting in more strongly, and fuck, that was it. Sparks burst all along Corin's spine, and he groaned aloud. "Oh, fuck, yes."

"Yeah? You like that?" Adam was pistoning in and out with confidence now, and fuck, Corin was going to die from this. Every other stroke dealt a hammer blow to his sweet spot, overwhelming him with pleasure.

"Harder," he gasped, almost without knowing he did so.

"Fuck, you're gonna kill me. You're amazing, you know that? So fucking perfect for me." Adam sped up, and now he was nailing Corin's gland with every stroke. "You want me to . . . ?"

A hand left Corin's hip to take a loose grip of his cock. Corin howled and came harder than he'd imagined possible, raw pleasure shooting like a cannonball down his spine and out through his dick.

"Oh, Jesus, fuck, that's so—" Adam's strokes grew erratic, and just as the sensation was getting too much, Adam groaned and collapsed on Corin's back. "Fuck, fuck, you're so fucking perfect. Fuck," he gasped into Corin's neck.

Corin's spent dick gave one last feeble twitch of pleasure that was close to pain.

They lay there in a sweaty tangle while Corin's brain slowly rebooted itself, optimising memory and checking that all essential functions were still operational after the storm of electrical activity that'd swept through his wiring. It was bliss.

He moaned in disappointment as Adam carefully slid out of him.

"Sorry. Didn't wanna squish you."

"You're not that big." Corin rolled over and pulled Adam back on top of him. "Except in one important area."

"Hey, I told you, it's what you do with it."

"You win on both counts, then."

Adam seized Corin's face between his hands and kissed him sloppily. "Have I mentioned you're perfect?"

Corin's heart swelled. "I'm really not. But feel free to keep saying it."

Adam snuggled in with his head on the un-inked side of Corin's chest, and Corin started to drift off to sleep.

Then Adam roused, breaking Corin's loose hold and pushing himself up on one elbow. "Hey, no going to sleep before we've looked after your ink. Come on, let's get it washed and rewrapped." Adam tugged at Corin's arm until, groaning, he heaved himself out of bed and let himself be led into the bathroom.

CHAPTER TWENTY-EIGHT

Corin blinked, unsure what had woken him. The skies outside were beginning to lighten. It felt too early to be awake, after the late night before. Warmth flooded through him as he remembered *why* it'd been a late night, and he rolled over with a smile.

It disappeared as he gazed at the dimly-lit and still-sleeping face on the pillow next to him. His heart gave a sickening lurch. There was nothing—*nothing*—he could latch on to, to be certain of who lay beside him, wound up tight in the duvet. It could have been anyone. Corin swallowed. He was being ridiculous, he knew he was, but knowing it didn't stop the icy surge of panic in his breast.

Should he prod Adam? Wake him up to hear his voice? Would that be a reasonable thing to do? *No.* No, it really wouldn't. *For God's sake, it* has *to be Adam; he was there when you fell asleep. Think.* Corin took a deep, shuddering breath. Willing himself to be calm, he cautiously pulled the duvet down to bare Adam's shoulder. A swirl of dark ink became visible, and Corin's head swam with relief. It was Adam.

Who was now stirring, because of course Corin had managed to wake him up. "Mm, 's it time to get up already?"

Corin put the duvet back over Adam's shoulder. "No. It's early. Didn't mean to wake you."

"C'mere?" The duvet slid down again as Adam reached out blindly.

"Not sure I—"

Adam's questing hand found his arm. "C'mon. Back to bed."

There was a sleepy smile in Adam's voice, and his hand was soft and warm. Still half-convinced he was too jittery to relax, Corin let himself be drawn back into the cocoon of Adam's embrace. He took a deep breath, and Adam's male, musky scent flooded his nostrils, calming him beyond reason. How had he ever doubted that he knew this man?

"Y'okay?" Adam asked.

"Fine." Corin nuzzled into Adam's neck. It was a lot less conflicting than looking at his face.

"Sure? Cos you seemed a bit freaked out." Adam sounded more awake, now.

"Sorry. It's— I haven't done this before. Not since the accident," Corin added quickly.

"You mean, waking up with someone?"

Corin's chest went tight, because Adam *understood*. "Yeah."

"Gotta be a bit weird. Hey, you know it's me, right? Want me to tell you something only I would know?"

Corin breathed a laugh into Adam's neck. "What did I say when I first saw your bike?"

"Uh, that she was a thing of sleek, streamlined beauty and in no way older than you'd expected?"

"Close enough." Corin kissed him gently.

Adam kissed back, and somehow it now felt the most natural thing in the world to be here with him. Kissing turned into lazy frotting, their bodies pressing blissfully together, and when the urgency became too much, Corin reached down between them to take them both in hand. It didn't take long before they were both gasping out their pleasure.

After a hasty clean-up with a handful of tissues, they lay back down, duvet kicked to the floor. Corin drifted into a pleasant half doze.

"What time do you have to start work?" Adam murmured, as a weak winter sun began to shine through Corin's thin curtains.

"Nine." Corin glanced at his phone by the side of the bed and groaned. "Twenty past eight. I'll have to get up soon. How about you?"

"No rush for me. Studio doesn't open till eleven, although I need to get there around half ten."

Corin smiled. "Slacker."

"Hey, I don't see you working Saturdays, do I?"

"Point. Do you get a day in lieu?"

"No, I was kinda tight for cash when I moved back here, so I signed up for a six-day week. But Sasha's always good if I want to take a day off. If I haven't got a booking, that is, and I'm booked up for Saturdays for, like, months. Weekdays are easier, but then I'm missing out on walk-ins."

"You do walk-ins? Then how come I had to wait weeks?" Corin gave an exaggerated pout.

Adam laughed. "Cos you were a newbie. It's a rule Sasha has. If someone comes in who's never been inked before, we give them a cooling-off period. In case it's just an impulse and they're gonna regret it. Anyone else, we assume they know what they want. And cover-ups, we always try to do those soon as. Gotta look after people's mental health. But if it's a bigger piece, more than a couple of hours, or a custom design, you're gonna have to book anyway." He nuzzled into Corin's neck. "Think you'll want another? I could design you something special."

"That sounds great." Of course, it wouldn't be so great if they split up, would it? Corin was surprised by how painful that thought was already. "But I think I'll see how I get on with this one first. And I really do have to get up," he added, disentangling himself reluctantly from Adam's embrace. "Especially if you want breakfast. Mind if I shower first? That way you can stay in bed longer."

"Hey, it's no fun on my own. But yeah, you go ahead. I'll lie here and mope." Adam grinned.

"My heart's breaking for you." Corin climbed out of bed and padded to the bathroom.

"Don't forget to change the cling film!" Adam called after him.

Corin had a quick, not-too-hot shower to avoid irritating his new tattoo and dutifully taped on fresh cling film. The butterfly was a little red and swollen around the edges, but it made him smile to see it there. Steeling himself, he glanced in the mirror.

The face was still that of a stranger—one who badly needed to put some product in his hair—but the body was his. Marked as his.

Warmth flooded through Corin, even as he shivered in the chill air coming in through the open bathroom window. He grabbed the tub of gel and quickly styled his hair. Better. Now all he had to do was resist the temptation to slip back into bed with Adam.

When he padded into the bedroom, though, Adam was already getting up. He sent Corin a glance of pure appreciation. "Save me any hot water?"

Corin widened his eyes. "Oh, you wanted a *hot* shower? Sorry, you should have said."

Adam laughed. "Right, that's a star off your TripAdvisor rating already."

"Breakfast?" Corin grabbed a pair of boxer briefs from a drawer and pulled them on. "I'll make sure to burn your toast. Seeing as I'm getting tanked in the review anyway."

Adam loped to the bathroom, grabbing Corin for a quick kiss en route. "Burnt toast I can handle, but there'd better not be salt in my coffee or I'm calling in Trading Standards."

Corin finished getting dressed with a smile on his face. Then he headed to the kitchen and got started on breakfast. They ate their toast (miraculously not burnt, despite Corin being somewhat distracted today) and marmalade standing at the kitchen counter, so Corin wouldn't forget he needed to log in to work soon. It was harder than he'd thought it would be to end the cosy togetherness. But eventually Corin had to say, "Sorry, but—"

"I know, I know," Adam cut him off with a smile. "I'll get going. But I'll see you soon, yeah?"

"Definitely." They kissed, and Corin entertained brief thoughts of pulling a sickie before drawing back. "Soon," he promised, and Adam gave him another blinding, lopsided smile.

Five minutes later he was letting Adam out of the front door. As they stepped onto the metal staircase, Corin couldn't help glancing over at the corner by the street. There was no one there, thank God.

"I hope you're not worried about being seen with me," Adam said, his tone light.

Damn it—had he really been that obvious? "Of course not," Corin said, and pulled him in for a kiss. "Thought I might have seen something. But it was nothing."

"Huh. Not seeing ghosts like me, are you?"

Corin's blood ran cold, and he released Adam from his embrace more abruptly than he meant to. Adam didn't seem to notice anything odd about his behaviour, though. Thank God. "Drive safely," Corin forced out, and watched as Adam jogged lightly down the stairs to his motorbike.

If he sent the corner another wary glance as Adam rode off, at least nobody saw it.

CHAPTER ❧ TWENTY-NINE

As Adam rode away from Corin's flat, it felt like the Yamaha had sprouted wings and was flying over the streets. Familiar shops and landmarks were a barely seen blur, his mind filled with visions of Corin's face as they'd fu— *No.* Made love. He wanted to punch the air.

How had an evening that'd started out so crap turned out so utterly, fucking brilliant? He laughed to himself. The morning had been pretty great too. Okay, there had been an odd note when they'd said goodbye . . . The fizz in Adam's blood flattened for a moment, then rallied. *Nah. Corin was startled by something, that was all. Nothing to worry about there.* And they'd definitely be having another night like that. Tonight would be good. And all the other nights, come to that.

He parked his bike outside Mum's—*his*—house, and jogged up the steps whistling. Yeah, they'd see the band tonight, he mused as he opened the front door, then tomorrow there'd be the Samhain celebrations, and then—

Adam stepped into the living room and stopped dead.

"*Evie?*" She was lying on the sofa in her clothes from last night, more rumpled than he could remember ever seeing her before. His chest tightened.

She roused with a start, rubbing her eyes. "Is it morning?"

"Too right. What are you *doing* here? I mean . . ." Adam wasn't sure *what* he meant, but he did know he didn't want to argue with her. Not today. Not after last night.

Evie rubbed an eye, smearing her already badly smudged mascara even further. "I was worried about you."

Her words banished any lingering anger. "Me? Why?"

"I thought— I don't know what I thought. I'm sorry. I was horrible to you last night."

"No, you weren't." Okay, so it was a lie, but she seemed so miserable he didn't have the heart to be truthful. Adam sat down beside her on the sofa. "Won't Paul be going spare, you not coming home all night?"

"He knows where I am." Evie frowned at the black smudges on her hand. "Oh God, I must be a total mess."

"Weeellll . . ." Adam shrugged. "Nothing a bit of soap and water won't fix. Unless that shit's waterproof, in which case you're stuffed."

She raised an eyebrow. "Voice of experience?"

"Oh, hell, yeah. Ghosts of Prides past." He winced. Yeah, mentioning ghosts—like that was going to go down well.

To his surprise, her expression softened. "I wish I'd known you better then. I've never been to Pride."

Well, duh, he didn't say. It was sweet of her to suggest she'd have gone with him, though. "Eh, you might not like it. It's not really meant for straight people. They can find it a bit much, sometimes."

She raised an eyebrow. "Think I'd be clutching my pearls at the sight of someone in a leather harness or puppy-play gear?"

"Uh, not so much now you've said that?"

"I did go to uni in Manchester, you know. I met all sorts of people there."

Adam grinned. "Yeah, but that was back in the Dark Ages, wasn't it? Don't s'pose Pride had been invented yet."

"Remind me why I care about you?" She ducked her head, a faint flush on her cheek.

Yeah, she did care. Adam should have remembered that last night. "So, are we good now?"

"Um. I want us to be?" She hugged herself. "Paul asked me what it was all about, after you'd gone, and you know how sometimes when you explain things to someone, you get a whole new perspective on them? I didn't like what I was seeing." She huffed a small laugh. "Everyone always wants to think they're the reasonable one, don't they?"

Adam winced at a short, sharp stab in the conscience. Here she'd been agonising over their row all night, while he'd been having a fucking ace time with Corin and not thinking about her. "You weren't unreasonable. Opinionated, maybe." *Close-minded too*, but he wasn't about to kick the argument off again by saying that.

"It's just . . . I know you like the idea of Mum still being here in some way, but I want her to have some peace at last. You don't know what it's been like, these last few years." Evie drew in a breath that was more of a sob. "Don't hate me, okay? It's horrible, I know it is, but I was almost relieved when she died. Because now she could rest. Stop worrying about whatever it was that plagued her."

Adam slung his arm around his sister and drew her in for a hug. *Shit.* No wonder she'd been so against the idea of Mum's spirit hanging around. "Hey, wanting Mum to be at peace isn't horrible. I'm sorry too. I shouldn't have flown off the handle like that. I keep forgetting this is a shed load of stuff for you to deal with all at once, especially right now."

Evie leaned against him with a sniff. "It makes sense that she was the way she was, after what you told me about Dad. She must have felt guilty about the affair."

"Yeah. Exactly. That's why she might feel she had unfinished business here on Earth? I'm guessing, anyhow."

There was a pause. "Maybe," Evie said in the end. "Look, don't take this wrong, but it might be a good idea for you to talk to someone. Someone objective."

Shit, did they have to start the argument all over again? Adam was too tired for this. "You mean like a shrink? Because I'm seeing things that aren't there?"

"No!"

Her tone wasn't convincing.

"All I meant was," she went on, "you've got a lot to work through, here. Regardless of whether Mum's . . . you know. It might help to talk to someone who's not family."

"Like Corin?" he asked drily.

"Um. Maybe someone you're not emotionally involved with?" She paused. "You were at Corin's last night, weren't you? You smell nice."

Adam blinked and huffed a laugh, relieved that she didn't seem any keener to rehash their fight than he was. "Yeah. Top-notch taste in shower gel, that bloke. So he's gotta be a good'un, right?"

"M-must be. I would like to meet him." Evie drew away from him and grimaced. "Unless you told him what I said, in which case I doubt he'll want to be friendly."

Adam gave himself a mental pat on the back. "Nope. Didn't breathe a word. I said we'd argued, but I didn't go into specifics."

"Thank you. I'm sure he's good for you."

Yeah, he could accept that as an apology. "He is. He really is."

Evie took a deep breath, then let it out again. "I'm glad. I'd better go, now I know you're okay. Don't you have work today?"

Adam cocked his head. "Don't *you*?"

"I'll call in sick. I've got a splitting headache, and your sofa hates my back." She stood and rolled her shoulders with a grimace. "Any chance of a cup of tea before I go?"

Adam smiled and stood. "I'll put the kettle on. And I'll even make you some toast."

"Oh, no—I can eat at home."

"Don't be daft. I've still got an hour before I have to be at work. Plenty of time." And he didn't want her to have a literal blood sugar crash while driving home. Thinking of which—how come he hadn't noticed her car on the street? Huh. Maybe *he* was the one who'd been lucky not to have an accident on the roads this morning.

He made himself a coffee while he was getting Evie her breakfast, and sat down with it to keep her company. He could feel his brain moving faster as the caffeine made its sweet way through his system. Corin's instant might have tasted fine, but it didn't have the kick he preferred from his favourite drink.

"You're not eating?" Evie asked through a mouthful of toast and Marmite.

"Had breakfast at Corin's."

"So he's treating you well?"

"Yeah. He's great." Adam could feel his face stretching into what was probably the world's goofiest smile.

"I'm glad." She ate a few more mouthfuls. "I had a thought."

Adam tensed. "About Corin?"

"No, about Mum, actually. Or rather about your father. Your biological father." She hesitated. "You want to know who he was, don't you?"

Adam nodded, his heart racing. Bloody caffeine. "You've got an idea?"

Evie took a sip of her tea. "There's a lady who Mum used to be friends with. I don't know if you'd remember her? We used to call her Auntie Rowan, but she stopped coming round years ago. I think they had some kind of fight."

"When was this?" Adam wracked his brains. He couldn't recall Mum having a friend at all. And, Christ, how sad was that?

"You were quite young," Evie said. "It was before Dad left. I know that."

"Before I broke my arm?"

"No, she came to see you when you were in plaster and brought you some sweets. You know, those toffee ones you used to like?"

God, he hadn't had those in years. Did they even make them nowadays? Adam was hit with a vivid memory of a red packet and the taste of creamy, chewy caramel—and it brought with it a vague impression of someone tall with long hair and a warm smile.

"But anyway," Evie went on, "she was Mum's closest friend—up until she wasn't. So I thought—"

"She might know who Mum had an affair with." Adam's heart beat faster yet, and this time he didn't try to blame it on the coffee. Even if Mum hadn't actually told this Rowan lady about the affair, maybe she'd know enough to make a good guess as to who the bloke had been. But how the hell was he going to find her? "Have you got any idea if she stayed in Glastonbury? Do you know, like, her surname or anything?"

Evie gave a crooked smile. "That's just it. She's still here."

CHAPTER THIRTY

After Adam had seen Evie off with a hug, it was too late to do anything but head straight into work. What with the prospect of maybe finding out who his biological dad was and the memory of last night with Corin—Christ, he couldn't wait to tell Corin about Rowan—Adam was amazed he managed to keep his head in the game through the morning. The touch-up he had first thing didn't take a lot of concentration, thank God, and he'd regained a lot of his focus by the time his next client, a cover-up job, came in.

In fact, the woman was so pleased with his artwork, compared to the frankly tragic, misspelled song lyrics that had been there before, she'd left him a hefty tip.

Sasha raised an eyebrow after the woman had gone. "Gonna treat us all to lunch, are you?"

"Uh . . .'nother time, maybe? I've got something I need to do." He frowned. "Anyway, all two of us?"

"Scratch texted me he's coming over."

"Oh." Adam didn't like to be rude, but there was no way he was gonna put this off. "Tell him I'm sorry I missed him."

"You coming to the Prince of Wales tonight? Cos he's gonna ask."

Adam rolled his eyes. "He does have my number. Not sure. Me and Corin didn't exactly talk about that last night." *Shit.* His face was warm. Was he blushing?

Her eyes went wide, and yep, he was definitely blushing. "Last night, eh?" she asked meaningfully. "What happened to 'We're taking it slow'?"

"Hey, I said slow, not continental drift." He couldn't help giving her a goofy grin. "It was really good, yeah? But, listen, I gotta go. See you later." He opened the door.

"Fine. But I'm telling Scratch you blew us off for a lunchtime shag," she called after him as he stepped through.

"I'm not—" he started to say, but then the door was closing, and he didn't want to waste time on explanations anyway. Adam quickened his steps down the high street towards Magdalene Street, where Evie had told him that Auntie Rowan ran a shop called The Crystal Tree.

He had a vague idea where the shop might be, and it turned out to be right. Not far from the Market Cross, it was narrow and squeezed between a vegan café and a convenience store. He must have passed the shop dozens of times since he'd moved back to Glastonbury, but he'd never been inside. Not his thing, crystals. Of course, a month ago, he'd have said ghosts weren't his thing, either.

Adam took a deep breath and pushed open the door.

The shop might be tiny, but it seemed bigger inside due to the sheer variety of stuff that was on display. Not only crystals: incense, candles, and books with intriguing covers.

There were no customers inside at the moment, which was a relief.

A tall lady stood behind the counter, sorting a tray of crystal rings. She was middle-aged, but the sort who'd kept herself young at heart, with brightly henna'd, long flyaway hair kept under control by a thin plait worn around her head like a crown. Familiarity sparked. She'd been pretty in her youth, hadn't she? Like a princess? Or was he simply imagining what his younger self might have thought? She probably turned a few heads even now, with her laugh-lined face and comfortable waistline.

She smiled in welcome, and Adam found himself echoing that smile. "Auntie Rowan?" he asked, feeling about six years old.

"Adam! I didn't think you'd remember me," she said in a gentle, musical voice. "I used to babysit you when you were little. Haven't you grown up handsome?"

"Uh, thanks. You're looking good too," he said quickly. "How have you been?"

"Very well, thank you." She paused. "Is there something special you were after? I can suggest certain crystals if you let me know which area of your life you want to influence, or if you'd prefer, I can do a reading?"

She'd assumed he was a customer. Adam flushed. "Oh, no, actually I need to talk to you."

Rowan raised an eyebrow. She wore a long, floaty dress the colour of old ivy with a low V-neck that showed off her ample cleavage, and there was a thin line of kohl around her sharp green eyes. Was that the sort of thing she wore all the time, or was she just amping up the *Lord of the Rings* vibes for the punters? "That sounds more serious than wanting to reconnect."

"Sorry. I— You're right, I don't really remember a lot of my childhood, but Evie said you were there a lot? And you stopped coming around when I was seven or eight?"

Her smile faded. "After you had your accident. Yes. I'm afraid your mum and I had a falling out."

"Yeah. Uh, it's Mum I wanted to talk about. You know she died recently?" Shit, this wasn't news to her, was it?

Rowan was nodding, thank God. "Yes. I thought very hard about coming to the funeral, but I decided it would be going against her wishes. I lit a candle for her at home instead."

That was good, wasn't it? That she still cared? "You were close when I was little?"

"Oh, yes. And before that too. I remember your sister as a toddler—such a mischievous creature she was." She paused. "You were such a happy baby. Everyone always said you were born laughing."

It did weird things inside Adam's chest to hear himself spoken of like that. But of course, babies *were* happy, weren't they? As long as they had food and shelter and someone who loved them. They hadn't learned to want anything else yet. *If I was happy as a baby, Mum must have loved me back then.* It was like a knife twisting between his ribs. "So, you'd know who her friends were? Anyone who was, maybe, more than friends?" He wiped his palms on his jeans.

Rowan frowned. "More than friends? I'm not quite sure what you're asking me."

"I know Mum had an affair," Adam blurted out. "Me and Dad did a DNA test, and I'm not his."

She stilled. Had she gone pale? Her skin, behind the freckles, was so white already it was hard to tell. "I'm sorry. That must have been difficult for you to learn."

Adam swallowed. "So that's why I'm here. To ask you if you know—or have any idea—who my father was."

With a hand motion weirdly like a chicken pecking at grain, Rowan plucked a mauve—amethyst?—ring from the middle row of the display and set it in the top row. Then she moved a silver ring set with a rough-hewn black stone into the place the first ring had come from.

"Does it really matter all that much, who your biological father was?" she said without looking at him. "'The blood of the covenant is thicker than the water of the womb,' as they say."

They did? That wasn't the phrase Adam was used to. He wasn't even sure what it meant. "Uh . . ."

She raised her head then and smiled. Was it only his imagination, or was there something brittle about her expression? "The person you are today—they're not just the creation of one man and one woman. All the people you've ever known have shaped you into who you are. The people you grew up with. Your friends. Your teachers. Your lovers. Even chance acquaintances can have a profound influence on our lives."

What, like old aunties who insist on being mysterious? "Heredity's real, though. If it was you, wouldn't you want to know who gave you half your genes?"

Rowan spread her hands wide. "Why? It wouldn't change anything about me. We are who we are."

"And maybe who I am is someone who wants to know who his dad is." He couldn't keep the impatience out of his voice.

She sighed, fiddling once more with the black stone ring. "I'm sorry. But I can't tell you about Isla having an affair."

"Can't or won't?" Adam bit out.

"You'll have to interpret it as you see fit, I'm afraid. But I am glad to see you and looking so well. I hope you'll drop in here again."

Right. Adam could understand *Piss off* however politely she said it. Still, as he opened the door, chimes ringing, Adam turned and threw back over his shoulder, "Why did you and my mum stop being friends?"

Rowan froze, for an instant. Then she smiled, and there was definitely something forced about it this time. "We had a difference of opinion, that was all."

"About what?"

"Oh, I don't think that's important after so many years. I think there's someone trying to get in, so would you mind . . .?"

Adam realised he was blocking the way for a woman in a wheelchair and hastily stepped off the doormat to hold the door open for her. She rolled past him into the shop, her *Thank you* only slightly pointed, and immediately got talking to Rowan.

Shit. Rowan knew more than she was saying. Adam was sure of it. Nevertheless, he let the door fall gently closed and stomped back down the street.

When he got to the studio, Scratch was still there. Adam glanced at the time—still half an hour of his lunch break left. He ought to get food at some point, and why the hell hadn't he thought about that when he was passing all the sandwich shops just now?

Right. Two birds; one stone. "Oi, Scratch?" he called out. "Wanna come to the caff with me? I need to talk to you."

"Sorry, mate. I gotta go." Scratch squinted at his phone. "You're back a bit soon though, ain't you? That bloke of yours must be easily satisfied."

Sasha cackled.

"I wasn't with him," Adam said, exasperated. "I went to see— It doesn't matter. I'll tell you about it later. I need to get some food. Meet you for a pint after work?"

"Yeah, all right." He glanced at Sasha, then back at Adam. "This a general invite, or just you and me?"

Adam gave Sasha a guilty look, but he wasn't sure he was ready to tell the world about his mum and dad yet. "Uh . . ."

She rolled her eyes and gave him the finger. "Don't worry, I'm busy anyway. Washing my hair."

Shit. That sounded really pointed.

"Aaannnd I'll be going now." Scratch shoved his phone into his back pocket and flung open the door. "See you at six."

"See you later," Adam called as the door closed behind him. Then he sighed. "Sash, if you want to come—"

She laughed. "Just messing with you. You go and have your manly pints and talk about men's stuff. And make sure you go back to the doctor if the cream doesn't work."

Adam winced. "It's not an STD, okay?"

"Hey, am I judging?" She spread her hands wide. "This is me, not judging. Now bugger off and get your sandwich so you don't get the shakes later and screw up some poor bastard's ink."

She had a point. "Okay. You want anything?"

"Nothing you can afford. Now piss off."

Adam pissed off.

That evening, Adam plonked Scratch's pint on the table in front of him and sat down with his own drink. "Right. I hope you're not in a hurry to get home." They were at the Isle of Avalon for a change, so it wasn't like it would be far for him to go.

Scratch frowned. "If you'd said that earlier, I'd have asked you to get some snacks."

"Thought of that." Adam reached into his jacket pocket and drew out a couple of bags of pork scratchings, slinging them on the table.

Scratch's eyebrows hit the ceiling as he fielded one of the bags. "You hate them things. This is serious, then, is it? Something up with you and Corin?"

"*Everyone* hates pork scratchings. They're literally the most disgusting snack known to man. And no. This is about my dad. Uh, my biological dad."

"You found 'im, then?" Adam had told Scratch about the DNA test years back, when they'd both lived in London. "Thought you weren't bothered about that."

"I know I wasn't before, but lately I've been thinking more about where I came from. And I reckon my mum wants me to find out who he is. That's why she hasn't moved on."

Scratch nodded and crunched a pork scratching. "Makes sense."

"But I'm kind of . . . I'm not sure what to do. See, Mum hasn't, like, said anything, or left any clues. I went to see an old mate of hers today, and it was weird." He gave Scratch a quick run-down of what had happened with Rowan.

"Sounds like she knows stuff she ain't saying." Scratch stroked his beard between his finger and his thumb, leaving it greased and lightly salted from the pork scratchings.

"Yeah, and it's bloody frustrating. Why's she being so cagey? I don't get it."

"Sounds funny to me. 'Er and your mum having a break up like that. 'S more like lovers than mates." Scratch's eyes went wide. "Could be something in that, and all."

Adam frowned. "I guess? Always thought of Mum as straight, though. And it still doesn't tell me who my dad was."

"*Don't* it?" Scratch said, eyebrows up to his hairline, as if he was in some cheesy drama and there ought to be music going dum-dum-*duuummm* right now.

"Uh?"

"Your Auntie Rowan could be trans, couldn't she?"

Adam hadn't read her as trans, but that meant bugger all, didn't it? "No," he said uncertainly.

Scratch clipped him round the ear.

Adam's eyes flew wide. "Oi! What was that for?"

"You, looking like a wet festival weekend at the idea your dad might be trans."

"No, I'm looking like that because I hate the thought that she stood there and didn't bloody *tell* me." And maybe it was daft to feel so betrayed, seeing as he'd forgotten her existence until Evie had reminded him, but he couldn't stand thinking Auntie Rowan had let him down like that. Then he shook his head. "It's not all that likely, though, is it? Think of all the bloody hoops people have to jump through to transition nowadays—it must have been even worse nearly thirty years ago."

"Don't mean it didn't happen."

"No, but we've got no real reason to think it *did* for Rowan." For a moment, though, Adam wondered what it might have been like being brought up by his mum and Rowan as a couple. He snorted. He'd have had the shit teased out of him at school, most like. Section 28 had still been in force back then, bless Maggie Thatcher's dried-up, homophobic heart. Then he shook his head again. "No. Can't be. Evie was, like, sixteen when they had their fight or whatever. You're not telling me she wouldn't have noticed if they were more than friends."

"Come up with any suggestions for who the bloke might be, then, has she?"

Adam threw his face into his hands. "No. Shit. I could maybe give it another shot with her. She really didn't want to tell me anything, though."

"How's about you go back to the source, then?"

"What source? *Evie*?"

"Nooo. Your mum."

"How? She doesn't show up on demand, you know." And it'd been a while since she'd shown up at all.

"That's cos you ain't doing it right. You wanna, like, *pierce the veil*, you gotta have the proper veil-piercing equipment. Like a Ouija board."

"That's rubbish," Adam said, but it ended up sounding like a question.

"How do you know? More things in heaven and earth, mate. 'S gotta be worth a try, ain't it?"

"I guess . . ." Adam frowned. "Have you got a Ouija board?"

"No, but I can borrow one from Esme."

"Your landlady?" Scratch lived over the shop she owned that sold dream catchers, incense, and tie-dyed clothing to all the wanna-blessed-bes.

Scratch nodded. "She's into all that spiritualism. Got a crystal ball too. Nearly had my bollocks when I knocked the cover off it one time and didn't put it back."

"Why? Cos she thought you'd be letting the spirits out?"

"No, they catch the sunlight, see? Like a magnifying glass. Coulda burned the whole place down, she reckoned. So anyhow, I'll get the stuff, and we can set it all up at yours. Be perfect, cos that's where she'll be haunting."

Adam wasn't sure he liked the word *haunting* applied to his mum. And anyway—"I saw her on the tor the first time."

Scratch rocked his head from side to side. "Well, if it don't work at yours, we can try up there." His voice deepened dramatically, and his eyes went comically wide. "Course, might get more than we bargain for, a place like that. Could rouse the Wild Hunt—the proper one, mind—and send 'em after our souls." Then he added in a lighter tone, "Be a bugger explaining all that to Sash," before popping another pork scratching into his mouth.

"My house is fine," Adam said hastily. Scratch was just yanking his chain, right? He couldn't actually believe in a literal wild hunt. But maybe it'd be better not to chance it. "Can you do it with only two people, though? Don't you need, like, a group to sit round a table and hold hands— No, wait, that's a séance, innit?"

"Could get Corin to join us, and then we could do the whole séance thing if the Ouija don't work. Or do you reckon it's too soon for him to be meeting your parents?"

Adam sat back heavily in his seat. "This is way too weird."

Scratch shrugged. "Wanna get your answers, though, don't you?"

And that was the trouble. Adam really did.

CHAPTER THIRTY-ONE

C orin had found the afterglow of his night with Adam effectively dimmed by that offhand comment about seeing ghosts. He was almost glad to glance at his phone and see he had barely enough time to get ready for work before an online meeting first thing. At least it'd stop him brooding on—

No. Not going to think about it. Corin ran a hand through his hair and clicked into the meeting.

Thankfully, this time, Claire had her screen correctly labelled. They discussed a few new client issues with one of their products for a while—Peter had been trying to replicate them without success— and somehow moved seamlessly into office gossip. Corin let his attention drift but was pulled up sharply by the mention of a familiar name.

"Sorry, Claire—what did you say?"

"Oh, just that I saw Tyler the other day, when I was out in town. You know, Blair's boyfriend."

Corin's heart lurched.

"He looks as good as ever," she went on, "but you can tell he's still in mourning—I mean, he was inconsolable at the memorial service. It must have been terrible for him, poor lad."

"Yes. Terrible," Corin ground out, wishing he hadn't asked. Then he felt guilty. It wasn't Claire's fault. She didn't know what Blair had been to him.

"Did you know Tyler? With you and Blair being friends? We were all so surprised in the office, seeing him at the service." Claire shrugged. "But then, Blair always was such a *private* person, wasn't he?"

"Yes. He was. And no. I didn't. Have you got plans for the weekend?" Corin asked desperately.

"Well, it's Halloween, isn't it?" Claire rolled her eyes. "Sophie's old enough to be really into it this year. She keeps changing her mind about what she wants to dress up as to go trick-or-treating. So far we've had a skeleton, a ghost, and Peppa Pig, although I told her Peppa's not scary. I'm trying to persuade her to go for a ghost, and then I can cut eye and arm holes in a pillowcase and put her in a white top and tights. Those supermarket costumes are a total waste of money, *and* they're bad for the planet."

"What about a ghost Peppa?" Peter's voice lit up with enthusiasm for the first time this morning. "Same outfit but draw a snout on it? Which would be really meta—you know that Reddit fan theory that she's actually the spirit of a human child? She was seriously ill, and her parents couldn't bear her suffering and pulled the plug. You could turn it into a whole family costume—Daddy Pig is supposed to have killed himself and the rest of the family through guilt, and—"

"I'd rather *not* traumatise my three-year-old, thank you!" Claire's tone was sharp. "That's horrible. Why do people always have to ruin things?"

A flush spread up Peter's face to encompass his bald head. "Oh, you're fine with her dressing up as a ghost, but the ghost of a fictional talking pig is taking it too far?"

Corin was getting a headache. "Can we—"

"Have you got plans for Halloween, Corin?" Claire asked loudly. "I hear they're very into it in Glastonbury. Except they call it Samhain there."

"It's pronounced *Sowin*," Peter corrected her in a surly tone. "Not *Sam Hayne*. And it's a religious festival, not a dressing-up party."

"Actually—" Corin tried again.

Claire snorted. "Oh? I didn't know you were a practising Satanist, Peter. Or, what do they call it? Wiccan?"

"Satanism has nothing to do with Wicca," Corin snapped. "Even I know that. And can we please get back to work?"

"Oh," Claire said, sounding wounded.

"Fine." Peter's tone was surlier than ever. "But in case it's slipped your mind—which would be totally understandable; I'd be the last person to judge—I *am* actually team lead . . ."

When the meeting finally ended, Corin shoved back his chair and stomped to the bathroom cabinet for some headache pills, downing them with a mugful of water from the tap. God, he needed a coffee. A *proper* coffee.

One cup of Starbucks won't kill you, he told himself guiltily as he jogged down the metal staircase to the street.

The unaccustomed caffeine in his Americano hit hard, and Corin spent an unexpectedly productive morning—but by lunchtime he was jittery and tense, and his headache was coming back.

Damn it.

A brisk walk in his lunch hour helped clear his brain a little, but the ache was still there, pounding in his temples when he moved his head. Corin struggled to focus on his afternoon's work and was heartily glad when it was time to down tools for the day.

As usual, when he looked in his fridge after finishing work, the contents were sadly lacking. He should probably do something about that. After all, he was seeing Adam tomorrow night, which meant there was a good chance he'd be staying for breakfast again. Corin straightened, smiling at the memory of this morning. At least, the part after he'd got over his embarrassing meltdown over waking up in bed with a stranger.

And before anyone had mentioned ghosts . . .

Corin's smile fell. At least his head had finally stopped aching, he realised with relief. He should get some eggs in, and bacon. They could have a leisurely morning— Except Adam would be working on Saturday, wouldn't he? Oh well. There was always Sunday. Corin pulled on his jacket and headed out to the shops.

As he made his way down the street in the twilight, the sound of drums caught his ear. When he rounded the corner, he was confronted by a troupe of morris dancers performing in front of the church. Corin stopped to watch them—a small crowd had gathered, which would make it hard to proceed in any case. These dancers weren't the cosy, white-clad morris men he'd seen at Avebury summer fetes, with bells on their legs and flowers in their hats. These dancers were of all genders, clad in rags and tags of black, and their top hats were adorned with ravens' feathers. Their faces, too, were smudged in black—or was it a very dark green? Corin couldn't tell in the twilight. All save for one, whose face was a stark white death's head.

They could have been evil spirits risen from the graveyard. Corin half expected the St. John's clergy to come out and perform an exorcism. He shivered, tempted to walk away, but it seemed rude, somehow.

And ridiculous. What was there to be frightened of in a motley assortment of folk dancers? Corin forced himself to stay and watch until the drums stopped and the dancers lined up to take a bow as the audience clapped.

A woman with an *entire* black bird on her top hat, its wings spread as if about to take flight, stepped forward. "Thank you! We've been the Ragged Ravens; please check out our Facebook page. Thank you for watching our rehearsal, and make sure you come along on Saturday to see the real thing!" There was applause, and the *chink* of donations as a hat was passed around by one of the dancers. As Corin rummaged in his pocket for some change, he cast an idle glance at the crowd.

They were a diverse bunch; one of the things he liked about Glastonbury. An Asian woman in bright colours had her arm around a tall white man in a long fur coat. The small child on his shoulders wore a princess dress, the skirt bunched up around her hips, and devil horns. A white woman with purple hair was laughing with a bald man in biker leathers, while a couple in matching harem pants held hands and smiled at everyone indiscriminately.

And a man with short, light brown hair was gazing directly at Corin. He froze as their eyes met and held one another for a long moment—then the other man looked away.

Corin's heart pounded. If only he could see how the man was dressed—but there were too many people in between them. Could this be the man he'd seen outside his flat?

No, he was being paranoid. Maybe it was someone he'd met here? It probably wasn't Adam, as he hadn't smiled and he'd looked away. And it certainly wasn't Scratch, unless he'd had a radical makeover. Fed up with uncertainty and tired of unwillingly being rude, Corin gathered his courage and made his way towards the man. It was slow going against the crowd, some of whom had lingered to talk to the dancers. Although Corin only glanced aside for a moment as he dodged around a woman with a wide double buggy, when he tried to find the man again, it was in vain.

The man had melted into the throng as if he'd never been there. Corin shivered. He'd forgotten to check for the eyebrow, hadn't he? How could he have forgotten that? The one thing that might have told him if it was really Blair?

It *couldn't* have been Blair. The man had most likely been a random stranger who'd now gone home for his tea. Corin must have imagined the man's interest in him. Unsettled nonetheless, Corin turned his steps back towards his flat. Beans on toast would do for tonight, and he could shop another time.

He half wished it was Friday already and he'd be seeing Adam tonight. He *could* call him—but although Adam had seemed to accept Corin's damaged state, the last thing Corin wanted to do was to seem needy. Begging his boyfriend to come and hold his hand because he thought he'd seen a man looking at him wouldn't just be needy, it'd be downright pathetic.

And it wasn't like he could expect much sympathy from Adam on the subject of seeing ghosts, was it? Corin frowned. Was he being unfair to Adam? Corin wasn't sure he wanted to find out.

At least . . . At least when he stood at his front door and peered back down at the street, there was no shadowy figure on the corner gazing up at him.

Not tonight, at any rate.

CHAPTER THIRTY-TWO

Corin couldn't help feeling on edge as he left his flat Friday evening. Adam had suggested via text that they go for a meal at The Huntsman, a pub Corin hadn't been to yet. Adam had also suggested that he could pick Corin up on the way and take him there but, feeling he needed to learn his own way around town, Corin had declined. He'd looked the place up online, and it *should* be simple to get to, although his damaged brain sometimes made the simple complex.

To reach The Huntsman, Corin had to walk down the high street to the Market Cross—that was easy—and turn right, down a street he hadn't explored yet. He would definitely have remembered the shop that claimed to sell all things Viking and had a fully-armed Norse warrior as part of its window display. Corin paused for a moment to admire the rest of the items on show—more weapons, jewellery, and statues of the Norse gods. His gaze fell on an impressive horned animal skull, the bones bleached white, and he shivered. Time he moved on. He didn't want to be late.

He found the pub a few doors down. It was an imposing building, half-timbered, and well kept up, most likely for the last three hundred years or so. It looked like the sort of place that would feature on ghost tours. Corin shook his head at himself and pushed the door open. He needed to stop being so bloody morbid.

Corin had to stifle a groan when he stepped inside. The pub, as he should have expected, was decked out for Halloween with pumpkins on the bar, skeletons in the corner, and ghostly bunting hanging between the light fittings. One of the skeletons was wearing a top hat at a jaunty angle, and another wore an orange feather boa. The effect was rather tacky than spooky, for which he was grateful. It was a reminder not to take it all too seriously.

A man leaning on the bar facing the door straightened and gave Corin a lopsided smile and a wave.

Corin smiled back and joined him. "Adam?"

"Yeah. Good to see you. You found the place okay, then?"

"No problem. Had a good couple of days?" *Since we woke up together, and had to part.* Heat rose in Corin at the anticipation of another night like that—and hopefully, a much more leisurely morning after.

Adam made a hand-wavy gesture. "So-so. Want to order some food, then we can sit down?" He handed Corin a menu card. "The lasagne's great here, almost as good as home-cooked. The pies are all puff pastry crust, though."

"What about the curry?"

"Varies. The chef gets heavy-handed with the spices sometimes." Adam grinned. "Are you feeling lucky today?"

Not especially, but sod it all to hell. Corin ordered the curry, and they sat down at a corner table with a pint of beer each. "So what was the bad part of your day? Unless you don't want to talk about it, of course."

"Nah, it wasn't that bad. Caught up with an old mate of my mum, but it was frustrating. I reckon she knows something about who my biological dad might be, but she's not telling."

"But why wouldn't she?" Corin frowned. "Do you think she promised your mum she'd keep the secret?"

"Could be. Still annoying, though. It feels like I'm so close to finding out. And there she is, trying to convince me it doesn't bloody matter."

"That doesn't sound good." Corin caught himself. "Sorry, but I can't help thinking, maybe she's trying to protect you as well as your mum? Maybe she thinks you might regret finding out who he is?"

"What, like he's a serial killer?" Adam took a long drink of his pint and sat back. "Ah, I dunno. I just wanna *know*, you know? And I can't help thinking Mum wants me to know too."

"Right," Corin said uncertainly. "Have you, uh, seen her again?"

Adam shook his head and drew in a breath, but at that point their food arrived.

Corin couldn't say he was sorry.

The curry turned out to be a little on the hot side, but nothing Corin couldn't handle. When he sneaked a forkful of Adam's lasagne, though, he had to admit he should have taken his advice. The rich, meaty sauce was seriously tasty, the oregano and basil complementing the garlic and tomatoes. Corin stared at Adam. "And you said this is only *almost* as good as homemade? Are you secretly a cordon bleu chef?"

Adam laughed. "Cooking's not that hard."

"You've clearly never watched me attempt it," Corin muttered, and cast around for a new subject before Adam could dig out any embarrassing particulars of his culinary incompetence. The pub décor came to his rescue. "Given all this lot, I'm surprised they haven't got a special menu on with pumpkin in everything."

"Yeah, Samhain's pretty big in Glastonbury." Adam pronounced it pretty much as Peter had said it should be: *Sowin*. "Coming out tomorrow to see the dragon procession? There's going to be stuff going on at the tor too. Music, morris dancing, and there's a whole pagan ceremony to celebrate the Winter King coming to replace the Summer King. Loads of people dress up for it in horns and cloaks and stuff, but don't worry, I'm not planning to."

Corin blinked. "It's a religious thing?"

"Oh, yeah. Totally." Adam shrugged. "I mean, not for me. But a lot of people round here really believe in it all. Gwynn ap Nudd as a literal horned god, leading the Wild Hunt."

"Gwynn ap . . .?" It'd sounded like *niece*, or maybe *neath*.

"Nudd. Spelt *N-U-D-D*—it's Welsh, so nothing to do with having your kit off." Adam grinned. "He's the Winter King. The Wild Hunt is when he comes to collect our souls."

Corin shivered and put down his fork. He'd had enough of his curry. "That sounds dark." He was wishing now that he hadn't changed the subject.

"No, it's cool. The celebrations are supposed to be really fun. At least, that's what Sash and Scratch tell me. I've never actually been. Mum . . . didn't like pagan stuff. I used to get books out of the library with all the old stories in, but I had to hide them from her." Adam frowned, then shook his head. "This is the first year I've been in Glastonbury for it since I was sixteen."

"So everything you've told me about it is just hearsay?" Corin teased, in an attempt to lighten his own mood.

Adam laughed, pushed his empty plate away from him, and slung his arm around Corin's shoulders. "What is this, a court of law? Hey, come with me and you can make your own mind up about it."

Warmed by his embrace, Corin couldn't say no to that smile. It would be fine. It was simply a celebration of folklore, that was all. And surely he'd be safer in the middle of a crowd, rather than on his own on Halloween night.

A chill washed over him. Was he really worrying about his *safety*? From, well, spirits? That was crazy. He had to stop dwelling on death. For the sake of his own sanity. Corin forced a smile. "Will your sister be going too?"

"Evie? Oh, I doubt it. She's not much into that kind of thing. I think she reckons she's grown out of fairy stories. She wants to meet you, though. Maybe you could both come round to mine for dinner one night? Or we could eat out, if you'd rather. We won't go to hers. Her husband's dead boring and he doesn't like me much. Especially at the moment."

"Because of the rows?"

"That, and he generally doesn't trust me cos I was out of touch all those years. Like, he assumes I'm after something, wanting to reconnect with Evie now. And Mum leaving me the house can't have helped."

"But you've sorted things out with her?"

"Pretty much. I dumped too much on her all at once, and it's taken her a while to get her head round it. It's not just about my dad. It's about me seeing Mum after she died. Evie's convinced I'm hallucinating."

Corin bit his lip. Evie had a point. "Do you truly believe it's her? Your mum? Watching over you?" God, if that was the case, maybe Blair really was watching him too.

And not in a good way.

Adam shook his head. "See, what gets me is, Evie won't even consider it. Mum being real, I mean. Shit. There was me, starting to think I— So anyhow, me and Scratch, we're going to do, like, a séance tomorrow."

Ice-cold water filled Corin's veins, and he forgot to breathe. It wasn't only *what* Adam had said, it was the way he'd thrown it out so casually. *We're going to watch a parade, and then we're going to call up the dead.*

"After we've been to the tor," Adam was saying. "Me and Scratch, but I'd love it if you came along too? Cos I reckon if there's ever gonna be a chance to contact Mum, to speak to her properly, it's on Samhain. Like, the veil's thinner then?"

Corin felt as though he was going to throw up. "You *want* to call up spirits. Invite the dead in."

"Well, yeah? I think my mum needs to tell me something. Before she can rest."

Oh God. Corin's mind conjured up an image of Blair as an unquiet spirit, unable to rest until he'd twisted the knife in the wound he'd left in Corin's heart. "That's horrible," he blurted out. It *couldn't* be true. He refused to believe it.

Adam jerked backwards as though Corin had slapped him in the face. "Why does it have to be *horrible*? If someone loves you, and they want to stay with you even after they're gone, you think that's a *bad* thing?"

"How the hell could it not be? And you're missing the point. *Ghosts don't exist.*" Corin's palms were slick with sweat. Ghosts *couldn't* exist. Because if they did . . .

"So what, you're saying I'm crazy? Christ, you haven't even met Evie yet, and it's like you're ganging up on me with her! Just because stuff doesn't fit in with your neat little world view doesn't mean it's not real. You're not the one who makes the rules. You can't programme life—or death—to do what you want."

"Is that what you think? That I want to be some kind of . . . of puppet master?" Corin threw himself back in his chair.

"Well, you seem to think you've got the right to tell *me* what to do!"

Corin stared at Adam's unfamiliar face. "Only because what you want to do is *insane*. You honestly think it's reasonable to, what, attempt to overcome death itself so you can have a chat with your mum?"

Adam shifted his chair back. "Right. Fine. So I take it you won't be coming tomorrow." His tone was tight and angry.

"You're mad if you go ahead with this," Corin countered, his hands shaking as he put down his drink. He opened his mouth to beg Adam to reconsider, but Adam was already standing.

"Good to know what you think of me. Hadn't pegged you as so bloody judgemental, but hey, what do I know? I'll see you around."

Adam walked away, to be lost in a sea of unfamiliar faces.

CHAPTER THIRTY-THREE

Adam stomped off down the street. He couldn't believe it. He'd thought Corin was on his side. Turned out that, given half a chance, the bloke would probably get together with Evie and Sash and send a priest to Mum's to get busy with bell, book, and bloody candle. It'd *hurt*, hearing Corin call him mad. Call his mum *horrible*. What the hell had changed since they'd first met on the tor? He hadn't been so bloody anti back then.

Course, back then he hadn't got his leg over yet, had he? Adam kicked at a beer can someone had left next to a litter bin. It arced away, sending fuck knew what liquid spraying everywhere.

Why the hell hadn't Mum been around lately? He hadn't seen or heard her since that time with the painting shortly after he'd moved into the house. That was *weeks* ago. Maybe she hadn't stayed to tell him about his dad, after all? Maybe she'd only lingered to make sure him and Evie were getting on okay. And now they'd made up, he'd never see her again. There was a tight, painful knot in Adam's chest. If only he'd been here more while she was alive . . .

Fuck.

Adam had calmed down a little by the time he'd walked home. He wasn't so angry now, but there was a hollow ache in his chest that wouldn't subside. He'd really thought him and Corin were good together, and he still couldn't understand why Corin had been so . . . so like *that*.

When he pushed open the front door, the house was dark and silent. Adam hesitated to turn on a light. "Mum?" he said, hopefully. "I believe in you, okay?"

Nobody answered. Adam waited for a minute, then flicked the light switch with a sigh. Trudging into the kitchen, he put on the kettle, then changed his mind and pulled a beer out of the fridge.

He sat on the sofa to drink it and found himself staring at Mum's Scottish painting. This time, though, Mum didn't have a word to say about it. Not even in his head. *Shit.* Adam jumped up again. His whole body itched to move, to do something. *Anything.*

There was stuff he'd been planning to do, to make the house *his.* Somehow, though, he didn't wanna do that right now. It was like it'd be disrespectful to Mum.

There was the attic, though, wasn't there? He still had plenty of boxes to go through.

Adam had jogged upstairs before he'd finished the thought, and pulled down the loft ladder. It fell with a *clang*, narrowly missing his toes. He climbed it, the ridged surface of the rungs biting into his sock-clad feet.

It was colder in the attic than the rest of the house, and the single bare light bulb cast deep shadows. Were there more boxes in here than last time he'd looked? Maybe they were breeding. Adam went to open up a box next to the one he'd found his books in, then, on a whim, made his way carefully to the farthest reach of the attic instead.

Ducking under a beam, he found a small box right in the corner and pulled it out to where he could get at it more easily. It had a damp feel to it, although it might simply have been the cold.

A musty smell tickled Adam's nose as he opened the cardboard flaps to see what the box held. His heart beat a little faster as he saw a baby record book. His or Evie's? Inside, he found a picture of a newborn all in blue. His, then. Underneath the picture was his name, written in Mum's neatest handwriting: Adam James Merchant. Date and time of birth were also recorded, and his birth weight: a respectable 7lb 14oz. Adam flicked through the pages—apparently his first word had been *bic*, for *biscuit*—and put it down with a sigh. So, yeah, when he'd been little Mum had cared enough to fill in a book for him, but it didn't tell him anything about who his dad was.

He gave a bitter laugh. Apparently it was more important to know the date he'd cut his first tooth than who'd contributed half his DNA. Adam laid the book to one side and sorted through the rest of the box's contents. Most of them consisted of packs of photos, printed out in six-by-four glossy. He looked through the first one, but seeing Mum's beaming face as she held baby Adam made him feel weird, so he put the rest aside for later. How come she'd been so loving back then but not later, when he was old enough to remember? Had it been to do with Dad leaving?

It was some comfort that she'd kept all this stuff. Then again, maybe she just hadn't bothered to chuck it away. Adam turned his attention back to the box, which was almost empty now. There was a tiny pair of shoes, his vaccination records, and something that rattled around in a corner when he picked up the box to turn it to the light.

It was a tiny wristband, not much wider around than his thumb, snipped in half. A newborn baby's ID tag from the hospital. Adam shook his head. She'd kept that all these years? He turned it over to read the faded biro, and his breath caught.

The date of birth was right, but it said *Baby Hendricks*, not *Baby Merchant*.

Why would Mum have kept the wristband from someone else's baby? And wait, there was another one in there too. Also cut off, this one said, as expected, *Baby Merchant*.

Adam rocked back on his heels, almost braining himself on a beam.

What the hell?

CHAPTER THIRTY-FOUR

Adam woke up way before his alarm on Saturday. Good. It meant he'd have time to visit Auntie fucking Rowan before he was due in at the studio. She had to know something about the wristbands. She *had* to. He threw on some clothes and dashed out of the house without bothering about breakfast.

Then his phone alarm went off. Eight thirty. Shit. The shop wouldn't be open yet, would it? And the chances were she didn't live there. Probably used the top floor for storage, or rented it out to someone like Scratch, who didn't mind the noise of living in the town centre. Adam sighed and headed back into the house, where he managed to force down a slice of toast and jam.

Dead on nine thirty, Adam marched into The Crystal Tree. Rowan was behind the counter, dressed in jeans and a tight-fitting top. The lone customer who'd beaten him to the shop, a short man losing the battle against middle-aged spread, took one look at his face and scurried out without buying anything.

"Who's Baby Hendricks?" Adam demanded, dropping the ID tags onto the counter in front of her. "And why did my mum have his wristband?"

Rowan went absolutely still for a moment—then she slowly reached down and picked up the tags. She was wearing a heavy amethyst ring today, and one with a deep blue stone. "I didn't know. Not for sure. Not until you told me about that test. She might have imagined it, or dreamed it, and convinced herself it was real. After all those years, memory wouldn't have been reliable." She fixed him straight in the eye. "You mustn't blame her. She did what she thought was right. It was only after your accident that she realised she might have been wrong all along. That was when she told me about it."

Adam's head was spinning. "What? What did she do?"

Rowan hugged herself, the gesture making her look years younger. "She had some difficulties on the day you were born. It was a long labour—it was breech—and she was exhausted by the end of it all. She hardly knew what was happening anymore. And it wasn't like when she had Evie, she said. She had to be stitched up, and I think there was some worry about the baby's breathing, although it was nothing, in the end. So she didn't get to hold her baby until sometime after the birth. And . . ." Rowan took a deep breath. "They put it in her arms, at last, and she felt nothing. *Nothing.* Not the rush of love she'd felt for Evie. It was a scrunched-up little thing, howling already, and when she tried to feed it, it wouldn't latch on. Just grizzled."

It, Adam thought numbly.

"When they took her to the ward, there was another woman, who'd been in the delivery suite next-door. The baby in the cot next to her was sleeping, and Isla looked at him, and she *knew*, she told me. This was her baby. The hospital had made a mistake. Had given her the wrong baby. So she waited until the ward was quiet and the other woman was asleep . . ." Rowan took a deep breath. "And she swapped them back. She couldn't get the wristbands off without cutting them, so she hid them in her bag. When the other baby cried, the woman fed it, still half-asleep, and nobody seemed to notice the change. So she kept you and brought you home."

Ice-cold water seemed to wash through Adam's veins. "How long have you known all this?"

"She didn't tell me anything until after that blood test that caused all the trouble with Joe. And she was still convinced it had to be a mistake—or at least, she wanted to think that." Rowan gazed at him sombrely.

"She told you all this and you *kept quiet* about it?" Adam's legs felt weak. If this was true . . . He wasn't Dad's kid. He wasn't Mum's kid either. Who the fucking hell *was* he?

Rowan's expression sharpened. "You were seven years old. Isla was the only mother you'd ever known. She loved you. Was I supposed to drag you from her arms and thrust you into the hands of strangers?"

"You mean, my real parents? And what about the other kid? The real Adam Merchant?" Adam's voice cracked. Except he wasn't Adam, was he? He was whatever his real mum and dad had called him. He didn't even know his own *name*. "And what about my dad? He doesn't know he's got a son—a real son." It hurt. It hurt like *fuck*. "It doesn't have to be true. Maybe I really was her baby. Just not Dad's."

Rowan shook her head slowly. "No. She didn't have an affair. I'm sure of it. She was too in love with Joe. So if you're not his, then you're not Isla's either."

"Maybe she did, and you didn't know about it? She didn't tell you about swapping babies for years." Adam's temper rose, and his voice did too. "Maybe you're the one who's lying. Maybe you're making all this up."

She straightened her back and folded her arms. "You can believe me or not, as you choose. Ask yourself though, why would I lie? It isn't like you can't find out the truth."

The truth. Christ. It'd be simple, wouldn't it? All he'd have to do would be to take another DNA test. He wouldn't even need to find the Hendrickses, whoever they were. All he'd have to do was get Evie to do one with him.

And then he'd know. Both of them would know he was nothing to do with her family. Just some fucking cuckoo in the nest. Paul had been right to be suspicious of him all along.

"There's more to family than blood," Rowan said quietly, as if she'd read his mind.

Adam took a stumbling step back.

"She regretted telling me," Rowan went on. "I'm sure that was why she stopped wanting me around. Knowing that I knew—it was a reminder of the whole thing. And what was worse, I think she was afraid, deep down, that she'd got it wrong, but she tried to deny it to herself. It affected her. Damaged her mental health." She sighed. "And I was angry with her too. For putting me in that position. I didn't want to be her secret keeper."

"But you did. Keep it." His voice was hoarse.

"Who would it have helped if I'd spoken out?"

"Me, maybe? I left home at *sixteen*; you ever think there might have been a reason why?"

"I didn't know." Her regret sounded honest. "We weren't in contact by then. But I suppose it's only natural her relationship with you suffered, after what she'd found out."

Yeah, that was one way of putting it. "And what about the other kid? The—the real me?"

Her face softened. "You're the real you. This changes nothing about who you are."

Fuck that. It changed *everything*.

Adam pushed blindly out of The Crystal Tree and stumbled down the street towards Furious Ink. Something of what he was feeling must have shown on his face, as the other pedestrians scurried out of his way like mice.

It all made sense now. Mum being so distant with him. Had she accepted he wasn't her kid, in the end? Or had she kept on telling herself it wasn't true, like she'd always insisted to Dad that the tests were wrong? *"She tried to deny it to herself,"* Rowan had said. And all the time, the terrible doubt had eaten away at Mum. Poisoned their relationship.

And the good days . . . maybe those had been the days she'd been able to forget about it for a while. Pretend she hadn't taken the wrong baby home from hospital.

Had she ever gone looking for the real Adam? Seen him living his life with a family of strangers? But then, if she'd found him, wouldn't she have left her house to *him*? Or was the legacy a *Sorry I stole your life* present?

He had to find him. The other him. Find out what life might have been like.

Christ, should he *tell* him? Adam stopped dead in the street, a few doors down from Furious Ink. He'd been mad as hell at Rowan for not telling him—but it wasn't so simple, was it? What if this other bloke was happy in his life, and Adam would fuck that all up for him by telling him the truth?

If it *was* the truth . . . Fuck it. Adam couldn't deal with all this now. It must be time to get to work, right? Sasha wouldn't care if he got there early. He set off again, this time paying a bit more mind to his fellow pavement users.

Sasha was busy cleaning when he got in, thank God, and by the look of her, suffering from a late night last night. She raised her head briefly to greet him and didn't seem to notice that he'd just had the rug pulled out from under his whole fucking *life*.

It was a relief to lose himself in his work. Because this was *his*, this was him. Whoever he was. *Don't think about it.*

Two o'clock rolled around quicker than Adam could have imagined. They were closing early due to it being Samhain and the celebrations starting at three. Adam washed the floor down with disinfectant and tried not to think about how little he had to celebrate. He didn't have Corin—shit, he didn't even have *himself* any more.

He'd thought he wasn't doing too bad at hiding how he felt, until Sasha put a hand on his arm. "Adam? Are you okay? Cos you've got a face like a puppy that's had a kicking."

Adam looked at her, and Christ, he could feel tears welling up. "Fine," he choked out.

Sasha's eyes widened. "Babe, come here."

Adam let himself be enfolded in her arms and pressed against her chest. She was soft, and she smelled of roses and antiseptic. He didn't cry. He fucking *didn't*, okay?

"Wanna tell me?" she said gently.

"No." Adam drew in several deep breaths. "Had a fight with Corin," he said in the end, because it was true and because he couldn't talk about the other thing. Not yet.

"Do I need to beat him up for you?"

"No— Fuck, no. It was my fault too." It had been, hadn't it? All his bloody babbling about his dear old mum watching over him from beyond the grave, when she'd sodding well stolen him from his real parents. No wonder Corin had got fed up with him—although what he'd said still stung like fire.

"Then tell him you're sorry, give him a bunch of flowers, and get onto the makeup shagging."

Adam let out a laugh, but it sounded more like a sob.

"Oh, fuck, babe, it's not just that, is it?"

"You been using Scratch's crystal ball?" He tried to smile.

Sasha snorted. "Scratch has a crystal ball? What's the other one made of?"

Adam laughed again despite himself, then sniffed. "You'll have to ask him that. Me and Scratch's balls aren't that well acquainted. Sash, what would you do if you found out you weren't who you thought you were?" Adam held his breath, too late to stop the words coming out.

She drew back to gaze at him, her eyebrows raised. "Huh. You too?"

"Me too what?"

"You found out you're adopted?" She went on without waiting for an answer. "My mum and dad completely ballsed up telling me. Waited until my seventeenth birthday, sat me down and said they had a surprise for me. I totally thought, *Fuck me, I'm getting a car*. I mean, come on, my seventeenth? Then they tell me they're not my biological parents, and they wonder why I spend the next year drinking and getting my face pierced. Turned out they'd meant to tell me on my sixteenth, but they'd wimped out when it came to it."

Adam blinked. "You're adopted?"

"Well done that, man. A-star for listening comprehension." She sent him a gentle smile.

"How did you get over it?"

"What, you mean apart from the booze and this?" She gestured at her face. "Grew up, didn't I?" Her eyes widened. "Fuck, shit, I didn't mean it like that. You've got every right to be in shock about it if you've only just found out. But for me it's been years, ain't it? And I'm over that 'rebellious teenager' phase." She did ironic air quotes. "So how'd you find out? Did you find the adoption papers?"

"Something like that."

"Shitty way to find out. Parents, eh? Who'd have 'em?"

"So . . ." Adam took a deep breath. "Did you ever find out who you really are?"

She cocked her head. "Yeah. I'm me, ain't I? If you mean, did I go looking for my birth mum, then no. Thought about it. Then I thought, where was she when I fell off the swings and got a concussion? Where was my bio dad when I had a bee in my bonnet about having a tree house? It wasn't him up the apple tree with a hammer and nails and a two-by-four, despite knowing bugger all about carpentry."

It wasn't the same, but it still felt better hearing her say that. "Yeah. You're right. But it rocked me, you know? Finding out Mum wasn't my biological mum."

"Oi, she chose you, didn't she? That means a lot."

Christ, more than Sasha knew. Adam gave a despairing laugh. "Yeah. Guess so."

She gave him a quick squeeze, then stepped back. "Now are we gonna let Samhain happen without us, or are we heading down to the Market Cross to meet Scratch and have a fucking good time?"

Fuck. *Scratch.* He'd still be expecting Adam to hold that bloody séance today. Screw that. Why the hell would Adam want to talk to someone who wasn't even his mum? He'd have to say he'd changed his mind, that was all. "Let's go," he said, grabbing his jacket.

Sasha hesitated. "Do you wanna call Corin first?"

Adam didn't have to think about it. "No. I just wanna chill. Hang out with my mates." The wounds from Corin's words were still too raw, and the thought of seeing him, of admitting to the bloke how fucking wrong he'd been about his mum . . . Would Corin even listen, after the way they'd parted?

Adam couldn't face trying and failing. Not while his head was still spinning with the whole fucking shambles.

Sasha nodded. "Fair enough. You come and have some fun, relax, and let him stew for a while, cos it takes two, yeah, and I bet you're not the only one whose fault it was. Make him realise how much he misses you. Maybe he'll be the one turning up with a bunch of flowers."

Adam cleared his throat. "Yeah." *Maybe.*

CHAPTER THIRTY-FIVE

Walking back to his flat after the argument with Adam had been a nightmare. Corin had seen faces in every shadow. Adam had sounded so certain he'd be able to contact his mum. So confident that spirits existed—and were closer than ever at Halloween. Samhain. Whatever. How could he be so bloody blasé about something so risky? How could he blithely talk about unquiet spirits as if they were a *good* thing? Just because this particular spirit was his mum's didn't guarantee she meant him well. They'd been estranged before she died, so why would she be so caring now? What if the very fact that she'd lingered had twisted her, turned her malevolent?

When he'd rounded a corner and almost literally bumped into a crowd of teenagers dressed in spooky costumes a day early, Corin had jumped a mile. He'd hurried on, only to slow his steps when he'd finally got back to his street, scared he'd see Blair waiting for him by his flat.

The corner had been empty, thank God. Corin had jogged up the stairs, let himself in, and poured himself a large slug of vodka. It had been hours before he'd felt able to try to sleep.

Adam hadn't called or texted. *Should I call him? Beg him not to hold the séance?*

No. Adam had made it clear what he thought of Corin's concern for him. Corin turned out the light and did his best to be comforted by the faint glow that found its way through his curtains. Eventually, he managed to sleep, but his night was marred by terrifying dreams of evil unleashed.

Saturday morning, Corin struggled out of bed close to noon with a headache he wished he could put down to the vodka. In the light of day, his fears seemed absurd, but he was still on edge. Anxious for Adam, even if logically, a séance couldn't possibly pose a threat. With the same illogic, he was anxious for himself, with Samhain upon him. If there was one night of the year Blair was likely to be haunting him . . .

Maybe he shouldn't stay here this weekend. It wasn't like it'd be much fun, now he and Adam weren't . . . Corin's heart clenched painfully. He could visit Declan and Lori—they wouldn't mind him turning up at short notice. Probably. Corin grabbed his phone and hit Dial.

"All right, mate?" Declan's voice wasn't as relaxed as usual.

Corin's grip tightened on his phone. "I'm fine. You?"

"Uh, gimme a mo?" There was a pause, and then the sound of a door closing. "Sorry about that. It's, uh, Lori? She's had some bleeding. I'm gonna take her into hospital, get her checked out. Trying to keep it low-key, not get her too worried."

A chill ran through Corin's chest. "Is the baby okay?"

"Yeah, I'm sure it's fine." He didn't sound sure. "Listen, I gotta go."

"Keep me posted," Corin said quickly. "And call me if there's anything I can do." He felt scared and helpless—but how much worse must Declan and Lori be feeling, after the excitement of the scan? They must be terrified. To lose the baby now would be devastating. "Tell Lori I'm thinking of you both. All three of you."

"Will do. Cheers, mate. I know you'll be there for us whatever." Declan hung up.

Oh God. Had their parents been right all along about it being a risky pregnancy? Corin struggled against a rising sense of dread. If Samhain was a time when the world of the living drew closer to that of the dead, did that mean the baby—

No. He was letting his fears run away with him again. The baby would be fine. Or they *wouldn't*, and it would be terrible, but it would be nothing to do with any pagan celebrations that happened to take place at this time of year. Corin scrubbed both hands through his hair and went to make a cup of coffee. Decaff.

After that, there was probably some shopping he needed to get. Or surfaces in the flat that needed cleaning.

He'd find something to do.

Caught between his worries about Lori and the baby, and the game he'd begun playing after lunch in an attempt to distract himself, Corin only gradually became aware of a change in the sounds coming through his open window. The roar of traffic dimmed while the noise of people rose.

Then drums started up, their slow beat resonating like a death march.

Corin checked the time. Just gone three. It must be the Samhain parade. Adam would be there to watch it, wouldn't he? With Scratch and Sasha, whom Corin had started to think of as friends. Were they lost to him now too?

He felt horribly alone and missed Adam so fiercely it hurt. He should have told Adam why he was so worried about his plans to contact the spirit world. Told him about his own haunting—if that was what it was.

Which it wasn't. It was his guilty conscience making him see things, that was all. Or making him read too much into coincidences, into random people he saw on the street. In all likelihood, the man he'd seen watching his flat was simply a neighbour, out for a smoke or something. Probably it wasn't even the same man every time—it wasn't like Corin would know, was it? The man on the street the other night had most likely been different again. Just someone whose eyes happened to rest on Corin. Maybe he'd fancied him. Maybe Corin's hair had been weird. Who knew?

And by the same token, Adam's mum's "ghost" was most likely a trick of a grieving mind. But Corin had been wrong to call him out on it. *If thinking his mum's still around is a comfort to him, who are you to tell him it's a lie?* Corin should have been more supportive. Agreed to go to the séance—

No. The idea made him sick to his stomach. But he could have declined politely. Or at least given the reasons for his objections to it.

Maybe, if he'd found the right words to say, he'd have been able to talk Adam out of holding the séance?

Could he have? With the pounding drums an ominous backdrop to his anxious thoughts, Corin could barely think straight, let alone come up with a reasoned argument.

There was so much *death* in Samhain, in Halloween, whatever people celebrated, and Corin's gut churned again at the thought of the festivities going on while his brother's baby's life might be slipping away. There were catcalls now, too, in among the drumbeats. Was Adam there right now? Corin stepped to the window, but although the sounds were louder, there was nothing he could see. The parade would be starting at the Market Cross, and there were too many buildings between here and there. If he stayed at the window, though, he might catch a glimpse of them as they passed down the high street. It wouldn't be dark for hours yet.

He returned to his game, but his mind wasn't on it. It was back in Swindon, with Declan and Lori—and when it wasn't, it was out there, in the streets of Glastonbury, with Adam and the Wild Hunt.

Was no one he cared about safe?

CHAPTER THIRTY-SIX

Adam stood at the side of the street with Sasha and Scratch and what seemed like the entire population of Glastonbury, plus a few thousand more who'd travelled in special for the celebrations. Fuck, the drums were loud. Almost like gunshots. Corin could probably hear them in his flat—if that was where he was. Underneath them sounded the ritualistic calls of the paraders and the melancholy bleat of a single horn.

First came the king, Gwynn ap Nudd himself in his velvet robe and his antler head-dress. He was carried on a throne shaped like a Roman chariot by bearers in a medley of costumes—some in death's head makeup and some wearing animal heads. Marching alongside him and behind him were people in cloaks, long gowns, and wild headdresses. Young and old, many wore face paint, and horns were definitely in fashion this year. Adam had never seen so many people in headgear—top hats, bowlers, even a pointy wizard's hat. All of them were decorated: with leaves, flowers, feathers or, on one of them, a pair of steampunk goggles.

An old bloke held up a banner showing a red dragon wreathed with green leaves, and behind him followed the red dragon itself. There were two dragons in the parade, a red one and a white one, each of them consisting of an enormous head worn by one man, trailed by a giant cloth body-slash-tail worn by a load of other people. They were a bit like the dragons he'd seen in Chinese New Year parades in London, except the styling of the heads was totally European. And they didn't dance around so much, just walked solemnly on, their big golden eyes staring into the souls of the onlookers. The Wild Hunt, they called the parade, after the legends and myths Adam had read when he was a kid. Every step took them closer to the tor—the Isle of Avalon. The underworld home of the fairies, or so they said, ruled over by Gwynn ap Nudd.

Black-clad Border Morris men and women danced along, leaping and twirling, sticks flying. There didn't seem to be much room for error, with the crowds pressed tightly on either side, but somehow no one got hurt. It looked like fun. Adam wondered how much hard work it was, learning the dances, and how much Sasha would rip the shit out of him if he joined a side.

It felt weird that this was his first time seeing the Samhain celebrations. As if he was a tourist, not a Glastonbury lad born and bred. Which he *was*, for fuck's sake. Whoever he really was. He'd been born in the same hospital as the real Adam Merchant, hadn't he?

Christ. If only he could stop thinking about it all for a few hours. Enjoy the celebrations.

Scratch nudged him. "Shame your Corin couldn't make it, eh?"

Adam's chest tightened, and he cleared his throat. "Yeah. Shame." He'd told Scratch that Corin had had a family thing come up. And yeah, he felt like shit for lying to his best mate, but he just *couldn't* tell him the truth. Not yet. He needed time to get his head in gear, first.

Scratch was right, though. Corin ought to be here. He should be seeing this. With him.

Adam wrapped his arms around himself, and wished it was Corin hugging him. Then he remembered Corin saying, *"You're mad,"* and hated himself for being so weak. Why did Corin have to be so close-minded?

The worst of it was that Adam wasn't even sure anymore what he thought about Mum hanging around. Because she wasn't really his mum and never had been. Maybe he'd been fooling himself.

He certainly felt like the biggest fool out here right now.

CHAPTER THIRTY-SEVEN

When the call came, the loud ring startled him. Corin almost dropped the phone in his haste to pick up. "Yes?"

"She's okay," Declan's voice told him. "They both are."

The wash of relief that ran through Corin made him light-headed for a moment. "Thank God. Did they say what it was about?"

"Not as such. One of those things that happens, doesn't have to mean anything bad, but she's to take it easy for a week or two and not to worry. I'm telling you, mate, I could've kissed that bloody doctor."

"And Lori's okay?"

"They're gonna keep an eye on her, but yeah, she's good. Baby's good. Got a strong little heartbeat. Head definitely still attached."

"Oh God. I'll never joke about that again."

"Yeah, we're never letting you forget that one. Lori's waving at you, by the way. And by waving, I mean with one finger."

Corin laughed helplessly, and there was an echo of laughter down the phone. "You look after her, okay? And I'll come and visit you soon."

"Yeah? Thought you were busy with your Glastonbury guy."

Corin took a deep breath. "I am. I hope. But I'll make time. Family's important."

After he'd hung up, Corin took a moment to gaze out of the window at the darkening sky. The man reflected dimly in the glass was smiling. Lori and the baby were fine. Life had won, even at Samhain.

The sounds from the street had long since passed on. Corin checked the time. After the good news about the baby, he could finally think clearly again. It was five o'clock, and the parade would have reached the tor by now. Adam would be there. Scratch and Sasha too, no doubt. Corin still wasn't sure how he truly felt about the séance—was it actually dangerous or simply a waste of time?—but he knew how he felt about Adam. He needed to find him and tell him he was sorry. That he'd been wrong to be so . . . What had Adam called him? *"So bloody judgemental."* God. What was he going to say to him?

He'd just have to think of a plan on the way. And hope it would be enough.

Corin thrust his feet into his shoes and grabbed his jacket. Not pausing to put it on, he hurtled down the steps and out onto the street, thinking only of Adam. Would he listen to what Corin had to say?

Please God, Corin hadn't ruined things between them.

Although the parade had passed on, the streets were still busy, presumably with people who'd turned up to watch the procession but had no interest in going further than the nearest pub or two. Despite Corin's bravado, it was a relief to be amongst people once more. In a crowd, surely he was safe from whatever Blair's spirit might seek to do? Even as he thought it, he knew the logic was simply not there. If a ghost had any power to harm, what could mere mortals do to stop him? But Corin *felt* safer, and he clung to that feeling.

Desperate to find Adam, Corin did his best to hurry through the streets, but his progress was impeded by meandering groups. As he neared the path to the tor, indistinct voices came through speakers, their rhythmic quality suggesting a poetry performance. Corin shivered as he made out the repeated refrain, "Die amongst the crows."

Was he being rash, hurtling out into the dark to find his lover? For all he knew, he could have already passed Adam on the street. Maybe Adam didn't want to be found.

"Die amongst the crows . . ."

Corin swallowed and hurried on—not sure any longer what he wanted most: to find Adam or simply not to be alone.

Kai—or someone of similar colouring and build—was by the gate again, their seated figure hooded and bundled in a dark sleeping bag. This time, there was an upturned hat in front of them, no doubt in hopes of generosity from a good-humoured crowd. Corin tossed a couple of pound coins into it, and they toasted him with a Starbucks cup and wished him "Blessed Samhain!" in a familiar voice, both stronger and more animated than the last time Corin had seen them. Relieved, he smiled, awkwardly wished them the same, and hurried on.

At the base of the tor, a crowd had gathered. When Corin got nearer, he could see that it ringed a roped-off area where the performances were taking place. The poetry performance was still going on, and black-clad, animal-masked performers stalked around the arena darting baleful glances at the audience. Several of them used walking sticks that were purposely too short. Corin had once seen a video of a man using sticks to imitate how a pterosaur might have walked on land, and their gait was just like that: halting, awkward yet somehow still menacing. They chanted as they walked: "Will you, won't you, will you, won't you, walk along death's road . . ."

Corin watched, mesmerised. As the performance went on, the chanting grew faster and was joined by drums, interspersed with ritualistic, demoniacal laughter, building up to a final deafening shout of "Die amongst the crows!"

The echoes rang for a long moment—and then the silence was broken by applause, laughter, and wolf whistles from the crowd. Small children on shoulders as though at a firework display cheered with their parents. In front of Corin, two young women with flowers in their hair shared a passionate kiss. He looked away hurriedly, feeling oddly voyeuristic.

Now the morris dancers were centre stage. But instead of the formal dances Corin had watched the other evening, they whirled around seemingly at random while playing instruments—clarinet, recorder, tambourine, and the strangest violin he'd ever seen, not much more than a bare skeleton with no soundbox. It was a mystery to him how they could possibly follow one another and keep to a single tune, but somehow the music made by each individual came together into a frenzied, atmospheric whole, pitch and volume leaping and falling like the flames of the huge bonfire at one side of the arena.

All around him, families, couples, and small groups watched, rapt, some in high street clothing, others in a bizarre variety of outfits. Amid the crowd, Corin felt more alone than ever.

As the light faded, so did his chances of finding Adam. Corin cast his gaze around hopelessly, his heart pumping.

And then it skipped a beat. There, not ten feet from him, stood a small group he knew well. A woman with bright red hair; a biker type with a beard. And a lean man with dark hair and the hint of a lopsided smile.

Corin's heart swelled, beating so hard it was like the drums all over again.

Adam. It had to be.

CHAPTER THIRTY-EIGHT

"Don't look now, but your boyfriend's here," Sasha said in a low voice.

Adam's heart gave a painful leap. "Where?" Even as he said it, he was turning, scanning the crowd—and there Corin was. Gazing straight at Adam as though he knew it was him. Adam's chest tightened, and he took a step towards Corin as though drawn by a line—then a hand on his arm stopped him going any farther.

"Oi," Sasha said. "What happened to letting him stew?"

"Who's stewing?" Scratch butted in. "Oh, hey, there's Corin. Guess that family thing's over, then." He gave him a cheery wave, then frowned. "Why ain't he comin' over?"

"Face blind," Adam said quickly. "He's not sure it's us."

"Oh." Scratch stroked his beard. "All right. I'll go tell him."

Adam grabbed his arm. "We had a bit of a row last night. Sorry. Should have told you. Didn't want to talk about it."

"Oh. So you gonna go make up with him, then?"

Adam ducked his head. "Wish it was that simple."

"You wanna make up with him?"

Adam ran his hand through his hair, and Christ, that was what Corin did, wasn't it? Messed up his hair and then got mad at himself when he realised what he'd done. Adam's chest hurt with a fierce ache. What was even keeping him from going to Corin? From making up with him?

Well, Sasha, for one, but mostly, if he was honest, it was pride. And Adam didn't have a leg to stand on there, did he? He'd been so cocksure of himself, so sure his mum was still around, when it turned out she wasn't his mum at all.

There was hurt too, but Corin wasn't one to be cruel. Adam knew him better than that. There had to be something behind what he'd said. Some reason why he'd reacted so badly to the idea of contacting spirits.

At least, Adam hoped so. Because otherwise . . .

He sneaked a glance in Corin's direction, suddenly terrified he'd gone.

He hadn't. He was still there. Still gazing at Adam—although now there was hopelessness in his posture. Adam took a step towards him, and then another, and this time, he didn't let Sasha hold him back. Shaking off her grasp, he closed the distance between them with a few quick strides.

"I'm sorry," Corin blurted out as soon as he was near. "I know it means a lot to you, seeing your mum again. I shouldn't have said what I did."

"It's okay," Adam said, although it wasn't. "Lots of people think it's daft, believing in ghosts."

"It's not that. I should have told you . . ." Corin took in a deep breath, his body tensing. "I was scared."

A chill ran through Adam. "Of my mum?" Did Corin think she was, like, evil or something? A nasty little voice inside him whispered, *What would* you *call someone who stole a baby?*

"No, it's— Oh God." Corin covered his face with his hands.

Adam didn't even think before slinging his arms around Corin. "Hey. It's okay. I'm here. You can tell me."

Corin's body was stiff with tension. "I think my ex is haunting me."

Adam frowned, confused. "What? You mean like stalking? That bastard who dumped you when you had your accident?"

Corin looked up, his eyes wide. "Oh God. No. I shouldn't have let you . . . He died. In the crash. Blair."

Adam's head was spinning. "Your ex is dead? And you think he's really haunting you? Like, his ghost?" Fuck, had Adam done this with his talk of seeing Mum's spirit? Made Corin think he was seeing ghosts too? "But the crash was months ago. Wait—he's been haunting you all this time?"

Behind them, a man was singing now, an eerie tune Adam didn't recognise, with words he couldn't catch.

"No. Only since I moved here." Corin swallowed.

"But that doesn't make sense." Off to one side, a female voice joined the man's in a lilting, plaintive counterpoint.

Corin shook his head. "Yes, it does. He's here now because . . . because I met you." He gave a shuddering sob. "It made him angry. Angry I've moved on when he c-can't."

"That's crazy— Shit, I didn't mean you." Fuck, now it sounded like he was after payback for what Corin had said to him. "But why would he blame you for that?"

"Because it's my fault he's dead."

Adam stilled. "Wait, what?"

"The car crash—it was my fault."

CHAPTER THIRTY-NINE

Corin stood there in Adam's arms in the gathering dark, the noise of the celebrations all around them, and somehow the words came rushing out.

They'd been driving back from a conference together, Blair at the wheel of his BMW and Corin in the passenger seat. It'd been good, spending two nights in comfortable college accommodation in Oxford, with expense-account dinners and no one else from the company there to care if they shared a bed at night. Corin was fine with keeping their relationship a secret in the office—it was none of their colleagues' business, and it was well-known that there were those in senior management who held annoyingly old-fashioned beliefs—but it was good to be able to relax a little, away from it all.

He was only sorry it had to end, which was why he said impulsively, "No need to bother driving on to Avebury. Why don't I stay at yours tonight and go into work from there? I've got a spare shirt in my bag." He'd have to get a bus back from Swindon in the evening, but it was less than half an hour. Not an issue.

Blair took his eyes off the road to flash Corin a startled look. "What? No. Out of the question."

His flat refusal irritated Corin. They *never* went to Blair's place—he always insisted on going to Corin's to avoid any chance of their workmates spotting them together—and Corin was sick of humouring him on it. "Why not? It wouldn't make any difference to you, and I don't mind living out of a suitcase for another night. You can drop me off a couple of streets from the office if you're worried about being seen coming in together."

"Not going to happen."

"Oh, for God's sake. Why the hell not? You had a good time in Oxford, I know you did. So what's wrong with having one more night before we're back in the closet?"

Blair's hands tightened on the steering wheel. "It's not going to happen," he said slowly and clearly, "because I very much doubt my boyfriend would be okay with it."

There was a long second while Corin's head refused to believe he'd heard correctly. Then he exploded. "Your *boyfriend*? What the actual fucking *hell*?"

"Oh, come *on*." Blair's voice was dripping with contempt as he changed gear to overtake a slower car. "Don't tell me you had no idea. All this secrecy, never going to my place . . . You had to have known."

"I thought you were worried about appearing *professional*, you arse." Corin's chest was tight, his limbs cold. "Does this *boyfriend* know about me?"

"No. And he's not going to." Blair stared at him, eyes narrowed.

"You utter tosser. And keep your eyes on the bloody road!" For fuck's sake—they were on an A road, with oncoming traffic only a few feet away. "If this boyfriend means so much to you, what the hell have you been doing with me?"

"Stop being such a bloody girl. We were having fun, that's all. We never said we'd be exclusive."

"I *thought* it was implied." Had he been cold, before? Corin's blood was boiling now. "You can drop me off at the next town. I'll get a taxi back. Oh, and I think maybe I *will* tell this boyfriend of yours the kind of man he's living with. After all, I've got your address, and he deserves to know."

So it was petty. So what? Blair deserved it. And the unknown boyfriend deserved better.

Blair turned to fix Corin in the eye with an icy gaze. "You say one word to Tyler about us, and I'm reporting you for sexual harassment."

"You'd have the fucking nerve to— God, watch out!"

Blair hit the brakes, but it was too late, and the car spun.

Right into the path of an oncoming truck.

CHAPTER FORTY

"That wasn't your fault," Adam said, gripping Corin tightly, as though he could squeeze the truth into him. "He treated you like shit. You had every right to get mad about it."

"I still distracted him. Made that stupid threat—"

"Which he turned straight back on you. Corin, listen to me. There's one villain in this story, and it's fucking well not you."

"That doesn't mean . . . Oh God. What if he still wants revenge?" Corin's eyes were wide and terrified.

An iron band tightened around Adam's chest. Christ. He'd done this, hadn't he? With all his oblivious talk about his mum's spirit. He'd fed Corin's fears, his survivor's guilt. And what had he *really* seen or heard of Mum, in the month since she'd died? A half-glimpsed figure in the mist and a voice that could easily have been a memory from his childhood.

That was it. He'd been living in her house for weeks now, and there had been nothing. Only his own stupid hope that his mum had loved him and stayed on this plane for him, and that had all been based on a lie, hadn't it?

"Corin, listen to me. I'm sorry I got so bloody carried away about talking to Mum. I guess I wanted to believe she was still here? Like, if she'd hung around, it meant she actually cared about me. But just cos I thought I saw something, heard something, that doesn't make it real. I know that now. So you seeing your ex could be the same. And, sorry, but how would you even know it *was* him? I mean, it could have been anyone—could have been several different people—and you, uh, you wouldn't be able to tell, would you?" *Which fucking sucks*, he didn't add out loud.

Corin drew in a deep, shuddering breath. "That's what I've been trying to tell myself. But it's . . ." He waved a hand. "Look at where we are. Look at everyone, dressed up to celebrate spirits, and the supernatural, and *death*."

"Not a real death," Adam said gently. "It's symbolic. It's more we're celebrating the cycle of life? A death, yeah, but followed by a rebirth? And I know, if you ask ten people here what they think about ghosts, you'll get ten different answers and maybe, here and now, a lot of 'em will be on the side of *yes*, but that doesn't mean you're being haunted by your dead boyfriend. Why would you be? I get you're feeling guilty about him dying, but it *wasn't your fault*."

Corin sobbed out an almost-laugh and stiffened in Adam's arms. "Does he know that?"

"If he doesn't, he bloody well ought—" Adam stopped. He'd assumed Corin was being rhetorical, but his eyes were wide and staring over Adam's left shoulder.

Adam turned and a chill ran through him as he followed the track of Corin's horrified gaze.

There was a bloke staring at them. Lean build, arrogant expression, way too smartly dressed for the occasion . . . Adam had no clue what that cheating bastard Blair actually looked like, but this guy fit the image he'd conjured up in his head to a T. In his fashionable coat and crisp trousers, he stood out like a Young Conservative at a protest march next to the festival-goers, whether in fairy gothmother chic or layered up for warmth as the sun went down.

Instinctively, Adam cast about for a friendly face, but Scratch and Sasha must've buggered off tactfully after they'd seen him and Corin embrace.

Adam glared at the stranger, but he didn't stop staring in their direction. Didn't smile, or duck his head in embarrassment at being caught. Didn't do anything *human*.

"Corin?" Adam said softly. "The posh git in the dark coat, staring at us—you think he's your ghost?"

Corin flinched. "You can see him, then? Maybe? I don't *know*." His voice was despairing.

All at once, Adam had had it with this bastard, and he didn't give a damn if the guy was alive or dead. Who the hell did he think he was, scaring Corin? "Wait here. Don't go anywhere." Adam didn't wait for a reply; he fixed the stranger in the eye and marched towards him.

Right now, he was gonna get some fucking *answers*.

As he neared the man, he realised Corin had ignored him and was by his side. Ah well. Strength in numbers. The stranger stood there, waiting for them, and somehow that made Adam even madder. "Oi! You. You're gonna tell us what this is all about, and then you're gonna piss right off and stop bothering my boyfriend."

"Why?" the stranger shot back, his chin up like he was ready for a fight. There was a tremor in his voice, though. "He never stopped fucking mine. Not till he was dead, and how come *he* got to live and Blair didn't?"

"You're Tyler?" Corin gasped. "Oh, Jesus, I'm so sorry."

"You *know* this guy? And what are you sorry for?" Adam's voice came out sharper than intended, but Christ, he was confused.

"I didn't know about you, I swear it." Corin took a step toward the stranger—Tyler—his tone earnest. "I only found out when— Oh, God." He turned away, his head in his hands.

"Corin?" Adam took hold of him. Answers could wait. "Hey, it's okay."

"No, it's not," Corin half sobbed.

Maybe answers couldn't wait, after all. Still holding Corin, Adam rounded on Tyler. "What the fuck is going on here?" Understanding began to dawn even as he spoke. Blair had been Corin's ex, right? So this guy, Tyler, he had to be—

"Ask him," Tyler said in a broken voice.

The guy was young, baby-faced, maybe twenty. Fuck, he looked like he shouldn't even be out on his own at this time of night.

Tyler went on, "Ask him what he was doing with my boyfriend."

Corin flinched.

Adam's anger spiked. "He's *told* me what happened. And it wasn't his fault. Your precious Blair was a cheating bastard, and you and the world are better off without him." A fist came out of nowhere, a lightning bolt of sharp pain bursting on his cheekbone, and he staggered back as much from shock as from the force of the blow.

"Leave him alone!" Corin yelled, grabbing the kid by the shoulders and pulling him bodily away from Adam.

Corin works out, Adam remembered muzzily, a hand to his cheek. It hurt like a bitch.

"Do you want me to call the police?" Corin said curtly, still holding on to Tyler.

Adam looked at the kid, who was wide-eyed and cradling the hand that had thrown the punch, and his anger drained away. "No. It's okay. But you," he added, jabbing a finger at Tyler. "You piss off right now and we never see you here again, you got that?"

"I didn't . . . I was never going to hurt anyone," Tyler stuttered. "I just wanted him to know I knew what he'd done."

"How did you find out about me?" Corin asked suddenly. He let go of the kid but stayed by his side, still eyeing him warily.

"Why do you even care?" Tyler demanded petulantly, then huffed in resignation. "It was Blair's phone. I kept it—and then my gran broke her phone a few weeks ago, so I thought I'd give her his. But I couldn't bear to delete everything without going through it first. It would have felt like I was throwing away a part of Blair." He swallowed. "That's when I found the dating app, the messages . . ."

"So it wasn't that I'd met Adam?" Corin asked, frowning.

"You ruined my life!" Tyler wailed, ignoring the question. "First you stole Blair from me, and now you've forgotten him! Why did he have to die, when you survived?"

Corin reeled back. "Tyler, I swear I didn't know about you. If I had, I'd have turned Blair down flat. I'm so sorry you had to find out about it."

"You're lying. You wanted him all to yourself, and if you couldn't have that—" Tyler took a step towards Corin.

Adam had had enough. "What, you're gonna accuse Corin of causing that accident now? You don't know what the fuck you're talking about. It happened cos your precious Blair picked a crap time to come clean about his cheating and didn't keep his eyes on the road while he did it."

Tyler flinched like Adam had hit him.

Corin was shaking his head. "I know it's not much, but he was always going to choose you over me. *Had* chosen you over me. I don't get why you've been following me around."

Tyler's face hardened. "Because I wanted you to suffer. Like I have."

Adam threw up his hands. "You think Corin got off *easy*? What about *him* finding out the bloke he trusted had been playing him all along?" Adam didn't miss Corin's flinch at his words.

"He knew," Tyler said, but he didn't sound so certain anymore.

"And all those months in hospital? He's got lasting brain damage!"

"I saw him in hospital." Tyler glared at Corin. "I wanted to see the man who'd survived when Blair had died. I felt *sorry* for you, and then it turns out all the time you'd been fucking him behind my back! And this brain condition that all Blair's colleagues talked about like it was so terrible, it hasn't stopped you getting on with your life, has it? Hasn't stopped you *living*."

Corin let out a curt laugh that was more like a sob.

His heart clenching, Adam rounded on Tyler again. "I bet you got off on it, didn't you? Hanging around a man with a *brain injury* and making him think he was seeing things. I s'pose you found that *funny*." Shit. He was gonna have a lot to apologise to Corin for, but this little prick needed to face up to what he'd done.

Tyler took a step towards him, his fists balled. "None of this is *funny*!"

"No," Corin said firmly. "It's not. And if you try throwing any more punches, you'll find it gets even less hilarious. This is your last chance before I call the police. Go home, and try to move on from Blair. He's not worth screwing up your life for. Believe me, I would *never* have been with him if I'd known about you. He treated us both badly, and you have my sympathy, but that's not going to stop me pressing charges for stalking if you don't leave me and Adam alone. And I don't suppose an assault charge would look good on your CV, either."

Tyler stared at him for a long moment. "You really didn't know Blair already had a boyfriend?" he asked in a low voice.

Corin shook his head, and when he spoke again, his tone was gentle. "No. And you visited me in hospital? Back before you found out I was— I didn't know who you were. I'm sorry." It must have been him—the visitor whose identity Corin had never worked out, back when he was first struggling to come to terms with his condition. To be fair, he'd stayed only minutes, and said barely a word, and none of it about himself.

The kid swallowed and turned to Adam, his chin up. "I'm not sorry I hit you. You shouldn't have said that about Blair. Even if he was—" He choked.

Adam rolled his eyes, which, okay, wasn't exactly mature, but it'd been a long day. "Are you going to leave us alone, now?"

Tyler nodded tightly, spun, and strode away towards the town.

"Thank God that's o—" Adam broke off with an *oof* as Corin fell into his arms. He stroked Corin's hair for a minute, then whispered, "Take you home?"

"Please," the almost inaudible reply came.

"Uh, yours or mine?"

Corin pressed his face into Adam's neck, then pulled away to gaze at him. "Either. It doesn't matter. Wherever you're going to be."

Adam patted Corin's shoulder, his heart swelling.

"Yeah," he said hoarsely. "It's the same for me."

CHAPTER FORTY-ONE

Adam's place was closer, so that was where they ended up turning their steps towards, Adam shooting off a quick thumbs-up message to Scratch.

"You were amazing back there," Adam said as they walked along the streets hand in hand. Screw anyone who had an issue with that. With his free hand, he cautiously prodded his battered cheek. "Ow."

"Didn't stop you getting hurt, though," Corin said ruefully, gazing at him in concern.

"No, but you stopped things getting out of hand. Not sure I'd have been so understanding, in your shoes." Christ, Corin had actually apologised to the fucker. "Even if the guy is just a kid, he was well out of line."

"I thought he was young," Corin said uncertainly. "I'm not so good at judging ages anymore. But it wasn't his fault, not really. He'd been badly hurt."

"Like you weren't? You did nothing wrong, you got that? He had no business blaming you for anything." Especially when Corin had suffered far more lasting consequences from getting mixed up with that total bastard.

Corin ducked his head. "I'm trying to tell myself that. Maybe it'll sink in one day."

"Still, you kept your head and calmed everyone down. Pretty impressive, after everything you've been through." Fuck, Adam was proud of him. He'd gone from almost sobbing on Adam's shoulder to taking control of the situation—and all while being sympathetic to the other guy.

"I'm not sure I deserve that much credit. You know what the worst thing's been, since the accident? The uncertainty. Not knowing who people are. Not being able to trust my own brain." Corin smiled and squeezed Adam's hand. "Finding out what's been going on was such a relief. Knowing for sure that the man I've been seeing is real, and he's not Blair. Not a ghost."

Adam winced. "Yeah, listen, I'm really sorry about the stuff I said back there. About you being brain-damaged. You know that's not how I think of you, right? I just wanted the kid to realise it wasn't all about him."

Corin took a deep breath. "It's okay. You didn't say anything that isn't true. I have got brain damage. Pretending I haven't isn't going to help anyone, least of all me. And I know that's not how you think of me."

He darted a quick kiss to Adam's cheek. It was the undamaged one, but somehow the pain seemed to go away in the bruised one anyhow.

Adam didn't glance into any of the car windows they passed, but if he had, he'd probably have seen a big, daft grin on his face. But there was more he needed to say to Corin, so he should stop feeling soppy and get on with it. "I'm sorry I kept going on about my mum, too. And then flying off the handle when you tried to tell me you weren't okay with all the ghost stuff."

"To be fair, I could have done a better job of explaining myself," Corin said.

They'd rounded the corner into Adam's street now, and the cool glow of the street lamps gave Corin's face an unearthly luminosity, like a figure from one of Adam's old books of myths come to life. "Not like I gave you a chance, was it?" Adam told him. "I'll do better in the future. Promise."

Corin's smile was like an early dawn. "Me too," he murmured, and Adam wanted so much to kiss him properly.

But, fuck it, they were almost at his house now, and they had plenty of time. He could wait.

As Corin closed the front door behind him, Adam realised he hadn't really thought this through. "Fuck, it's weird walking in here now."

"Why?"

Adam stared at Corin, and his stomach dropped. *He didn't know.* Corin had no clue that Adam's whole life had been a lie.

Or had it? Sasha's words—Rowan's too—came back to him.

"Adam?" Corin was frowning at him in concern.

"Sorry." Adam rubbed his face. "Sort of forgot about it for a while there. I found some stuff out today. About my parents."

"You know who your dad is?"

"Um. Kinda?"

The words came spilling out. About finding the hospital bracelets, and what Rowan had told him.

Corin held him throughout. Somehow they'd made it to the sofa, and Adam was wrapped in Corin's strong, safe arms.

"So yeah," Adam finished. "Not exactly sure who I am, now."

Corin hugged him tightly for a long moment. When he spoke, his tone was thoughtful. "It's . . . I know it's not the same, but when I became brain-damaged, I didn't feel like the same person anymore. Being disabled—that wasn't part of my identity? At least, not as I'd known it until then. And then suddenly, it was. So I had to get used to the new me." Corin paused. "And you know what? I finally realised he's not that different from the old me. Yes, there are certain things I find more difficult now, but I still have the same likes and dislikes. The same way of looking at the world. Sorry. I don't know if that helps at all."

Adam nodded. "Yeah. Yeah, it does." It wasn't the same, but it was enough to know that Corin *got* what he was talking about.

"Have you worked out what you want to do yet?"

"You mean, am I gonna try and find my biological parents?" Adam stared at the opposite wall with the stag picture still leaning against it, waiting for him to hang it. His mum's picture.

She had been his mum, hadn't she? She'd been the one who'd fed him, clothed him, and brought him up. Okay, there had been plenty of issues, but he couldn't deny the influence she'd had on his life. And, in the end, she'd left him her house and everything in it. *That* was the message she'd wanted him to have from beyond the grave—whether it was *sorry* or *I loved you* or some mixture of the two. And what about his dad, who'd known they weren't biologically related but who'd been a great father to him anyway? "I'm not sure," he said slowly. "I think . . . I wanna think about it. It's not just on me. This affects my dad too. I'm gonna need to talk it over with him before I do anything."

"Whatever you decide, I'll be there with you, if you want me to be," Corin said firmly. He sent Adam a crooked smile, his arms still tight around Adam's waist. "You helped me lay my ghost to rest. The least I can do is help you with yours."

"God, you're perfect," Adam murmured, his heart full to bursting, and kissed him.

Dear Reader,

Thank you for reading JL Merrow's *Face Blind*!

We know your time is precious and you have many, many entertainment options, so it means a lot that you've chosen to spend your time reading. We really hope you enjoyed it.

We'd be honored if you'd consider posting a review—good or bad—on sites like **Amazon, Barnes & Noble, Kobo, Goodreads, Twitter, Facebook, Tumblr,** and your blog or website. We'd also be honored if you told your friends and family about this book. Word of mouth is a book's lifeblood!

For more information on upcoming releases, author interviews, blog tours, contests, giveaways, and more, please sign up for our weekly, spam-free newsletter and visit us around the web:

Newsletter: riptidepublishing.com/newsletter
Twitter: twitter.com/RiptideBooks
Facebook: facebook.com/RiptidePublishing
Goodreads: tinyurl.com/RiptideOnGoodreads
Tumblr: riptidepublishing.tumblr.com

Thank you so much for Reading the Rainbow!

RiptidePublishing.com

ACKNOWLEDGEMENTS

I am truly grateful to the kind members of the Glastonbury Crow Morris, whose enthusiastic help was invaluable when I was writing about the Samhain celebrations they conduct to honour their ancestors.

Any errors or misinterpretations are, of course, mine alone, and artistic licence has been employed. Some of the words of the dancers in the climactic scene on the tor have been based upon my own initial mishearing of *die* for *fly*. I decided that Corin, in his heightened emotional state, might well have made the same mistake!

Many thanks also to Larissa, Elin Gregory, and Kristin Matherly for their valuable feedback.

ALSO BY
JL MERROW

ABOUT THE AUTHOR

JL Merrow is that rare beast, an English person who refuses to drink tea. She read natural sciences at Cambridge, where she learned many things, chief amongst which was that she never wanted to see the inside of a lab ever again. Her one regret is that she never mastered the ability of punting one-handed whilst holding a glass of champagne.

She writes across genres, with a preference for contemporary gay romance and mysteries, and is frequently accused of humour. Her novel *Slam!* won the 2013 Rainbow Award for Best LGBT Romantic Comedy, and her novella *Muscling Through* and novel *Relief Valve* were both EPIC Awards finalists.

JL Merrow is a member of the Romantic Novelists' Association, Crime Writers Association, International Thriller Writers, Verulam Writers and the UK GLBTQ Fiction Meet organising team.

Find JL Merrow on Twitter as @jlmerrow, and on Facebook at facebook.com/jl.merrow

For a full list of books available, see: jlmerrow.com or JL Merrow's Amazon author page: viewauthor.at/JLMerrow

Enjoy more stories like
Face Blind
at RiptidePublishing.com!

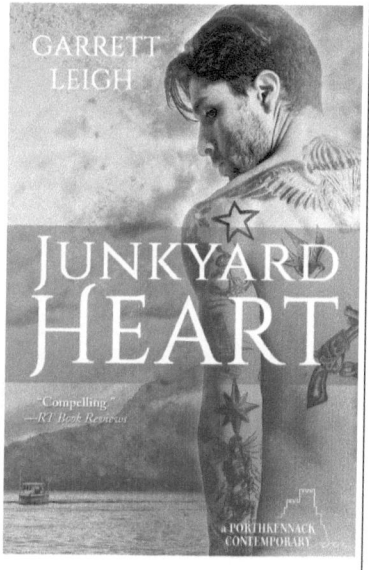

Sundays with Oliver

Two empty-nesters. Two bruised hearts. One chance to make things right.

ISBN: 978-1-62649-549-4

Junkyard Heart

Sometimes a carefree existence isn't as simple as it appears.

ISBN: 978-1-62649-964-5